I0630070

RAILS INTO HELL

A FARADAY NOVEL BOOK 6

ROBERT VAUGHAN
BRENT TOWNS

WOLFPACK PUBLISHING
— EST 2013 —

Rails Into Hell
Paperback Edition
Copyright © 2025 Robert Vaughan and Brent Towns

Wolfpack Publishing
1707 E. Diana Street
Tampa, FL 33610

www.wolfpackpublishing.com

All rights reserved. No part of this book may be reproduced in any form or by any electronic or mechanical means, including information storage and retrieval systems, without express written permission from the publisher, except for the use of brief quotations in reviews. Any use of this publication to train generative artificial intelligence (AI) technologies is expressly prohibited.

This book is a work of fiction. References to historical events, real people, or real places are used fictitiously. Any similarity to real persons, living or dead, is purely coincidental and not intended by the author.

All brand names and product names used in this book are trademarks, registered trademarks, or trade names of their respective holders. Wolfpack Publishing is not associated with any product or vendor in this book.

Editing by My Brother's Editor

Paperback ISBN 979-8-89567-809-1
eBook ISBN 979-8-89567-808-4
LCCN 2025946522

RAILS INTO HELL

CHAPTER 1

"It's ready."

Moving his gaze toward the man who had spoken, the boss outlaw turned up the collar of his wool coat, pulling it higher on his shoulders against the biting cold of the Iowan morning.

"Get every—" His gravelly words were suddenly no longer audible, cut off by the distant but shrill whistle from a 4-4-0 American locomotive.

"That would be it, the Iowa Flyer, right on time," the first outlaw said with a yellow-toothed grin.

The leader's scarred face twisted into a cruel smile. "All right, get the boys into place. Once the engine stops, I want them to take control so we can start unloading."

"Sure, boss."

Reversing slowly, five men made their way down the ballast-covered slope, taking refuge at the tree line. Behind the group, further back in the timber, tethered horses began snorting, making clear their unease as the metal monster drew closer.

Louder now with narrowing proximity, the whistle

blew again, signaling the five to draw their weapons. Six-guns slithered from holsters as the group of bandits held their collective breaths through the final moments of their long-awaited plan.

* * *

The huffing and puffing of the 4-4-0 was loud in the crisp air.

From the cab of the loco, neither driver nor engineer noticed the missing rails ahead, a one-length gap in the tracks.

Owned by Brown and Brown from St. Louis, the train contained cargo being shipped back east. Most noteworthy, however, was the $50,000 worth of gold secured in the express car. With no passengers, this trip was goods and gold only.

Once more, the mournful whistle howled through the Iowa morning, as though lamenting its coming demise.

The rumble of steel on steel, pistons pumping, steam blowing, drew to an almost deafening roar. With the absence of guiding rails, a calamitous derailment occurred, the noise blood-chilling. The scrape and screech of twisting metal was the locomotive's plaintive cry of excruciating pain. The cowcatcher dug in, sending a shower of dirt and ballast through the air.

The train's unfettered momentum had it twisting violently as it plowed down the embankment, reminiscent of a headless snake writhing in its death throes. The driver and fireman were killed instantly.

Reaching the bottom of the embankment, the train came to an ungraceful stop, a mangled heap under a cloud of dust. Steam erupted from the boiler right before the catastrophic explosion. Heavy steel parts were torn from the locomotive and flung through the air like shots from cannons on a battlefield, spreading deadly metal rain through the trees.

* * *

Hearing one of his men scream in pain, the outlaw leader turned to see who it was. Blackie Turner, once a butcher, now part of the Jim Kendall bunch. Or had been. A rivet from the exploding boiler had opened his head like a ripe watermelon.

"More for us," Jim Kendall growled, lifting his weapon into the air. "Right, get to that express car."

The remaining outlaws, followed by Kendall, stumbled along the wreckage toward the rear of the train where the express car sat. It was upright, though barely just. The wheels had come free of the tracks, and the front ones were in the air a few feet.

"Get that door open," Kendall ordered.

Short in stature but long on ornery, Billy Quinn, a former cowhand from Kansas, climbed up and tried the door. With a loud screech, it slid back on its rollers. Gunfire erupted from within, many rounds hammering through the opening.

"Hell, Jim, some varmints just don't like sharin'. Especially when they got more'n what they need," he called down.

"Stop messin' around," Kendall growled.

Quinn snaked his Colt around the edge of the door and opened fire. A cry of pain punctuated the gun thunder, and the short outlaw stopped shooting. He disappeared inside, and moments later came the sound of another shot.

3

Quinn's head reappeared with a wide grin and he said, "I guess we can start unloadin' now, Jim."

Kendall looked at the man beside him. "Bring up the horses and the pack mule."

Lefty Nelson nodded. "Sure, Jim."

Kendall climbed up into the express car and looked around. There were three men inside, two of whom were older and appeared to be rail workers. The other man, the one shot by Quinn, wore a gray suit with a string tie. "Who you figure he is?" Quinn asked.

Kendall shook his head. "Don't much care, the same as him."

The outlaw boss frowned as he watched the short outlaw squat beside the dead man.. "Now what in the hell are you doin'?"

"He's got me curious," Quinn replied. "It gets to be like an itch I can't scratch."

Rummaging through the suit's pockets, Quinn had soon accumulated a few items. With a frown, he opened a small wallet. "Far—Faridy—Far—"

"Hell, give me a damn look," Kendall growled and snatched it out of Quinn's hand.

After just a moment, he said, "It says Faraday, you pinhead."

"What's a Faraday?" Quinn asked, looking up at his boss.

"Hell, I ain't got no idea."

"Detectives," piped up Pete Turner, the fourth member of the gang. "Faraday Detective. They are goin' to come after us for that."

Kendall glared at him. "Have you got that strongbox open yet?"

Turner pulled his six-gun and shot the lock off the box. He leaned down and flipped open the lid to reveal one sack seated in the bottom of the strongbox. Turner glanced at his boss. "That don't look like no fifty thousand I ever saw."

"Ah, shut up," Kendall snarled. He kneeled beside the box and opened the sack. Reaching inside, he pulled out a fistful of cut paper. "We've been had. That son of a bitch telegrapher lied to us."

Kendall came erect and let out another curse. He walked toward the door. Behind him, Quinn asked, "What are we goin' to do now, Jim?"

"Why don't you follow me and find the hell out."

They jumped down from the express car and looked around. It was Quinn who asked, "Where are the horses?"

Kendall looked down the ballast slope toward the trees. Lefty should have arrived by now. His eyes narrowed as he thought he caught a flash of movement. Turner said, "Where is L—"

A bullet tore out his throat, sending a warm spray of blood across Kendall's face. The outlaw leader brought his gun up and fired at a puff of blue smoke. Beside him, Quinn drew his second six-shooter and started shooting at unseen targets.

Kendall felt a bullet tug at his coat. "Come on, Billy. Let's get."

"Where?"

Kendall glanced behind him and saw the gap under the express car. "This way."

He threw himself down and began clawing his way across the rocks beneath the car. Quinn was close behind. Bullets hammered into the wood and steel car above them as they crawled through. Once on the other side, both outlaws plunged down the ballast slope toward the tree line.

They could hear shouts behind them. More gunshots clipped small branches from the trees around them.

Then the shooting stopped.

"Did you see which way they went?"

"No, did you?" asked another voice.

Slowly, the sounds disappeared in the distance as Kendall and Billy Quinn kept running.

* * *

Lightning flashed, followed immediately by the crash of thunder overhead, causing Mort Gray to jump. Just as well he wasn't sending a message because his finger would have slipped off the key. Setting in just before dark, the storm had been going now for an hour and showed no signs of abating.

Storms after dark were a pet hate of his. Especially this time of year, when they brought the possibility of concealed twisters. He remembered one night that such a storm had ripped through. He'd emerged from his lonely telegraph office on the siding the following morning to find his outhouse gone. Not only that, but the barn had vanished.

The next clap of thunder made Gray jump again. He reached for the small flask of sippin' likker he kept in his coat pocket. The cap rattled as his trembling hand unscrewed it. The opening rose to his lips and the raw liquid burned as it slid down his gullet.

"Ahh."

"That looks mighty good, Mort," a voice from the doorway said.

Alarm on the telegrapher's face soon turned to horror. His heart flipped even more when he identified the speaker. "Jim! What are you doin' here? You need to get out of here."

Kendall and Billy Quinn, water sluicing from their hats and slickers like a waterfall, filed into the telegraph office, each holding a six-gun.

"You and me need to be havin' a talk, Mort," Kendall said, his voice full of menace. There was evil in the killer's eyes as he stepped closer.

Gray said hurriedly, "They're lookin' for you, Jim. Since you wrecked that train and killed those people. The law is crawlin' all over. Even the Faraday men. You don't want to get on the bad side of them."

"What happened to the gold, Mort?" Kendall demanded.

"Didn't you get it?" Gray asked desperately.

"It wasn't on the train, Mort. Nothin' in that strongbox except cut paper. It's like they knew we was goin' to hit it. Do you know anythin' about that, Mort?"

Mort paled. "Wait, Jim, no. You can't think that I had anythin' to do with it."

"Who else, Mort? You were the one who told us. Unless they were suspicious of you, but here you are."

"That—that's right," Gray nodded vigorously. "I did tell you. You paid me for the information."

"Who gave you that information, Mort? It was a damn trap, I tell you." The hammer came back on the killer's Colt. "I lost three men at that blamed train. Now you are goin' to pay for it."

Mort took a step back. His hands came up in a defensive gesture. "No, wait, Jim. They made me do it. I had no choice. You have to understand," he begged futilely.

"I understand all right, you traitorous son of a bitch," Kendall snarled.

He lurched forward and began bringing his six-gun

7

down with brutal force on the telegrapher's head and face. Blood began to flow like the rapidly rising streams outside. Red droplets combined with those from the rain on Kendall's face, his lips curled back in a wicked grin. Not content with the beating he had administered, he pointed the bloody gun at the man on the floor. Then he fired. All six rounds in the wheel.

* * *

"Take another step to the left," Sam Roberts called out to young Jimmy Lewis.

The fourteen-year-old student had been chosen to assist the surveyor because of his avid interest in trains and all things railway. His parents had given him permission to miss school for several weeks for the duration of the survey because of the small stipend on offer.

The kid did as ordered. "Mr. Roberts?"

"Yes, my boy?" the middle-aged man called back.

"We're a long way out. What if some Indians come by?"

The surveyor for the Chicago, Rock Island and Pacific Railroad chuckled. "There are no Indians out here in this valley, boy. Maybe the odd cow or cowhand, but I assure you, there are no Indians."

They had been in the valley for the past two days surveying the right of way for the new spur into Sagebrush Creek. Presently, they were on open range, but soon, over the next ridge, they would be moving into ranching country. Therein lay a problem because not all the ranchers wanted rails crossing their land. Not that Roberts was expecting trouble, but you never could tell.

The spur would bring not only people to Sagebrush

Creek but also provide a way for the ranchers to get their cattle to market without having to drive them for days on end. The town would boom, providing a win for everyone.

"Are you sure?"

"Quite certain, Jimmy, quite certain."

"Then what was the rider I saw on the ridge near the trees?"

Roberts lifted his eyes from the theodolite toward the ridge. He narrowed them against the glare but saw nothing. He shrugged, concluding that the boy's imagination was running wild because he lived in the town and had never been so far afield.

The surveyor leaned back down. "Hold the pole still, Jimmy."

It kept moving.

Roberts looked up again and saw the kid glancing toward the ridge. "Jimmy!"

"Huh?"

"I said hold the pole still." A hint of annoyance had entered the surveyor's tone.

"But I saw him again, Mr. Roberts."

"How can you see anything in that glare?" Roberts asked the boy.

"I tell you—"

An audible thump was followed by the crack of a rifle in the distance. Roberts staggered and looked down at his white shirt. There was a small red splotch just left of the second button. But it was rapidly growing as blood streamed from the bullet hole at its center.

Roberts looked up at the kid. "Goodness me, Jimmy. I think I've been shot."

That was when the rifle fired a second time.

9

* * *

The rider let his blue roan choose its own pace along the main street of Hog Town. The animal balked as one of the town's namesakes trotted across the street in front of it, making a snuffling sound. Beneath a black hat, the rider's blue eyes watched its passage before patting the animal on the neck. "Take it easy, boy. Don't let the folks upset you."

The roan snorted before setting off once more.

There were no boardwalks in Hog Town. No solid structures either. All were false fronts with canvas tents hidden behind the dry, weather-battered wooden boards.

People stopped to run a curious eye over the newcomer. Like the hat, the clothes he wore were black. His face was tanned a walnut color from long days in the harsh weather, even though he was only in his late twenties.

A crude hand-painted sign identified the saloon as *Hog's Wallow*. The rider said, "Interesting."

Out front was a painted woman dressed in a green dress. She was talking to another girl wearing red. They stopped and looked the stranger over, working out their prospects. Painted was a bit much. They had nothing on their faces except lines of hard wear.

"You want a drink, honey?" Green Dress asked.

The rider ignored her.

"Maybe you'd like some fun?" Red Dress asked, raising a suggestive eyebrow.

He kept riding.

Both women shrugged their shoulders and returned to their conversation.

Up ahead, the sign above a corral gate said, *Livery*

Stable. The rider eased the roan up to the pole rails and stopped. Within the pen were three horses. Maybe horses was a bit of a stretch. Crowbait would have been a more appropriate term to describe them.

Dismounting, the rider stretched out his solid 6'4" frame. Removing his hat, he rubbed at his light-colored hair.

"You want a bed for the animal tonight, stranger?"

Turning to face the speaker, the rider found himself confronted with an older man with gray hair and a mustache to match. The rider nodded. "Just for tonight."

"Cost you a dollar," the man said, sending a stream of tobacco juice to the dry ground.

"Seems mighty steep for what it is."

The livery owner nodded. "I wouldn't put an animal like him in with these broncs. I have a barn at the other end of town for special animals."

The rider stared at the old timer. "Somewhere it's easy for your partner to steal him after dark?"

The livery owner stared at the stranger. "Are you callin' me a thief, stranger?"

A shake of the head and then, "Not callin' you a thief, old timer. Just questionin' your business practices."

"My what?"

"Just put the horse in with the others. He'll be fine there."

"If you insist." The old timer hesitated. "You got a name?"

"Jack Quade."

"I usually take payment up front, Mr. Quade. The name is Cully, by the way."

Quade reached into his pocket and took out a couple of coins. He tossed one to the livery owner and then the second. The man looked confused. "What's the second one for?"

"Information."

Cully watched as Quade reached down and tied off the cords on the holster around his thigh. The gun was a Colt with walnut grips.

Gunfighter!

"I don't know much about nothin'," Cully said.

"I haven't asked you anythin' yet," Quade said. "Is there any law in this town?"

"Hog Town?" Cully sounded as though he was about to bust out laughing. "No law within fifty miles."

Quade nodded. "Figured as much. I'm lookin' for two men. Big man with a woolly head and a smaller one with a fiery temper. Jim Kendall and Billy Quinn. I tracked them this far."

"I, ah—"

"You know them?" Quade asked.

"Well—" The liveryman was being evasive.

"Seems to be a simple enough question, Cully," Quade said. "Yes or no."

"You lookin' to kill them boys?" Cully asked, looking up under bushy gray eyebrows.

"Not if I don't have to," Quade replied.

"You're a gunfighter, ain't you?"

Quade reached into his shirt pocket with his left hand and withdrew a small wallet. He opened it and showed his credentials. Cully frowned as he tried to read what it said. He glanced up. "I can't read."

"It says Faraday Security Service," Quade told him.

"Faraday?"

"That's right."

"You a Faraday man?"

"I am. And the men I'm after are wanted for murder and derailin' a train."

Cully nodded. "You look like you've ridden a long way, Mr. Quade. Maybe you might like a drink to wash the dust from your throat."

Quade stared at him. Then he nodded slowly. "All right. Maybe I do at that."

"And don't worry about your horse. He'll still be here when you come to collect him."

The Faraday man went to his saddle and slid his rifle from the scabbard. Cully stared at it. "Is that the new Winchester?"

"It is."

"The Eighteen Seventy-Six?"

"Sure is," Quade said.

The rifle was bigger and heavier than the more talked-about '73 model. It had an octagonal barrel and was chambered for a .45-75 caliber round. "Don't see many of them around here."

Along the street came the high-pitched sound of a hog shrieking. It was followed by the bawdy laugh of a man, then the crash of a shot. Cully said, "Looks like pig for supper."

"Town named after the hogs?" Quade asked.

"Sure is. Feller named Hurst brought them here. German immigrant. Lasted two nights before someone shot him."

"Why did they shoot him?"

"They wanted to eat one of his hogs. He made the mistake of trying to stop them. Shoulda just let them eat it. Was only a hog after all."

"Man's possessions are his," Quade pointed out.

"Yeah, but some things ain't worth dyin' over."

Quade turned and started walking away. "Matter of opinion."

* * *

Kendall knocked back another shot of whiskey and slammed the glass down onto the scarred table. The saloon door was merely a flap of canvas, and it flew back when two men stormed in. "Yeehaw, bacon for supper tonight."

"Maybe we could get us some of that, Jim," Quinn said. "I got me a hankerin' for some fresh bacon."

"Maybe," Kendall said, reaching for the bottle.

"When are you goin' to pay for that bottle?" the barkeep asked.

"When are you goin' to shut up?" Kendall shot back at him.

The truth was, they were a dry hole. Until some money came in, they had nothing. Being betrayed had taken its toll, and now they were looking to recruit for another job. But if the barkeep wanted to push the issue, Kendall decided he'd just shoot him.

The soiled dove in the green dress who had eyed Quade outside sat down next to Quinn. "You want to have some fun, Billy?"

He stared at her milky white breasts as they bulged over the top of her not-so-hidden corset. He licked his lips. "I would, Lou-Belle, but you know I got no money."

"I could let you have it on tick," she replied.

"Really?"

"Sure."

Quinn looked across at Kendall. "Save me some of that bottle."

"Sure, kid, whatever you say."

The boss outlaw finished his shot and poured another. The bottle made a clinking sound on the rim as the fiery liquid splashed in. Now that it was full, Kendall went to place the bottle on the table next to the glass but paused. The canvas flap had opened, and a man stood in the opening. A man he'd never seen before. But judging by the way he was dressed and the low-slung .45, he was a gunfighter, through and through.

* * *

Quade stopped inside the flap and looked around. The place stank of unwashed bodies and tobacco smoke. He picked out the outlaw boss almost immediately. However, he needed to know where Quinn was before he took action.

Quade walked across to the bar, which consisted of a row of boards balanced on wooden boxes. The bartender looked him over. "Get you somethin', stranger?"

The Faraday man nodded. "Whiskey."

"Comin' up."

The bartender came back with a bottle and a glass. He poured the drink, and Quade threw some money on the homemade counter. "Leave the bottle."

"Sure, stranger."

"Want some company, stranger?" Red Dress asked. She had come up on his left shoulder. Quade turned. Her grin revealed yellowed teeth.

"No." His voice was flat but firm.

"Suit yourself."

Quade took the bottle and found a table in the corner of the saloon tent. He sat down, keeping an eye on Kendall. Everything was fine until he heard a hushed voice say with urgency, "It's him, I tell you. I seen him in Briscoe."

"Keep it down."

"But it's him, I tell you. Jack Quade."

Showing no sign that he'd overheard the man, Quade poured another drink and kept watch. His senses, however, were now heightened.

The man continued. "He took down Hank Jolly and Nels Kent. Just as cool as you like out in the middle of the main street. They braced him, figurin' that the two of them could make him back down. But not Quade. He called their bluff and killed them both."

The man's companion shook his head. "That's just the whiskey talkin'."

"It's not, I tell you. That is Jack Quade."

The last sentence was spoken loud enough for the whole saloon to hear. To a person, they all turned their heads to look at the newcomer. Quade sighed.

Kendall began to rise slowly. He turned away from the table and took one step before Quade said, "Hold it, Kendall."

The outlaw froze.

"Turn around."

Kendall turned, his right hand hanging by the butt of his six-gun. "What do you want with me, Quade?"

"I guess you already know that," Quade said, coming to his feet. His right hand hung by his Colt, his left held the Winchester, finger through the trigger guard, hammer cocked.

Kendall spat on the dirt floor. "Takin' on a big job, Quade. There's more'n enough people in here to bring you down."

"No, there ain't," Quade said. "None of them will fight for you."

"You sound mighty sure about that."

"I am. Now, use it or lose it."

"You ain't quicker'n me, Quade."

"Let's find out."

Hands went for guns in a blur of motion. Kendall had never been faster as a surge of adrenaline coursed through him. He gripped the handle of his six-gun and started his draw. He never cleared leather.

The Colt in Quade's hand crashed once, and the bullet hit the killer dead center. Kendall reeled backward, falling across a table before hitting the earthen floor.

No one moved. An eerie silence followed. Quade looked around the saloon to see if anyone else would show their hand. They all remained unmoved.

The clamoring sound came from behind a second flap of canvas that led out the back. A high-pitched yelp sounded female. Then a voice said, "Billy, what are you doing?"

Taking long strides, Quade crossed to the doorway and threw the canvas aside. Standing there almost completely naked was the prostitute Quade had seen earlier.

"Where is he?" the Faraday man asked.

She glanced at the slit in the canvas room.

Quade pushed through. Beyond the canvas wall was just open terrain. Rolling grasslands. The Faraday man caught sight of Quinn running away in a blind panic. Quade holstered the Colt and brought up the Winchester. He sighted along the barrel and let out a steady breath. Then he squeezed the trigger.

The rifle kicked back against his shoulder and the target was obscured by a puff of gun smoke. By the time the breeze had cleared it, the outlaw had fallen forward onto his face in the long grass.

Quade didn't worry about checking him. He knew there was no need. His job was done.

* * *

Seated behind the desk in his Kansas City office, Matthew Faraday read the telegram again with sharp blue eyes. It was the second telegram he'd received that day. The other lay discarded beside a small statue of a 4-4-0 locomotive.

The telegram he held was from Quade, the man he'd sent after Jim Kendall. It was informing the Faraday boss that the job was complete, and he was awaiting further orders.

This brought Faraday back to the first telegram. This one concerned the murder of a surveyor for the Chicago, Rock Island and Pacific Railroad. But that wasn't the only problem. It seemed that a range war was brewing. One of the big ranchers was apparently attempting to push the smaller ones from their properties to have full access with the coming of the spur into Sagebrush Creek. Whoever controlled the land would become wealthier by negotiating the sale of the right of way. The railroad wasn't required to negotiate, but thought it more prudent to do so than to get a whole valley on the wrong side.

Faraday rose from his chair, walked over to the window, and peered out. From the outside looking in, he stood perfectly framed, like a lifelike portrait painted by an artist. Standing at a touch over six feet tall, with broad shoulders. The sunlight caught his silver hair, making it shine. From his present position, the Missouri

River was visible along with the large rail bridge that spanned it. A grand view for certain, but one that couldn't help with his current predicament.

"I just know I'm going to regret this," Faraday said in a low tone. "I just know it."

There was a knock at the door, and a thin-faced man wearing a brown suit entered. He smiled at Faraday and said, "You wanted to see me, sir?"

"Yes. Send a wire to Jack Quade. Tell him to come to Kansas City at his earliest convenience."

The man nodded. "Yes, sir, at once."

"Thank you, Morris."

The door closed, and once more, Faraday was left to his thoughts. And almost immediately, the ones of dread came back.

CHAPTER 2

Quade entered the Coates House Hotel carrying his rifle and saddlebags. When he walked over to the counter, the clerk gave him a direct stare and said, "You're one of his, aren't you?"

No welcome, hello, or how may I help you. Quade said, "Depends on who you're talkin' about."

"Mr. Faraday. One of his detectives. Mind, you look more like a saddle-bum than a detective. I cannot understand why a detective would choose to dress thus."

Quade let the insult go and lay the heavy Winchester on the countertop. "It's part of my disguise."

The clerk pulled a face at the weapon and turned the register around. "If you say so. Please sign the register."

Quade signed his name. "I'll be wantin' a bath and maybe a shave."

"The bath we can do. The shave you'll have to go to the barber along the street. I'll have someone come up to your room directly and take care of it."

"That would be mighty fine of you," Quade said evenly.

"No ladies in your room after six. The last time one of your kind stayed here, he went all night and upset the other guests."

"His name wouldn't have been Ken Jeffrey, would it?"

"I do believe it was."

Quade grinned. "You can't trust those tearaways from Britain."

"Just you don't tear-away."

"What about my horse?"

"What about it?"

"Can he come up?"

The clerk suddenly looked flustered. His mouth opened and closed, and Quade thought he was about to have heart failure. The Faraday man smiled. "Just funnin' with you. This place is too uppity for him anyway. He wouldn't like it."

The clerk stared disdainfully at him for a moment before placing a key on the counter. "Room twenty-four. I'll send someone along to let Mr. Faraday know you've arrived."

"Don't bother. I'll see him myself after I've cleaned up some."

"Yes, sir."

Quade picked up his rifle and headed to his room. It was quite large compared to those he'd stayed in before. The bed was spacious, and there was a sideboard, floral wallpaper, curtains on the windows, and a carpeted floor.

The Faraday man dumped his saddlebags and rifle on the bed, crossed to the window, and opened it. The view was overlooking the street, which was bustling with life.

There was a knock on the door. Instantly suspicious, Quade's hand went to his Colt. "Who is it?"

"We're here for your bath, sir?" came a voice from the other side.

"Be right there." He opened the door and found a man and a woman standing in the hallway. The man was carrying the bath while the woman had water. Quade stepped aside. "Come in."

* * *

Fifteen minutes later, Quade was immersed in the hot water with a bar of soap and a scrubbing brush. His gun hung in its holster from the bedpost, and his clothes lay in an untidy mess on the floor.

Another knock came on the heavy door. "Not now, I'm having a bath."

"Sorry, Mr. Quade, I've come to collect your clothes to launder."

It was the maid again. What was her name? Ellen? "Hold on, I'll be right there."

He climbed from the bathtub, dripping water and soap. Wrapping a towel around his lower half, he strode to the door and unlocked it. "It's open."

Ellen opened the door and saw him standing dripping all over the floor. "Oh—oh. I am sorry, Mr. Quade, I—"

"Don't worry too much about it. You wouldn't be the first female to see me this way, and you won't be the last."

Ellen blushed. He turned back to the bath, and she averted her gaze. The towel might have been one of the largest the hotel had to offer, but for a man that size, there was a clear breeze blowing around his nether regions.

Suddenly, Ellen grinned. "Would you like me to close the window, Mr. Quade. It feels a mite drafty in here."

"The window is fine," Quade replied. "And stop with the Mr. My name is Jack."

"Yes, sir. Ah—Jack."

"The clothes are on the floor. I have some more in my saddlebags that I can wear."

Ellen bent and scooped them up. "Is there anything else I can help you with?"

"No, thank you. But you will find a dollar in the pants pocket. Keep it."

Ellen left and Quade climbed back into the tub. It was a little more than tepid. "Son of a bitch."

* * *

It was late in the afternoon when Quade finally arrived at Faraday's office. He was greeted by the man's new secretary, a young redhead in her early twenties with a scattering of freckles on her cheeks.

"I'm here to see Mr. Faraday, Freckles," Quade said to her.

"My name is Ellie," the young lady corrected him with a warm smile. "And Mr. Faraday is busy at the moment. You will have to come back tomorrow."

"In that case, how about dinner tonight?"

"How could I possibly go to dinner with a ruffian I don't know?"

"Then I shall help you out. My name is Jack Quade."

Ellie's eyes widened. "Oh, fiddlesticks. Why didn't you say who you were when you got here?" she said testily. "Mr. Faraday is expecting you. Follow me."

"What about that dinner?"

"Can I bring my fiancé?"

"Lead the way."

Ellie knocked on Faraday's door and opened it. The security service owner was standing at the window for the third time that day. He looked over his shoulder and saw Ellie. "What is it, my dear?"

"Mr. Quade is here, sir."

Faraday turned completely and saw Quade filling the doorway. "Yes, he is. Come in, Jack. Thank you, Ellie. Why don't you go home to that young man of yours."

"Thank you, sir. I'll see you tomorrow." She looked at Quade. "Goodbye, Mr. Quade."

"Good evening, Ellie."

The door closed. Faraday pointed at a leather chair. "Sit down, Jack, and for God's sake don't let that damn gun scratch the wood. You don't have spurs, do you?"

"No, sir."

"Good."

Quade unbuckled his Colt and laid it on the floor beside him.

Faraday took a seat behind his desk and said, "Well done on that Kendall mess."

"It was straightforward," Quade replied. "I was a little surprised that it got that far."

"I was too," Faraday said grimly. "The trap was set, but the posse was held up. It gave Kendall all the time he needed to derail the train. That we weren't expecting."

Quade nodded.

Faraday sat forward, his elbows propped on the desk. "The Chicago, Rock Island and Pacific Railroad has come to me because they have a small problem they want solved."

"Yes, sir."

"One of their surveyors was murdered while working on a new spur line in Iowa." Quade opened his mouth to speak but Faraday raised a hand to stop him. "I know, I know. You were just up there."

"I'm beginnin' to think that you called me down here for a reason, sir. Where did the killin' take place?"

Faraday's eyes narrowed. "Sagebrush Creek Valley."

Quade showed no emotion.

"How long have you been gone, Jack?" Faraday asked.

"About nine years," Quade replied.

"And you've been with me for four. Now, it's time to go back, Jack."

"I'd prefer not to," he said quietly.

Faraday's face remained passive. "Let me lay things out for you and make up your mind. I'll not force you to go."

Quade nodded. "Okay."

"Apart from the murder of the surveyor, a range war has sprung up in the valley," Faraday explained. "The largest rancher in the valley is trying to force the others out."

"Why?"

"Money, of course. With all the others gone, when the line goes down, the last man standing will be sitting on a mountain of it."

"The railroad is negotiatin' a settlement for the land?"

"Yes. Once the surveyors find the best route, then they will negotiate a settlement."

"I still don't see why you are sendin' me," Quade said.

Faraday slapped his hand hard down on his desk. "You know exactly why I'm sending you, son. Because of who you are. Jack Quade, gunfighter. What better cover than a son riding home to help save the family ranch?"

"So that is my cover?"

"Yes."

"My father won't want anythin' to do with me,"

Quade said. "His exact words were, 'Don't come back,' the day I rode out. Possibly even more so now."

"Then you make him want you back."

"If I do, there's bound to be some shootin'," Quade pointed out.

"So be it. Just find out who killed the surveyor and make sure that it doesn't happen to the others."

Quade stared at Faraday. "Others?"

"That's right, they'll be arriving on the stage within the week. You make sure you're there by then."

"Yes, sir."

"And, Jack, keep them alive."

* * *

It was almost dark by the time Quade left his boss, and upon his arrival at the hotel, he decided to get a meal in the dining room. As he stepped through the doorway, he was immediately stopped by the waiter. "Excuse me, sir, guests only."

"Jack Quade, room twenty-four," Quade told him.

Taken aback, the waiter said, "Of course, Mr. Quade, follow me and I'll seat you at a table."

The waiter led Quade to a table in a corner where he was less likely to be seen. Quade didn't mind. The quieter the better. He ordered steak and vegetables with gravy and coffee.

The meeting with Faraday brought back memories of their first encounter. Just over four years ago, in a cow town in Kansas.

* * *

It was called Bison Flats. Just a small town which Quade had been called to because of a local rancher who was fighting homesteaders. When he arrived, the war had already begun. The homesteaders were fighting for their very existence against the Box D. Dennis, the owner, had originally settled the valley, but now, homesteaders had flowed in using the Homestead Act to take up public land.

"Not in my damned valley," Dennis had raged. "Not on my damned land."

Before long, there was an influx of guns, and the killing had begun. A month later, Quade arrived. He was hired to protect the homesteaders from Hank Robards, a fast gun from Texas. At first, the Box D guns were wary of Quade. They'd all heard the stories about him. However, that all came to a head when Robards and he had faced off on Main Street one rainy afternoon.

Quade had ridden into Bison Flats to find a homesteader who'd gone to town and not returned. It had all been a setup. The sheriff had the homesteader locked away in a cell. It was obvious from day one that the sheriff was a Box D man, but until now, Quade had stayed out of his way.

That all changed the moment Quade rode down the main street wearing a slicker against the drizzling rain that afternoon.

As he rode, Quade saw a figure step out into the rain from beneath an awning near the Cow Hide Saloon. The person stopped in the middle of the street and faced the oncoming rider.

Quade drew rein. The figure spoke. "Time you and me had us a reckonin', Quade."

It was Robards.

There was no way around what was about to happen. "You mind if I climb down first?"

"Die on your horse or in the mud, it don't make no never mind to me."

Quade climbed down and led his horse to the hitchrail. He wrapped the reins around it and walked back out to the middle of the street. Water dripped from the brim of his hat.

Robards said, *"Mighty appropriate, you wearin' black an' all. After all, this is your funeral."*

"You talk too much, Robards," Quade said.

"Then go for your gun, tenth rate!" the killer snarled.

Robards would have told you if he could, in spite of the rain, it was one of the best draws he'd performed. However, Quade's Colt was already out before the hired gun had cleared leather.

The Colt in Quade's hand crashed, and Robards staggered under the impact. Quade fired a second time, and Robards crashed onto his back.

Walking up to the fallen killer, Quade looked down. Robards's eyes were closed and his face splashed with mud. The fact that he was dead was beyond doubt.

"Drop your gun, Quade!" a voice called out.

The gunfighter turned and saw the sheriff standing on the sidewalk with a shotgun pointed in his direction. *"What are you doin', Hanson?"* Quade asked.

"I'm arrestin' you for murder."

"You have to be jokin'."

"Do I look like I'm jokin'?"

"It was a fair fight, Hanson. Everyone saw it. Robards left me no choice."

"A jury will decide that. Now, drop the gun."

Quade's Colt went into the mud.

The trial was fast. The jury, rigged. But instead of Quade being sentenced to hang, the judge sentenced him to ten years on the thought that Quade was being railroaded.

The very first week he was in the pen, Quade was taken

from the rock pile to the warden's office. When he arrived, there were two men there. One was the warden himself, the other was a gray-haired man Quade had never seen before.

The Warden came to his feet and said, "Quade, this could be your lucky day."

"You mean I get to go to solitary?" the gunfighter asked bitterly.

Ignoring the remark, the warden said, "This is Matthew Faraday. He has a proposition for you."

Faraday looked up at Quade. "Son, how would you like to get out of this hole?"

Quade was suspicious. "What do I have to do?"

"Just say yes."

"Yes to what?"

"Coming to work for me," Faraday had said.

"Doing what?"

"I have a security service, detective agency if you like."

"Like Pinkerton?" Quade asked.

"Something like that, only we take care of the railways."

"What if I don't want to?"

"Then you can stay here for the next ten years, and I lose what I think will be a good agent."

"Puttin' it like that, what can I say?" Quade said.

"One thing you should understand before we leave. If you cross me, disappear, I will bring the full force of my agents to bear, and you will be brought back here in chains."

"I guess we have an understandin'."

* * *

During the course of his meal, three young men came in and were seated at the table across from where Quade sat.

The Faraday man had finished his steak and was

using the leftover vegetables to mop up the gravy when one of the young men decided it would be sport to poke fun at the Westerner.

"Hey, cowboy, just come in off the range?" the young man asked with an Irish accent.

Quade glanced over at their table, taking in the black suits they all wore. The speaker had a square jaw and an air of arrogance about him. He was obviously the ringleader.

Quade ignored him.

"I'm speaking to you, cowboy," the young man persisted. "Where's your cows?"

Finishing the last of the meal, Quade reached for his coffee, still ignoring the obnoxious young man.

Suddenly, there came the moo of a cow from the table. One of the other young men reached over the table to his friend and shook his head. "Maybe you ought to leave it, Marion."

"What do you mean? I'm just having some fun. Isn't that right, Cowboy?"

Quade drank more coffee.

"I said, isn't that right, Cowboy?"

"Maybe you should leave it, Marion," Quade said softly. "It stopped being funny the moment you opened your mouth."

Marion pulled a fearful face, mocking the Faraday man. "I think he's trying to scare me. Look, he's carrying a gun. Are you a tough man, Cowboy?"

Quade finished his coffee and rose from the table. As he started to walk past the table where the young men were seated, Marion said, "See, these cowboys are all show."

With the lightning speed that had made Quade a fast draw, he reached out and grabbed a handful of Marion's hair. Then, in a blur of motion, he slammed the young man's face into the table twice, making the table decorations jump with the force of the blows.

On first impact, his nose flattened in a spray of blood. The second time it hit, a spray of blood splattered his friends. Without a sound, the unconscious young man slid from his seat onto the floor.

Quade glanced at Marion's friends. "Are we goin' to have a problem?"

They shook their heads. "No, sir. No problem."

"Good. Enjoy your meal."

As Quade left, every eye in the dining room followed him.

* * *

That should have been the end of the problem. But it wasn't. The young man was the son of a prominent crime kingpin who ran what was considered a black market in Kansas City. His name was Colin Doyle. And the Irishman commanded respect. He stared at the three young men standing in front of his desk. Off to the side stood one of his personal bodyguards.

"What the hell happened, boy?" Doyle asked his son.

"Some cowboy took me by surprise," Marion replied.

"What were you doing?"

"Nothing," he lied. "Just waiting for our dinner."

Doyle let his gaze roam across all three of the young men before settling on Marion, whose eyes were swelled up and his nose encrusted with dried blood across the bridge. The Irishman said, "In my experience, a man doesn't just attack another without cause. Did he have cause?"

There was a drawn-out silence before one of Marion's friends said, "Well, we might—"

"Shut up, Lester," Marion snapped.

"No," Doyle snapped. "Keep going. I insist."

"Ah—It was kind of like Marion was just having some fun with him. That was all. The stranger took it too far and attacked him like he said for no reason."

"It doesn't sound like no reason."

"Yes, sir."

Doyle stared at his son. "What do you plan to do about it?"

"What do you mean?"

"The bastard insulted you, son. If word gets around, more will try. We must put a stop to it, now."

"Then what do I do?" Marion asked.

"Let's go pay him a visit in the morning. I gather he is staying at the hotel?"

"I think so."

Doyle nodded and said, "Fine. In the morning, we'll go and show the saddle-bum the error of his ways."

* * *

The following morning, Quade made it as far as the hotel steps before sensing imminent trouble. He carried his saddlebags over his left shoulder and the rifle in his right hand. Standing on the top step, he took in the black buggy drawn by two horses before him. Standing in front of it was Marion Doyle, accompanied by his father, Colin, and two of the Doyle family enforcers.

"Is that him, son?" Quade heard Doyle ask.

"That's him."

Quade adjusted his grip on the Winchester so that his

thumb was on the hammer and finger on the trigger. "Can I help you gents?"

"Friend, it would seem that you owe my son an apology," Doyle said loudly.

The Faraday man looked around as a crowd began to gather. "I do?"

"Yes, you do."

"And who might you be?"

"My name is Colin Doyle." He spoke the words as though Quade should know who he was.

Quade shook his head. "Name don't mean nothin' to me, feller."

"That isn't important. The apology is. Make it, and we can all go on our way."

"Don't make a habit of apologizin' for somethin' that weren't my fault, Doyle. Maybe it's your son who should apologize to me for ruinin' a pleasant meal."

The Irishman's ire was beginning to build. "You don't seem to understand."

"I understand perfectly. You want me to apologize to your son to make his hurt pride go away. Can't do it, won't do it. Now, if you don't mind, I have somewhere I need to be."

"Stop there, saddle-bum," Doyle's voice cracked like a whip. "I tried to be polite and have good manners, but now, we'll do it the other way. Pat, Oliver, beat the apology out of him."

Quade stood his ground as the two enforcers started up the steps. He showed no sign of responding until the first of the two men reached him. The butt of the Winchester swept around and clipped the first enforcer on the jaw, which broke with an audible crack, and the man fell backward, tumbling down the stairs. The second enforcer, seeing the sudden demise of his friend, panicked and decided that he needed more backup. His hand slipped beneath his brown coat and came out with a Colt Sheriff's Model chambered for a .44-40 round.

The last thing Quade wanted was a shootout like this. He tried to avoid it, in fact. But with the appearance of the revolver, he knew there was no other option.

The Winchester came around, and Quade snapped off a shot. The large caliber bullet hammered into the enforcer's chest and punched him back hard. The man died on the sidewalk, trying to draw breath.

Quade levered another round into the chamber but left the Winchester pointed at the sky. His hard gaze settled on Doyle, and he said, "I didn't want this, but you pushed it. Now one of your men is dead. If you want to keep pushin', I can accommodate you some more. At least now I know why your kid is the way he is."

Marion glanced at his father. The young man had never seen anyone push back on his father like this before. People were normally too fearful to try. Those who did usually suffered the consequences. But this man was something different.

"Father?"

"Just shut up, Marion," Doyle snarled. He looked at Quade. "We're not done here, cowboy."

"Looks to me like we are," Quade replied.

"You may have won the battle, but you haven't won the war."

"Is that what this is?"

"Colin Doyle, mister. Remember the name. Come on, Marion. We're leaving."

"What about the men?"

Doyle gave them a look of disdain. "What about them? Move. Be seeing you, cowboy."

Quade touched the brim of his hat. "I certainly hope not."

* * *

Hunched over a plate of ham and eggs, Doyle sat in an out-of-the-way café that he usually frequented. His anger still burned deep inside and refused to abate. He was determined to make the cowboy pay. Just see if he wouldn't. No one disrespected Colin Doyle like that and lived.

A thin man wearing a suit entered the café and began moving toward Doyle's table. There was no need to look around because the kingpin always sat in the same place. The man pulled out a chair and sat. Doyle stopped eating and glared at the man. "Did I tell you to sit down?"

The man got back up. "No, boss."

Doyle forked more egg into his mouth. "Did you find out his name?"

"Jack Quade."

"And where does Mr. Quade come from?"

"Not sure, sir."

"It doesn't matter." Doyle reached into his pocket and took out a sack of gold coins. He threw it on the table where it landed with a dull clink. "Find Pike Miller. Tell him what I want done. Tell him if he brings me that bastard's head, there is a bonus in it for him."

"Yes, sir."

"And tell him, not to let me down."

"Yes, sir."

CHAPTER 3

Someone had fenced the creek. Not only that, but it was also on the wrong side. Quade drew rein and stared at the line running in front of him. Divide Creek was the border between the Broken J and the Double Q. As the name indicated, it was the divide. Quade was certain his father wouldn't have fenced the creek like that. So that meant that it had been the Broken J. But why?

Why would his father stand for that? Obviously, the Broken J was driving the range war. And they had no right to fence the creek like they had. As he approached, Quade saw the reason. The creek was almost dry. But still, it was a shared water source.

A gunshot sounded and Quade hipped in the saddle, dropping his hand to the butt of his Colt. There were two riders coming down the rolling ridge toward him. Both men were carrying rifles.

The Faraday man leaned forward and patted the roan's neck. "Looks like we've got company. I guess time will tell if they're friendly or not."

The two riders drew up in front of Quade. Both held their rifles across their laps. "You lost, stranger?"

The man who spoke was rail-thin and had a tight beard. Just looking at him, Quade could tell that he wasn't a cowhand. Neither was he a friend.

"Just passin' through," Quade replied.

"Then you'll need to go around," the second man replied. He was short and stocky with red hair.

"Can't remember this fence ever bein' here before."

"*You* been here before?" short beard asked curiously.

"Yeah. Passed through a few times on my way to town. Last time I was here, this was Broken J range."

"Not anymore. This is the Rockin' R now. Hasn't been Broken J for a couple of years."

"Be about that when I last passed through," Quade said.

"You got a name?"

"Yeah."

They stared at each other, but no information was forthcoming. Beard nodded. "Go around the fence."

Quade shifted in his saddle. "I'll do that."

The Faraday man turned the roan and started riding away, aware that the eyes of the two gunmen were watching his every move.

* * *

Quade sat on the rise overlooking the Double Q ranch house. From this distance, it looked much like it had when he left. Except that the surrounding land had been green on that day, and now it was a dry yellow color. A sure sign that much-needed rain had not arrived.

There was movement near the barn. One of the

hands, Quade guessed. He kneed the roan forward. "Let's go and see what kind of reception we get."

As he rode into the ranch yard, the first person he saw was Charlie Brown. The old cook was out getting eggs for the evening meal. He stopped halfway to the coop, watching the rider come in. In his left hand was a basket, but his right hovered near a handgun poked into his belt.

Quade drew rein and said, "You won't be needin' that, Charlie."

The old cook's eyes narrowed. "Do I know you, stranger?"

Quade removed his hat. "You should."

Charlie's eyes widened with recognition. "Jack, is that you?"

"It's me."

"Hell and tarnation, boy, get down here so I can get a better look at you. My dern eyes aren't what they used to be."

Quade climbed down. Charlie closed the gap between them and took the Faraday man's hand, pumping it vigorously. "Damn boy, it's good to see you. Damn good."

"Good to see you too, Charlie."

"What brings you back here?"

"Heard there was some trouble brewin'."

The old cook's expression changed. "You could say that."

Quade paused. "How is he?"

"Your Pa? Still as ornery and stacked with cussedness as when you left."

"I saw somethin' on the way in, Charlie. It troubled me," Quade said.

"The fence?"

"Yeah."

"It's not good, Jack. Not good at all. Without that water source, the Double Q can only run half the number of head the range can carry."

"But that creek has always been a boundary and a shared water source."

Charlie nodded. "Used to be before Tom Rafferty and his Rockin' R crew moved in."

Quade frowned. "I don't understand."

"He moved onto the old Broken J and the next day started puttin' up the fence. When your pa went to see him about it, he produced a paper from the land office that showed the boundary on our side of the creek."

"Did Pa fight it?"

"Wasn't nothin' he could do. The paper was all legal, and the Rockin' R had the guns to back it up."

Quade nodded. "I met two of them on the way in."

He described them.

"That will be Summers and Cable. Summers is the one with the beard. Rafferty has at least five of them on his payroll. The toughest of them is Harry Crosby."

Quade nodded. "I know him. He's good."

"Figured you might," Charlie said. "Jack, we been hearin' stories about you, boy. About you packin' a gun."

"Charlie, what the hell are you doin' standing around gabbin'?" a familiar voice called from the ranch house veranda. "Who is he? Tell him we've got no work and send him on his way."

Quade turned to face his father. "Howdy, Pa."

Vince Quade's eyes narrowed, and a dark cloud seemed to settle on his face. "What the hell are you doin' here?"

"I came home to see you, Pa," Quade said.

"This ain't your home," he snapped. "And I ain't your pa neither. Now get off."

"Pa—"

Vince's voice deepened. "Don't Pa me. I already told you. It's a good thing your ma ain't alive today to see her son turned killer."

His words burned. Quade's mother had been a fine and gentle woman. She had died in a buggy accident when Quade was ten.

Without another word, Vince Quade turned and walked inside.

The Faraday man took a step toward the house. Charlie placed a hand on his arm. "Leave it, Jack. Let him get used to you bein' back."

"Hell, Charlie. I just need to talk to him. Tell him how it is."

"He knows how it is, Jack. He's been hearin' about his son, Jack Quade, the gunfighter."

Quade nodded slowly. "Is Mary here, Charlie?"

"She ain't lived out here for nigh on two years, Jack. She lives in town now. School teacher she is."

Quade smiled at the thought. "She always was the smart one."

"If she ain't at the school, you'll find her at Mrs. Hamblin's boardin' house."

Quade glanced toward the house. "All right, Charlie. I'll go. But I'll be back. Tell him that."

"I expect you will, son. I expect you will."

"One other thing, Charlie. How bad is it?"

"It's bad, Jack. Real bad. Things will be better when the railroad comes, but he has to hang on until then. Even without the water, the money from the railway will help."

"Has the right of way been finalized?"

"Not yet, but the line cuttin' across your pa's land is the only way they can come. To get to it though, they have to come through Rockin' R. The way Rafferty is squeezin' the other ranchers, you would think that he knows the route already."

"You figure that's what it's all about?"

"Well, it's mighty strange that Rafferty arrives and a line is announced. Then he starts buyin' up all the land he can."

Quade nodded and climbed onto his roan. "Be seein' you, Charlie."

The old cook placed a hand on Quade's knee. "It's good to see you, boy. I'll keep an eye out for you."

With a cluck of his tongue, Quade turned the horse and pointed him in the direction of town.

* * *

Behind him, Charlie heard the screen door open and boots on the veranda. He turned and saw Vince Quade watching his son ride away. Charlie said, "You could have been decent to the boy."

"Don't you tell me how to treat my son, Charlie," Vince growled. "I can get another cook anytime."

"So, he's your son now?"

Vince glared at his friend. "Be quiet."

The old cook shook his head.

"What did he want?" Vince asked.

"Heard his pa was havin' some trouble. Maybe he figured he could help."

"I don't need his damn help," Vince snarled. "Nor his damn gun."

"Why not just talk to him, Vince?" Charlie asked.

Vince's eyes lit with fire. "You know why, damn it. You were here the day he rode out."

"Sure, I was. Two he-bulls buttin' heads. Then you hit him, and he hit you back. First time I ever saw the boy stand up to you the way he did when you was ridin' him. That was the first day he stood up and became a man. That's what you wanted, and that's what you got. It was one of the best damn days this ranch ever saw."

"Sure I wanted a man. Not a damn killer."

"You still need to talk to him, Vince."

"The hell I will. And if he comes back here again, I'll throw him the hell off again."

"You're a stubborn fool, Vince."

"I'm not discussin' it no more, Charlie. Now, if you want to stay on as cook on Double Q, get inside and start doin' what you're paid to do."

* * *

Sagebrush Creek was nestled at the base of two hills. There was a scattering of cottonwood and other trees on the outskirts of town. The creek for which the town was named was sited to the east. The main trail ran right into town before terminating at an intersection in front of the courthouse. There it branched left and right. Both led out of town. The stockyards to the west were new. Quade figured they would be utilized when the spur line reached the town.

It would be getting dark soon, so he took the roan along to the livery where he was greeted by a bald man sucking on a corncob pipe. "Help you, stranger?"

Quade had never seen him before. "Need a stall for the horse."

"How long for?"

"Couple of days to start."

The liveryman gave him a cautious look. "You goin' to work for the Rockin' R?"

"Why do you ask?"

"Feller comes to town, dressed like you, wearin' a Colt that way, kinda makes sense. All the others around here dressed like that are."

"I see. You got room, or not?"

"Sure. Cost you fifty cents per day. That includes feed."

Quade grabbed the rifle from the scabbard and his saddlebags. "Take good care of him."

"He's a mighty fine lookin' animal, Stranger. Say, I didn't get your name. Mine's Silas Holmes."

"Jack Quade."

"Pleased to meet—wait, did you say, Jack Quade?" There was shock on his face.

The Faraday man nodded. "That's right."

"I heard of you."

"I wouldn't believe half of it," Quade told him.

"They say you killed twenty men. Is that true?"

"The count has gone up by two since then," Quade said evenly. The truth was, he had killed nowhere near twenty men.

"Well, how about that," Silas said.

"Where is a good place to stay?" Quade asked.

"You could try Mrs. Hamblin's boardin' house. I'm not sure she'd want you there. The saloon has rooms upstairs."

"Which one?" Quade asked.

"There's only one. The Tall Grass. The owner is Jasper Foley. He bought the other saloon and closed it down."

"The Tall Grass it is, then."

43

* * *

Quade walked along the boardwalk toward the saloon. In the west, the setting sun had imbued the sky with an orange hue. The stores were beginning to close, and people were thinning out on the street itself. When Quade reached the saloon, he eased in through the batwings and stopped. It would not be the first time that a cautious entry into such a place had saved his life.

The place was half full, or half empty, depending on how you looked at it. Most of the customers were seated at tables, however, there was a line at the bar as well. Four girls flitted from table to table. The arm of a man in a suit wrapped around the waist of a girl in a blue dress and pulled her down onto his lap. He stole a kiss, and the soiled dove let out a squeal. "Oh, Judge, behave."

She leaped to her feet and hurried off. One of the three men seated with him said, "Judge, if Mrs. Hamilton could see you, she'd cut your pecker off with a blunt knife."

The judge chuckled. "It's a good thing the old bat is half blind then, isn't it?"

They all laughed and went back to their card game.

Quade walked up to the bar and leaned his Winchester against the hardwood front. He waved at the barkeep, who was talking to someone at the far end.

As the man approached, he asked, "Get you somethin'?"

"A room if you have one."

"Got two. One at the back and the other overlookin' the street."

"I'll take that one."

"Figured you would."

The barkeep got the key, and Quade gave him some money. "Where can I get a meal?"

The barkeep pointed at a door in the far wall. "Through there we have a dinin' room. Nothin' fancy but the food is hot."

"Thanks."

"Up the stairs, along the hallway on your right. Number four."

* * *

The room was a lot smaller than the one in Kansas City. It contained a narrow bed with a typically lumpy mattress. A sideboard held a jug of water, a dish, and a bar of soap. Dropping his gear on the bed, Quade poured some water in the bowl and washed up the best he could, then used the towel to dry himself. Taking the Winchester, he pushed it under the mattress and shoved his Faraday wallet inside his boot. Once he was done, he returned to the bar.

There were a few extra people in the bar. The judge and his friends were still playing poker, and one of the girls had disappeared. Probably with a customer. Quade walked toward the door to the dining area and opened it.

Before stepping into the room, he observed it briefly, taking in all the tables with cloths on them. Three tables were occupied, two by single men, the other by a couple. Another door opened out onto the street and was flanked by two large windows providing light during the day as well as a view of the street for the patrons.

"Find a table, mister. I'll be with you in a moment. Take your spurs off before you sit. We don't pay good money for chairs just to have them busted."

Quade looked to the counter where a young lady was

working, her dark hair pulled back from her face. "Yes, ma'am."

"I'm not no ma'am. My name is Lucy."

"Ma'am."

She stared at him for a moment and then shrugged. Quade sat at a corner table, as was his habit. He had no need to remove spurs because he never wore any.

The dining room was tidy, and the smell of cooking food made his mouth water. He hadn't realized just how hungry he was.

"What can I get you?" Lucy asked.

Up close, she was even prettier, even with the drab gray dress she wore over her slim frame. She had brown eyes and a small nose, and her almost flawless skin had not been affected by the weather...yet.

"You're staring, mister."

He blinked. "Sorry. My name is Jack."

"Well, Jack?"

"Ma'am?"

Lucy smiled. "What will you have?"

"What do you have?" Quade asked.

"Bacon and beans, steak and vegetables, venison stew, fried potatoes, bacon and eggs, and there is apple pie."

"What do you recommend?" Quade asked.

"The stew is good. I shot the deer myself, but so is the steak."

"A real-life markswoman," the Faraday man said with a smile.

"Just don't make me angry," Lucy said with a grin.

"In that case, I might try the steak and vegetables with fried potatoes, please, Lucy. Maybe a little apple pie and coffee to go with it."

"I'll get the cook to get it started."

"Thank you."

* * *

When the meal arrived, the large plate was almost overflowing. The food was good, and by the time Quade was finished eating, there wasn't anything left on the plate. The apple pie was unlike anything he'd ever tasted. He was almost done when Lucy came over to collect his plate. "How was your supper?"

"Very nice, thank you."

"What about the pie?" Lucy asked.

There was something in her eye that gave away her interest. Quade said, "It was very bitter. There must have been somethin' in it that didn't belong."

Lucy's face fell. "Oh."

The Faraday man smiled. "The pie was fine, ma'am. Like nothin' I've ever tasted."

Lucy glared at him. "Not funny."

Quade smiled. "Sorry, I couldn't help it."

"Would you like some more coffee?"

"Only if you would join me, ma'am."

"I don't take coffee with strange men. Especially ones that look like you," Lucy replied.

"Don't let my looks deter you," Quade said. "My intentions are all honorable, I assure you. Besides, my pa would be most upset if I offended a lady."

"Your pa?"

"Yes, ma'am, Vince Quade."

Her jaw dropped, and she was just about to speak when the door to the dining room opened, and three men entered, making a raucous sound. Two were those he'd encountered at the fence earlier in the day. The third was a bigger, broader man whom Quade had never seen before.

Lucy finally found her voice. "Oh, no. This just got

worse. Please, Jack, no trouble."

Lucy hurried away. She'd almost made the counter when the bearded man called out. "What's the rush, Lucy. You got three hungry men here lookin' for a feed."

"Take a seat and I'll be right with you. And take your spurs off."

"Don't keep us waitin' too long," the big man growled.

"Like I said, I'll be right with you."

All three men sat down, ignoring the request. Quade watched them over the rim of his cup. Then Summers caught sight of him, and right away, Quade knew there was going to be trouble.

CHAPTER 4

"Well, lookee here. If it ain't Mr. Passin' Through. This was the feller we told you about, Bren." Summers pointed at Quade.

The man named Bren said, "You got a name, stranger?"

"His name is Jack, Bren Holiday. Now what do you boys want to eat?" Lucy asked.

"Just haul rein there, Lucy," Holiday said to her. "I ain't done talkin' to our friend here. Seems he was trespassin' on Rockin' R range earlier today. Is that right, stranger?"

"Depends on what you call trespassin'," Quade replied.

"It's when rannies like you are on another man's range without their say so," Holiday stated.

"You mean like fencin' off another rancher from the water he has every right to?"

Holiday's eyes grew into slits and the smiles from his friends had disappeared. "Just who the hell are you?"

"You first."

"I'm Bren Holiday, foreman of the Rockin' R. Your turn."

"His name is Jack Quade. And you'd do well to leave him alone."

No one had noticed the man enter from the street and remain just inside the door. He was slim, dressed in dark pants and a blue shirt. But what made him stand out was the double-gun rig strapped about his narrow waist. Quade nodded. "Hello, Harry."

"Jack. Been a while."

"Yeah. Last I heard, you was in Colorado."

Crosby nodded. "That was a while ago."

"Just a minute, Crosby," Holiday said. "He was trespassin' on Rockin' R range earlier today. He needs to learn that he can't be doin' that."

Crosby looked at Quade. "Can't be trespassin', Jack."

"Point taken, Harry."

"Satisfied, Bren?" Crosby asked the foreman.

"Well, I—"

"Good." The gunfighter turned to Quade and pointed at the chair. "You mind?"

The Faraday man shook his head. "Free world, Harry."

"Lucy, could I get a coffee, please?"

Lucy had been watching everything unfold in silence. She blinked. "Sure, I'll bring the pot and a cup."

"You're looking well, Jack," Crosby said, turning his attention back to Quade.

The last time the two gunfighters had crossed paths was right before Quade had gone to work for Faraday. They were riding guard on a gold shipment that was hit by raiders. The fight had been brutal, and by the time the smoke had cleared, there were only two men still standing. Quade and Harry Crosby.

"Let's cut to the quick, Harry. We're cut from the same cloth, you and me."

A look of acceptance came to Crosby's face. "All right, why are you here, Jack?"

"Came to see my pa," Quade replied.

"Of course, Vince Quade."

"That's him."

"What were you doin' on Rockin' R range today?" Crosby asked.

"Just passin' through like I told your friends," Quade explained. "I had reached the fence when they found me."

"Ah, yes, the fence."

"It don't belong there, Harry."

Crosby nodded. "The boss has a piece of paper that says different, Jack."

"The paper is wrong, and your boss is a liar."

"If you say so."

"I do." Quade's voice was definite.

"Then you'll have to prove it," Crosby said.

"Maybe I will."

"That's your right, I guess."

Lucy brought out the coffee pot and the cup for Crosby. She poured the hot liquid in and looked at Quade. He pushed his cup over and she filled his too. Then Lucy walked away.

"What's he like, Harry?"

"The boss?"

"Yeah."

"He's a hungry man, Jack," Crosby said. "Land, money, cattle, he wants it all."

"Seems like I've come across the type before," Quade said. "Put a few in the ground, too."

"There is one thing different about Tom Rafferty, Jack," Crosby explained.

"What's that?"

"He has me."

Quade sipped his coffee. "Since we're talkin' plain, Harry, tell your boss to stay away from Double Q."

"I'll pass it on." Crosby climbed to his feet. "Been good talkin' to you, Jack. Just like old times."

Quade chuckled. "The hell it is."

Crosby touched the brim of his hat and turned away. He stopped at the table where the others were seated. "Remember, you were warned."

Then he left.

Quade went to the counter and paid for his meal. "It was better than Ma made. And she was a good cook."

Lucy turned a shade of red. "Are you staying around town?"

"Yes, ma'am."

"I told you to call me Lucy."

Quade was confused. Most females he came across treated him with fear and contempt. But Lucy seemed different. After she'd got over the shock at first, she seemed to calm somewhat.

"Lucy."

She handed him his change. "So, you know Harry Crosby."

"We've crossed paths before," Quade allowed.

"I could see that. In your profession..." she let her voice trail away.

"I get to meet all kinds," Quade finished for her. "And yes, in my profession."

"You don't seem like the rest of them," Lucy said.

"Other gunfighters?"

"Yes."

"Why would you say that? You hardly know me."

"I've seen a few in my time, Jack," Lucy explained. "I may be young, but I've been around."

Her words gave him at least one answer to his questions. The one about why she wasn't afraid. He nodded. "I'd best be goin'. I've got one more place to visit before I turn in."

"Goodnight, Jack."

"Goodnight, Lucy."

He started toward the door but was stopped by the bearded Summers, who stood up to block his path. "Goin' somewhere, Quade?"

"Out that door behind you."

"All in good time. First, we need you to understand that you're goin' to stay away from Rockin' R range."

"You really should listen to Crosby," Quade said quietly.

"Crosby ain't here, is he?" Summers sneered.

"Are you really goin' to push this?" Quade asked.

"Yeah, I am."

Quade sighed. "Fine. I will give you my assurance that I will stay away from the Rockin' R range."

Summers grinned at his friends. "See, that was easy."

"Now, if we're done, I'll be leavin'," the Faraday man said.

The smile on Summers broadened. "Sure, you can leave. Just crawl on out of here."

Behind him, Quade heard Lucy gasp. She knew there was no way that the man dressed in black was going to do it. "Deke, sit down or leave. Jack wasn't doing any harm. He's just going about his business."

"Shut up and stay out of this, Girl," Summers snarled.

A change came over Quade at the harshly spoken words. His eyes became pools of fire, and his face hardened like granite. "You called the party, Summers. Make your play."

"Jack, no," Lucy blurted out. "Don't do it."

"Him stirrin' the pot with me is one thing. I'll not abide by him addressin' you that way. There is no need."

"Do not make this about me," Lucy pleaded.

"It's not about you, Missy. It's about showin' him who runs things around here."

The tension continued to build until it was in need of a pressure release. That came in the guise of an older man carrying a shotgun and wearing a badge.

He entered through the saloon and stood just inside the door. In a loud voice, he demanded, "Is there a problem here?"

"This has nothin' to do with you, Carter," Holiday said. "Just teachin' Quade here how things are."

"Is that right?" the sheriff said casually. "Now I'm teachin' you how things are in my town. You and the two gunnies have one minute to leave, or I'll let you have both barrels. There will be no gunplay in my town."

Summers stared at Quade before glancing at the sheriff. The shotgun seemed to persuade the gunman of what he should do. "All right, Sheriff. This can wait."

Holiday and Cable got up from their seats and headed toward the door. Reluctantly, Summers followed them. Once they were gone, the sheriff said, "You come with me. I want to have a talk with you."

Quade nodded. "All right, Sheriff. If you insist."

The sheriff looked at Lucy. "I'll see you after."

She nodded. "Sure."

* * *

54

The sheriff's office was a small one-room affair with two barred cells and the sheriff's desk. On the wall was a typical gun rack, and in the corner was a wood heater for warmth and making coffee.

Closing the front door behind them, the sheriff said, "My name is Sheriff Lyle Carter."

"Jack Quade," Quade told him.

Carter had been about to sit down at his desk when he froze. "Vince Quade your old man?"

"He is."

Carter finished sitting. "What brings you back to Sagebrush Creek, Quade?"

"Just visitin'," the Faraday man said.

"I hope your father didn't send for your gun, Quade."

Quade shook his head. "I'm sure you have been around here long enough to know about me and my father."

The sheriff nodded slowly. "So, why here?"

"I heard there was trouble. We may not see eye to eye, but he's still my father. I'll stand by him through any storm."

"What was that in the dinin' room?"

"Summers thought he would push me into somethin'," Quade said. "He almost succeeded when you came along."

"Do you know him from somewhere?" Carter asked.

Quade shook his head. "First time I met him was today. Out at the fence along the creek."

"That damn fence."

"You do know that it isn't on the boundary?"

"The paper from the land office says it is."

Quade shook his head. "I lived on that land all my life, Sheriff, and the boundary has always been the creek. It gave access to both ranches."

"Well, accordin' to Amos Dent, that fence is in the right place."

"Who is Amos Dent?"

"Land agent."

"How long has he been here? I've never heard of him before."

Carter thought for a moment. "Maybe three years."

Quade nodded. "If you've finished with me, then I've somewhere else I have to be."

"Almost done, son. Almost done. Listen, I won't have any trouble in my town. I've seen what range wars can do, and it isn't pretty. I guess you have too. With the railroad comin' there'll be enough problems. My advice to you is leave."

"Are you orderin' me out, Sheriff?" Quade asked.

"No. But if you start any trouble, me and you are bound to butt heads."

"I'll remember that."

"See that you do."

The door to the office opened and Lucy entered the small space. Quade stared at her, but she ignored him. Instead, she focused on the sheriff. "I'm here for you to walk me home, Pa."

She was the sheriff's daughter.

Carter shook his head. "I've still to finish my rounds, Lucy, and Chuck is still out of town."

"I can do it if you like," Quade said.

"I thought you had somewhere to be," the sheriff said.

"A few minutes won't make any difference."

"It will be fine, Pa," Lucy said. "I'm sure Jack will be a perfect gentleman."

"It's not the gentleman side of him I'm worried about," Carter said dryly.

Lucy kissed her father on the cheek. "I'll see you when you get home."

"Don't wait up, girl. I could be late."

"Okay."

Once out on the boardwalk, Quade discovered that the evening had cooled markedly. Lucy pointed left along the street. "This way."

The first part of the walk was made in awkward silence, which was then broken by Lucy, who said, "If I knew you weren't going to talk to me, I would have walked home alone."

"Sorry, ma'am," Quade said.

"There you go again, calling me ma'am."

"Habit," he replied.

"Why are you here, Jack?" Lucy asked pointedly.

"I heard there was trouble at the ranch, and I decided it was time to come home and mend fences, as they say."

"You have fences to mend?"

"I do."

"With your father?"

Quade hesitated.

"I'm sorry," Lucy apologized. "I guess all the questions come from being a sheriff's daughter."

"Is that what you meant in the dinin' room when you said that you'd seen things? Gunfighters?"

"Yes."

"So it's just you and your Pa?"

Lucy nodded. "Uh, huh. Ma died when I was twelve. About ten years ago. She was shot down in a gunfight between railroad workers and cattlemen. Pa was the town sheriff. He blamed himself for not being able to stop it. It took him a while to get over it, but then he went back to work. Being a sheriff is all he knows how to do."

"I'm sorry."

"It isn't your fault, Jack. You weren't there."

They walked a little farther. Somewhere ahead of them, a dog barked but was silenced when a voice shouted at it.

"This is us just here," Lucy said.

The house was small and there was a picket fence out front. Quade said, "I'm guessin' the picket fence was you?"

"Yes. It gives it a homely feel."

"My ma liked picket fences. We had one once. When she died, Pa ripped it down because it reminded him of her."

"I'm sorry, Jack."

"Don't be. It was a long time ago," he said dismissively.

Lucy's eyes widened. "Say, something just came to me. Your sister is Mary Quade."

"Yes, she is."

"Mary and I are friends. She is a lovely person, Jack."

"Gets it from Ma. Not that I've seen her in a long time. The last would have been when Pa and I fought, and I rode away."

"You're going to see her tonight, aren't you?"

"That was the plan."

The sound of hoofbeats drew their attention. A rider was coming along the street on a tired horse. He saw the pair and turned the horse toward them. The rider removed his hat, and he said, "Hello, Lucy."

"Hello, Chuck," Lucy replied.

The rider adjusted his position in the saddle and Quade saw the deputy's star. "New friend?"

"You could say that. This is Jack Quade, Mary's brother. Jack, this is Deputy Chuck Tobin."

Quade nodded. "Deputy."

Tobin's face remained stoic. "Quade."

"Jack was just walking me home," Lucy said.

"I must say I'm surprised, Lucy. Keepin' company with a hired gun of his reputation."

"Jack is being quite the gentleman, Chuck. Besides, Pa knows."

"And he is okay with it?"

"Why wouldn't he be?"

"I'm surprised, Lucy. But now that you are home, I'm sure Quade can go on his way."

"I'm sure Jack can make up his own mind," Lucy said abruptly.

"Darn it, Lucy. He—"

"Goodnight, Chuck," she said dismissively. "I'm sure you have other things to do."

The expression on the deputy's face grew annoyed and he sawed on the horse's reins, making it back up. Then he said, "I'll see you tomorrow."

"Not if you're in that mood, you won't," Lucy shot back at him.

He glared at Quade and then gave his tired mount a sharp kick before disappearing down the street.

"I think I may have ruffled someone's feathers," Quade said.

"He'd like to think he has his brand on me, but he doesn't."

Quade reached up and touched his hat brim. "Good evenin', Lucy."

"Good evening, Jack."

* * *

Quade knocked on the door of Mrs. Hamblin's boarding house and waited for the door to be answered. A gray-haired woman with a round belly and an aversion to height answered and stared at the man in front of her. She tilted her head and said, "I figure I should know you, but a name escapes me."

"Jack Quade, Mrs. Hamblin."

Recognition came to her face. "Of course it is. How are you, Jack?"

"Fine, Mrs. Hamblin. I'm here to see Mary, if that is possible?"

"She's in her room. I have a rule, no male visitors in the rooms, but you don't count." She stepped aside. "Come in."

He entered the boarding house and stopped inside the door. Mrs. Hamblin closed it and nodded toward the stairs. "At the top of the stairs, turn left, it is the second door on the right."

"Thank you, ma'am."

"Um, Jack."

"Ma'am?"

"Your gun. Please leave it down here."

Quade nodded and unbuckled his gun belt. He hung it from the hat stand in the corner then asked, "Is that all right, Mrs. Hamblin?"

"Yes, fine, thank you."

Quade climbed the stairs and found his sister's room. He knocked on the door and heard her voice say, "Be right there."

Quade waited and then heard the key in the lock. He removed his hat as the door swung open. Mary stood before him, as pretty as he remembered her. Dark hair, brown eyes, slim waist. She stared at him. "Jack?"

"Yes, Mary, it's me."

Without hesitation, she launched herself at him. Her arms wrapped around his neck, and she pulled him close. "Oh, Jack. You're home. Let me look at you."

Stepping back, she studied him. "You've changed."

He nodded. "How about we get out of the hallway and talk some."

Mary grabbed his hand and pulled him inside. "Of course."

Her room was small and neat, and Quade soon found a chair. Mary sat on the bed. "Have you been to see Pa?"

He nodded. "Yes."

"How was he?"

"About as you'd expect. He ordered me off the ranch."

Mary looked sad. "Oh, Jack. I was hoping that time might have healed old wounds."

"Maybe while I've been gone another one has opened," Quade said.

"Why a gunfighter, Jack?" Mary asked. "Of all the things you could have done."

"I didn't choose to be a hired gun, Mary. It just happened."

"It's a terrible way to earn money." She paused. "Why are you here, Jack?"

"I thought you were glad to see me?" Quade asked.

"Oh, I am, but I can't help wondering why now?" There was concern in her voice.

He thought about lying to his sister, but he couldn't. Every time he looked at her, he saw his mother. "If I tell you, Mary, it must remain a secret."

Mary looked puzzled. "Of course."

Quade reached into his boot and took out the wallet. He passed it to his sister, and she opened it. After a brief moment, she stared at her brother. "What is it?"

"For the past four years I've been workin' as a detective for the Faraday Security Service."

"A detective?"

"Yes, we mainly investigate for the railroads."

"But why—" Mary stopped. She then answered her own question. "The surveyor?"

"Yes."

"I thought you were here because of what was happening in the valley."

"No. But while we're talkin' about that, tell me what is happenin'."

"Tom Rafferty and his hired guns are pushing everyone out of the valley. He's trying to get all the land before the railroad comes through."

"How long has it been public knowledge about the rail line?" Quade asked.

"A couple of years."

"About the same time Rafferty came to the valley, Charlie told me."

Mary's head bobbed. "Yes. Since then, the smaller ranchers have been pushed out. It's only the bigger ones that are left."

"I saw the fence," Quade told his sister.

"It's terrible. He's blocking Pa from water so he can't run the cattle he needs. Meanwhile, the bills are piling up and he's behind in payments."

"What is the bank sayin'?"

"They've given him three weeks to get it caught up."

"Can he sell some cattle?" Quade asked.

"We haven't had much rain. The cattle are in poor condition because of lack of grass."

"What about the free graze over by Bobcat Spring?" Quade inquired.

"Rafferty has claimed that too," Mary explained. "It's been fenced."

"But that's free range."

Mary shook her head. "Not according to the land agent who sold it to Rafferty."

"All of it?" Quade asked.

Mary nodded. "Yes."

Quade was beginning to realize just how bad things were in the valley. This was why Faraday had chosen him for the job. This Rafferty was taking up all the water to use it as a way of forcing the others out. "The creek that comes in from the north?"

"Ironwood Creek?"

"That's it."

"Rafferty is building a dam on his property on the creek. It's almost dry."

"Darn it."

They talked for a while longer before Quade decided it was time to head back to the saloon. "I'll try to see you tomorrow, Mary."

"Be careful, Jack," she replied, giving him a hug and a kiss on the cheek.

"By the way, I met a friend of yours tonight. Lucy Carter."

"Lucy? She's lovely, Jack. Shame that she can't shake herself of that deputy."

With a grunt, Quade said, "I met him too."

"Keep an eye on him, Jack. The man is a hothead."

"I promise."

After they said their goodbyes, Quade left the boarding house and walked straight into trouble.

CHAPTER 5

The evening air was cold and no longer carried the sounds of daily life he had heard before visiting his sister. Most of the citizens were now indoors. Quade remained aware of his surroundings as he walked along the boardwalk toward the saloon. As he drew closer to it, the noise filtering out from within grew in volume.

Quade's innate sense of danger, honed over many years, drew his attention to an alley opening between the saddlery and gunsmith across the street. It was bathed in shadow, and beyond the mouth, the darkness was total, impenetrable. The Faraday man frowned and stopped suddenly. A flash and crash of a shot came from the alley, the muzzle flame illuminating the shooter standing there.

Fanning Quade's face, the bullet passed in front of his nose. His life had been spared by the sudden stop. The Faraday man's hand went down and came back up filled with Colt. He fired at the alley mouth twice before running across the street.

There was no return gunfire, nor was there a bushwhacker. Quade guessed that whoever had fired at him had run off. Quade slipped into the alley, keeping the saddlery wall at his back, making sure to stay out of the middle. Behind him, voices could be heard growing louder as people were drawn by the sound of the gunfire.

When Quade was halfway along, the alley exploded with the roar of two more shots. The bullets burned through the darkness, missing Quade by a narrow margin. The Colt in his hand fired twice in response, and this time was rewarded with a cry of pain.

Quade paused, and when no more shots were forthcoming, he eased forward. The shooter was at the other end of the alley, lying in the dirt.

Behind Quade, a voice demanded, "What the hell is goin' on?"

It was Chuck Tobin. The Faraday man said, "Someone decided they wanted to take a shot at me."

"Is that you, Quade? I knew you was goin' to be trouble. You're under arrest."

"You're gettin' ahead of yourself, Deputy," Quade replied. "I was the one bein' shot at."

"By who?"

"Feller lyin' here in the alley."

"Damn it. Someone get a lantern," Tobin snapped.

"What's goin' on?" Carter asked as he pushed through the crowd.

"Someone took—" Quade started, but Tobin cut him off.

"Quade has killed a man. I told you it was a bad idea lettin' him stay, Lyle."

"Button your lip, Deputy," Carter snapped. "Is someone gettin' a lantern?"

"Yes," came the answer from the crowd. "Hector just went."

"Right, until then, Quade, tell me what happened."

Quade repeated what had happened after leaving the boarding house. Just as he was finishing, the man arrived with the lantern. Carter took it and lowered it over the dead shooter. "Deke Summers. Damnation. Just like somethin' he would do."

Both of Quade's bullets had taken the hired gun in the chest. Carter said, "All right, Quade, it looks like you're in the clear."

"You're not goin' to lock him up?" Tobin asked incredulously.

"No, I'm not." Carter turned to the gathered towns-folk at the opening of the alley. "All right, you lot. Go home."

As the crowd started to disperse, Quade stepped past Carter, but Tobin blocked his path. "I'll be watchin' you, killer."

"Don't crowd me, Deputy." There was a hardness in Quade's voice.

"Damn it, Chuck, go and find the undertaker."

With the deputy's departure, Carter said by way of explanation, "He's a little keen."

Quade nodded. "Just make sure he understands, Sheriff. I won't be crowded. Especially when I done nothin' wrong."

"He'll get the message, Quade. Just stay out of any more trouble."

"I'll do what I can."

* * *

The log fire in the Rocking R ranch house had burned low and Rafferty was seated in a large leather chair listening to Harry Crosby talk. Rafferty wasn't that old in years. At forty-two, he was still in the prime of his life.

"What is he doing here?" Rafferty asked Crosby.

"I figure he's here for his old man."

"I don't like that, Harry. He could interfere with my plans."

"From what I heard, he and old Vince aren't on the best of terms. He might not want anythin' to do with him."

"What do you suggest we do?" Rafferty asked.

"We wait and see. If we start any gun trouble, we'll have Carter snoopin' around."

"You can take care of Carter," Rafferty said.

"If I need to. But he's got issues lookin' for whoever shot that surveyor."

"Yes, mighty inconvenient, that."

"Look at it as a blessin'," Crosby said. "It gives you more time to acquire the land before you need it."

Rafferty was about to speak when Bren Holiday and Monte Cable burst through the living room door. Rafferty could see by their expressions that something was wrong. "What is it?"

"Deke is dead. Quade killed him," Holiday blustered.

"What happened?"

"Quade got under his skin and Deke didn't like it. We tried to talk him out of it, but—"

"I warned you what would happen if you braced Quade," Crosby said.

"He didn't brace him," Cable said.

"Son of a bitch," Crosby growled. "He tried to bush-whack him?"

"Yes."

The hired gun shook his head. "About what I would

expect from someone like him. So, Deke got what he deserved."

Holiday stared at Crosby. "He was part of the Rockin' R brand."

"He was a backshootin' coward."

"Enough," Rafferty said. "The man is dead. Now move along. Harry, I want you to keep an eye on Quade. Find out why he's really here. If he is going to interfere with my plans, he'll have to be dealt with."

"You're the boss."

"Yes, I am," Rafferty said. "Now, I want no trouble tomorrow. After all, it is an important day for me. Hopefully the stage will be on time. I can't have my future wife arriving to a mess of trouble. That is for you to control, Harry."

"You want me to watch Quade or ride herd on your men?"

"Both."

The man didn't want much. Crosby was a hired gun, not a nursemaid. "Isn't that what you have a foreman for?"

"I hired you to follow orders, Harry. So do it."

The hired gun nodded slowly. "Is there anythin' else?"

"No."

"Then I'll turn in."

* * *

The next morning dawned cool and clear. Quade had an early breakfast of bacon and eggs while the news filtered through Sagebrush Creek about the killing the night before. Lucy was working but seemed a little distant. He figured she was still coming to terms with the fact that he'd killed a man last night.

Once he was done, Quade went along to the telegraph office. He was greeted by a thin man with virtually no hair. "Morning, sir."

"Mornin'. I'm checking to see if there is a message for me. Jack Quade."

"Yes, sir, I think one—" the telegrapher stopped and looked at his face.

"Is there a problem?"

"You're him."

"Him?"

"Jack Quade. You shot Deke Summers last night."

"Only because he was tryin' to shoot me. Is that goin' to be a problem?"

"No, no." The telegrapher picked up a folded piece of paper from his desk and handed it over. "It makes no sense whatsoever."

Quade read the coded message. The surveyors would be on the noon stage. "I need to send a message."

The telegrapher passed Quade a small slip of paper and a pencil stub. "Write your message out and I'll send it for you?"

Quade wrote the message and passed the paper over. The telegrapher looked at it and frowned. "This makes no sense, the same as the other."

"It will to the receiver."

"Faraday Security—Oh, Lord."

"One last thing. That message is confidential. If I hear anythin' about it, I'll be back here, and I swear I'll take it out of your hide. Do you understand?"

The man swallowed hard. "Yes, sir. Do you expect there will be a return message?"

"No, but if there is, you find me, and only me." Quade placed some money on the counter. "Will this do?"

"That is a lot too much."

"Consider the extra a little more incentive to forget."

After leaving the telegraph office, enjoying the warms of the sunshine, Quade sauntered along the street to the schoolhouse. Class was in, and he climbed the stairs and peeked in through the door, trying to remain out of sight. He saw Mary engaged with her class. They were learning about math. Sensing his presence, she looked directly at him then held up a finger, directing him to wait. Then she spoke to one of the older girls in the schoolroom. "Jessie, can you run through the times tables with the rest of the class while I tend to something?"

Jessie rose from her seat. "Yes, miss."

Mary hurried over to where Quade stood and whispered, "What are you doing here, Jack?"

"I just wanted to see what you do," he replied.

She took his arm and guided him out onto the veranda. "Class has a break in an hour, I'll meet you at the dining room for a coffee."

"Sounds good."

"Fantastic. Now go before the class sees you, or I'll be answering questions about you all day."

"Yes, miss."

Mary slapped him playfully on the arm. "Go."

* * *

Mary was already in the dining room when he arrived. Lucy was sitting across from her, talking animatedly. Mary looked at Quade as he entered, a blaze of anger in her eyes. "When were you going to tell me?"

"If you're talkin' about the shootin', I haven't had time to tell you. And just so you know, he tried to bushwhack me from an alley." He stared at Lucy. "Didn't your father tell you that?"

Lucy turned red with embarrassment.

"Oh, Jack," Mary moaned. "I was hoping you being here would be different. But obviously not. When Pa finds out, he'll be even more against your presence."

"What would you prefer I do, Mary? Let him shoot me?"

"Don't be silly."

Quade went to get up, but Mary grabbed his hand. "Don't, Jack. Please stay."

He sat back down and turned his attention to Lucy. "It wasn't your father that told you, was it? It was the deputy that is keen on you."

He thought she was about to protest when Lucy nodded slowly and sighed. "Yes."

"Oh, Lucy," said Mary. "How could you—"

"Easy, Mary. It's not her fault."

Lucy said, "I'd better get back to the kitchen. I'm sorry, Jack."

Jack nodded. "Maybe you can show me by allowing me to walk you home again."

She smiled. "Maybe."

Watching her go, he then saw the expression on Mary's face. "What?"

"Jack, don't."

"Don't what?"

"She is a nice girl, Jack. She deserves someone just as nice. Not a..."

Her voice trailed away.

"Not someone who makes a livin' by his gun?"

Mary gave him a horrified look and turned red. "I didn't say that."

"I'm goin' out to the ranch this afternoon. Do you want to come?"

"To keep you and Pa apart?" Mary asked skeptically.

"He might be a mite calmer if you're there, Mary," Quade explained. "Maybe long enough for me to explain what I'm doin' here in Sagebrush Creek."

"I finish school at one."

"Horse or buggy?" Quade asked.

"Horse. I'm not that much of a lady."

"I'll see you at one then."

"What about the coffee?" Mary asked.

"I'd better order one."

* * *

On the veranda outside the saloon, Quade stood waiting for the stage, which was expected soon. The day was warming up considerably and the prospect of rain seemed incomprehensible. Looking around, Quade spotted Harry Crosby across the street outside the general store, leaning against an awning post, smoking. Crosby saw Quade watching him and reached up to touch his hat brim. The Faraday man nodded. He was certain now that the gunfighter was in town to keep an eye on him. He'd have to be careful.

The sound of multiple hoofbeats drew Quade's attention toward the end of the main street. He saw three riders and a horse-drawn buggy coming toward him. One of the riders he'd seen before. Monte Cable. Which, through a process of deduction, made the man in the buggy Tom Rafferty. The other two, Quade didn't know.

They pulled up across the street in front of where Crosby was standing. Climbing from the buggy, they started to talk among themselves. After a few moments, their gazes turned to Quade. A few more words were passed back and forth, then Rafferty started across the street toward where Quade stood, Crosby following him.

The rancher stopped in front of Quade and said, "You killed one of my men last night."

It was a statement, not a question. The Faraday man nodded. "Seemed like the thing to do at the time, considerin' the circumstances."

"I would have done the same thing had I been in your shoes, Quade. I'm just makin' sure that you understand, Summers was not in any way actin' on my orders. I'm just happy to live peaceful with everyone around me."

"Then take down the fence," Quade said.

"The fence? Oh, yes, the fence. That fence is on my land, marking the boundary."

"The boundary has always been the creek," Quade replied. "There was no need for a fence. It gave both ranches access to water."

"I'm sure if you check with Amos Dent at the land office, he will clear the matter up for you."

"The way he cleared it up for you?"

"I'm just exercising my legal right," Rafferty said. His smile was cool, mirthless. "Surely you understand that?"

"What I understand, Rafferty, is that you're up to something. But if you figure you can ride over my father to get it, think again. Like you, I don't want trouble. But if you push, I'll push back even harder."

"I do believe you would. From what Harry Crosby says, you're quite capable when it comes to using a gun."

"If Harry says so." Quade caught sight of the deputy across the street, watching on with interest. "Is there anythin' else?"

"No, I think that is all. Just so things are clear."

The Faraday man nodded. "They're about as clear as a muddy waterhole. But I guess you already knew that."

Rafferty smiled. "Be seeing you, Quade."

The rancher turned and walked away, but Crosby stayed. He said, "What he said was true, Jack. He had nothin' to do with Summers. He just got a burr under his saddle and tried it on for himself."

"What about the murdered surveyor?" Quade asked.

"What do you mean?" Crosby was confused.

"Your boss might not want the railroad to come across his land. Seems like he could stop that if he tried."

"By killin' the surveyor? You got that wrong. The boss wants the railroad. He can see it bringin' in a lot of money."

Quade thought for a moment. If what Crosby said was true, then Rafferty had no reason to have killed Sam Roberts.

"What's with the interest in the dead surveyor?" Crosby asked.

"Just figured if a man was bent on forcin' ranchers off their land, then he wouldn't want the railroad comin' across it either."

Crosby nodded slowly. "Stay out of trouble, Jack."

"You too, Cros."

The gunfighter turned and walked away.

Five minutes later, and running ten minutes late, the stagecoach pulled by a six-up team thundered into the main street of Sagebrush Creek, steel-rimmed wheels crunching on the rough surface.

And things became even more interesting.

CHAPTER 6

The horses were lathered with sweat, and when the driver managed to stop them on the correct spot, they stomped and snorted.

"Sagebrush Creek, folks," the driver called out as the shotgun messenger started to climb down. He went to the door and opened it.

"End of the line, folks—ma'am."

The coach rocked and a woman appeared. She was wearing a red and black dress and a wide-brimmed hat. Helped down by the shotgun messenger, once her feet touched the ground, she looked around. Quade took in a sharp breath when he saw her face.

Five years had elapsed since he'd last seen her. Where was it? Sharpe's Bend? He'd ridden into town with the intention of passing through. But that night, a trail crew had arrived in town and began whooping it up. Around midnight, all hell broke loose, and the sheriff and his deputy were killed in a shootout with the crew. By the following morning, they had the town treed with no one to do anything about it.

No one except for Quade. So, when the mayor of Sharpe's Bend had come to him for help, he'd refused. Then, in a desperate move, the mayor had sent his wife, hoping to persuade him. A pretty twenty-three-year-old former painted lady from Chicago. At first, Quade had not been moved, not willing to get involved. But she eventually wore him down and he relented.

By the time Quade was finished, six men lay dead, and the rest were run out of town. The episode became known as The Sharpe's Bend Cleanout.

Once the gun smoke had cleared, most expected Quade to ride out. But that didn't happen. Instead, he stayed on and took advantage of the situation with the mayor's wife. A month, it was about the longest he'd stayed in one place. At the end of that month, the mayor had come after him with a gun. Quade killed him in self-defense. Then he rode out of town, leaving Abigail Davis on her knees in the dust, begging him to stay.

Now she was in Sagebrush Creek. But why?

Abigail looked in his direction. She saw him. He saw the recognition in her eyes.

"Abigail?"

The woman turned her head and stared at Rafferty. He hugged her. "It is good to meet you. Finally."

"Hello, Tom," Quade heard her say. "I've been looking forward to this for the past month, since the wedding was all decided."

"I'm sure you'll be very happy at the ranch," Rafferty said. He hooked an arm through hers and started walking her across the street.

About halfway across, Abigail looked up briefly before continuing with her fiancé.

In the meantime, two men had climbed down from the stage. They watched as the driver passed their survey equipment from up top. The stocky man said, "Be careful with that. It's the only one we have."

The driver paused. "I been unloadin' this blamed stage for as long as I can remember. I don't need you to tell me how to do it." He spat a stream of tobacco juice, causing the surveyor to jump back.

"I say, watch it."

They gathered their things, and one of them looked at Quade. "Good afternoon, sir. My name is Dennis Franks. Could you tell me the best place to stay in town?"

"Quade. Here is good. Not much else."

Franks recognized the name. "Then here will do. This is my partner, Hamish Grimshaw."

Quade took one look and knew the man immediately. Grimshaw wasn't a surveyor, he was a Faraday man. Quade said, "Whatever."

Then he turned and walked back inside.

* * *

Meanwhile, across the street, the arrival of the surveyors had not gone unnoticed. Rafferty helped Abigail into the buggy, and on the way back around to climb in, he said to Crosby, "Have someone keep an eye on them. I want to know where they go."

"I'll take care of it."

Rafferty pulled himself up into the buggy and smiled at his wife-to-be. "Are you ready, my dear?"

"Yes, Tom. Take me home."

"I do like the sound of that," Rafferty said.

"Me too."

* * *

77

Quade heard them thumping up the stairs and along the hallway from his room. He waited until he heard them stop and poked his head out into the hallway. Both men looked at him and nodded. Then Quade went back inside.

Five minutes later, there was a soft knock on the door and Quade opened it. Franks and Grimshaw filed in, and Quade locked the door behind them.

"Good to see you, Jack," Grimshaw said. "You met briefly down on the street, but this is Dennis Franks. Franks, Jack Quade."

The pair shook hands. Quade asked, "What happened to the second surveyor?"

"Faraday figured that I'd be more suited for the job," Grimshaw explained. "What's the lay of the land like?"

"I'm still not sure," Quade said honestly. "The person I thought might be good for the killin' of Roberts don't exactly fit in the hole. He wants the railroad to come. Getting' the ranchers off the right of way has him standin' to make a lot of money."

"But no one knows the route until the survey is done," Franks pointed out.

"It doesn't matter. It'll have to come down the valley. Rafferty just needs to claim it all for himself."

"Many ranches?" Grimshaw asked.

"The Double Q, Lazy S, and the Rockin' R, which Rafferty already owns."

"Faraday said you had family out here."

"Double Q. It's situated between the Rockin' R and the Lazy S. I'm headed out to the Double Q to talk to my pa today. Give him a heads-up. What is the railroad offerin'?"

Franks said, "I've been told fifty dollars per acre plus free transportation for all cattle needed to be shipped."

Quade nodded. "There is always a little wiggle room, Franks. You can do better than that. Bring it up to a hundred."

"I can't do that, Jack. I can come up to seventy-five. And that's only because he is your family."

"Eighty-five and I'll make sure he signs when the time is right."

Franks nodded. "All right. Eighty-five."

"Have you got papers to draw up?"

"I've got them with me."

"Fine. Start on the Double Q tomorrow."

Franks nodded. "Then that's what we'll do."

* * *

If it was at all possible, the grass seemed to have browned off even more since he'd ridden through yesterday. The roan was happy to be out of the stall and showed it. Beside them rode Mary on a bay mare. Looking around at the dun landscape, she said, "Every time I come out here it seems to be drier and drier."

"Pa needs the water from the creek."

Mary nodded. "Yes, but with the fence, there is no hope of that."

"I'll have a word with the land agent," Quade told her.

"What can you do, Jack. It is all documented."

"What happened to Bob Jenkins?" Quade asked.

"The Broken J, owner?"

"Yeah."

"He died, Jack. He was out bringing in a small herd of heifers and they ran over him."

"Convenient," Quade said, shaking his head.

"That's what Pa said. Jenkins died and Rafferty

moved in. About the same time as the railroad was announced."

"And the Broken J at the mouth of the valley, right where the railroad will come through."

"All that's missing is the piece of string to tie it all together," Mary finished.

"However, Rafferty isn't the man who killed the surveyor," Quade said. "He wants the railway. He stands to earn a lot of money."

"What about Pa?"

"Him too if he'll allow it. Mind you, if he doesn't deal, the land can be taken anyway. So it is in his best interests."

"I hope he sees it that way."

The roan hopped sideways. Quade patted his neck. "Stop that."

The horse snorted.

"Mary, has Pa ever talked about it?" Quade asked his sister.

"You know Pa. He's never changed."

"Well, he'll need to talk about it now."

"Yes, he will," Mary said grimly.

* * *

Crosby rode into the ranch yard and tied his horse to the corral post. He strode purposefully toward the ranch house across the packed earth, worn hard by years of horse traffic.

Reaching the gate in the picket fence, he shoved it open, then stomped up the steps onto the veranda, spurs jingling.

With a push, the front door opened, and he walked inside. The doorway opened into a spacious living room with a large ornate mantel and fireplace. Crosby pulled up short. Rafferty and Abigail were lost in each other's arms, sharing a passionate moment. The rancher broke away from his wife-to-be and glared at the gunman.

"Haven't you heard of knocking, damn it?" he snarled.

"Sorry, boss, but I needed to see you."

"I thought you were meant to be in town?"

"I was, but the problem isn't."

Rafferty sighed angrily. He looked at Abigail and said, "Please excuse me, my dear. I'll be right back."

"Of course, Tom."

The two men walked outside and into the main yard, away from the house. "What is it?"

"Quade rode out of town with his sister. I'm guessin' they're headed toward the ranch."

Rafferty thought for a few moments. "I'm thinking it's time we paid Vince Quade another visit. Get some of the men together. Including Holiday."

"Boss, if Holiday goes, he's bound to try somethin' with Quade."

"Maybe. Let's see how tough he really is."

Rafferty went back into the ranch house and found Abigail waiting for him. He gave her a wan smile and said, "I'm sorry, Abbey, but I need to tend to some business."

"I hope there isn't any trouble, Tom?" she asked, concerned.

"No, no trouble. Just ranch stuff. While I'm gone, why don't you have a look around? Get acquainted with the ranch house and the yard."

Abigail smiled and kissed him. "Don't be gone too long."

"I don't plan to be."

81

* * *

Mary and Quade rode into the Double Q ranch yard under the watchful eyes of two ranch hands. Lefty Powers and Lucas Howard, the foreman, were working a young horse in the corral.

"Hello, Luke," Mary called over to him. "Is Pa around?"

"Howdy, Miss Mary. I think he's inside."

"Thank you."

"Who's your friend?" Howard asked.

"This is my brother, Jack."

The foreman's expression changed. "Figured it was."

"Jack, Luke is Pa's foreman," Mary explained.

"Pleased to meet you, Luke," Quade said.

Howard ignored him. "Your Pa left instructions to say that if'n he showed here that he was to be ordered off."

"We're here to see Pa, Luke," Mary said.

"He was mighty firm with his words."

Things might have taken a turn if Charlie Brown hadn't chosen that particular time to intervene. "Let it go, Luke. I'll take care of it."

Howard nodded. "Better you than me, Charlie."

Mary walked over to the cook and wrapped her arms around him. "Hello, Charlie."

"Hello, girl."

"I'm a grown woman, you know?" Mary said.

"To me, you'll always be that little girl I watched grow up." Charlie turned his gaze to Quade. "I was hopin' you'd come back, son. Always knew you weren't one to give up."

"We need to see Pa, Charlie," Quade said.

"Yeah. Follow me."

He stomped the dust from his boots and pushed

through the front door, escorting them inside the ranch house. The living room looked exactly the same as the day Quade had left. Hell, it had been the same ever since his mother's passing.

Squeaky floorboards in the dining room betrayed the passage of Vince on his way from the kitchen to the living room. Stepping into the room, he pulled up short at the sight of the two new arrivals. His top lip curling in a sneer, he growled, "You don't belong here. Get the hell out."

"Pa, he's here to talk," Mary said plaintively.

"I don't care what he's here for, Mary. He is never to step foot on this ranch again."

"Oh, Pa, I hoped things would have changed over time. But obviously not. Maybe Jack didn't hit you hard enough the first time."

The old man's face turned red. "I'll not take any lip from you, girl. If you don't like it, you can leave too."

"Damn it, Vince," Charlie snapped. "Just hear the boy out."

The old man looked at his son. "All right, speak your piece and then get."

"The railway is comin' through—"

"I already know that, damn it."

"They're comin' out to Double Q tomorrow to start surveyin'," Quade said.

"Are they now. Says who?"

"From what I can see, you could really use the money, Pa," Quade said.

"I need water more."

"They're offerin' eighty-five dollars an acre," Quade said.

"That much?"

"Yes. I figure they'll need around two hundred acres

83

between the Rockin' R and the Lazy S. It comes to seventeen thousand dollars."

"Seventeen?" Vince pondered the amount.

"The surveyor will have papers for you to sign tomorrow."

Vince gave his son a puzzled look. "Why are you here, Jack? You left here swearin' black and blue you'd never come back. Now here you are with that damn gun of yours, havin' already killed a man since your return."

"Summers was tryin' to kill me," Quade said.

"It's true, Pa," Mary said. "It's all over town."

"Still don't explain why you are here."

"Let's just say I'm workin'," Quade told his father.

"Workin' at what? Gunslingin'?"

"I can't tell you too much, Pa. Not yet."

"Jack—" Mary started, but was interrupted by the sound of approaching hoofbeats.

The Quade family turned to the window in time to watch riders coming into the yard. Rafferty was at their head, followed by Harry Crosby. Also with them was Holiday, Cable, and another gun called Toby Jones. The group drew up in front of the house, where the others now stood. In the corral, Quade saw Powers and Howard moving to see what was happening.

Vince Quade stared at Rafferty and said, "What do you want, Rafferty?"

"I came to talk, Vince."

"Fine. Say what you came to say and get the hell off my land."

"I came to renew my offer. Last time I'll do it, Quade. Five dollars an acre."

"You've said your piece," Vince said. "Now leave."

"You'll not even consider it?" Rafferty asked.

"No."

"I'm surprised, Vince. Will you be able to make payment to the bank?"

Quade glanced at his sister. The look of surprise on her face was enough. Vince said, "I'll make it."

"In a week?"

"Just sell it now, old man," Holiday growled. "It'll save us pushin' you off when the time comes."

"What the hell is he talkin' about?" Vince snarled.

Rafferty gave the smile of a snake. "I forgot to mention, I bought your loan from the bank. You either make the payment or you're off."

"It'll give me great pleasure to move you," Holiday said, joining his boss's smile.

Quade stepped forward. "Why don't you try it now?"

Holiday shook his head. "Uh, uh. You're mighty tough with that hog leg backin' you."

The Faraday man started unbuckling his gun belt. "If that's all you're worried about, I can accommodate you."

"Pa, stop them," Mary pleaded.

Old Vince shook his head. "Not my dance, daughter."

Quade passed his gun to Charlie, who was watching on from beside his boss.

He looked at Crosby. "I expect you to keep the others in check, Harry."

"It'll be a fair fight, Jack. As fair as it can be."

Quade turned to meet Holiday, but the big man was already out of his saddle and moving. His body crashed into Quade and knocked him backward. The foreman kept his feet, but Quade sprawled across the hard-packed earth of the yard.

Holiday came in to take out the Faraday man while he was down. His boot rose and came down savagely.

Quade rolled to the side as the boot struck in a puff of dust. Holiday grunted with anger as he realized he'd missed. Quade, however, lashed out with his boot and took the foreman's legs.

This gave him time to come to his feet.

Opposite him, Holiday rolled away and did the same. For a big man, he moved with catlike grace. Quade cocked his fists and closed the gap between them. Holiday welcomed him with a wild swing.

The Faraday man went under it and ripped a blow to the man's stomach. Holiday grunted, but it felt like hitting a tree. The blow jarred through Quade's arm and into his shoulder.

Quade struck again, this time to the jaw. Holiday staggered back, shook his head, and attacked.

He came in close and broke through Quade's defense. A blow landed on the Faraday man's jaw, and it was his turn to stagger.

Holiday stepped in and followed him, landing two more blows to the body. Then came another crunching blow to the jaw that knocked Quade down.

Stunned and with his hat dislodged, Quade was grabbed by the hair and dragged to his feet. He tasted blood in his mouth. Holiday hit him again, and this time, Quade staggered back to the water trough. His legs buckled on contact and he went in with a large splash.

Quade felt rough hands on him as Holiday worked hard to keep him beneath the surface. Mary watched on in horror at her brother's plight.

Through the tumult of the trough water, the Faraday man caught a glimpse of the grinning foreman. He raised his hand, fingers straight, and managed to poke Holiday in the eye.

The foreman reeled back with a howl of pain. Coughing and spluttering, Quade hauled himself out of the trough. Holiday was bent over, clawing at his face.

Quade stepped forward and kicked him hard in the stomach. The foreman sank to his knees.

Quade went to kick him again, but Holiday twisted and grabbed his boot. With a forceful shove, he sent the soaked Faraday man backward.

Holiday scrambled to his feet, blowing hard. He caught sight of Quade and let out a guttural growl as he charged forward, dropping a shoulder into Quade's stomach. His powerful arms enveloped him as he picked him up.

Holiday drove him back, slamming Quade into the rails of the corral. The Faraday man let out a grunt of pain, and when Holiday released him, he buckled.

Stepping back, Holiday looked at the man on his knees before him. He glanced at Rafferty, whose slight nod indicated his permission to finish it.

The foreman spat on the ground. "I'm goin' to beat you to a pulp, Gunslinger."

Quade, head down and seemingly beaten, muttered something that Holiday didn't catch. Inclining his head, the foreman bent down and asked, "What did you say?"

Quade lifted his head so they were face-to-face. "I said you talk too much."

The response from Quade was brutal. His head came forward, and his bony forehead smashed across the foreman's nose.

Blood splattered and Holiday staggered back. He came erect, but so did Quade, who followed the big man and belted him with savage hammer blows.

Off to the side, Vince watched his son respond and rode every blow with his facial expressions. Jones, the hired gun, dropped a hand to his weapon when he saw Holiday starting to be beaten.

He caught sight of Crosby, who shook his head in

silent admonition. Jones let it go. Rafferty watched intently, and as soon as he saw his man losing, he grew angry.

Quade finished the fight with two more solid punches, and Holiday lay bleeding in the dirt.

Sucking in gulps of air, Quade turned to Rafferty. "Take your trash and get gone, Rafferty."

"We're not done by a long sight," the rancher growled. "You have one week to pay your outstanding debt. After that, I'll move my cattle onto the range."

"The hell you will," Vince growled.

"You've been warned, Vince."

"Get off!" The roared order made Mary flinch.

The interlopers managed to get Holiday onto his horse and the Rocking R riders left the Double Q head-quarters.

"What loan, Pa?" Quade asked, turning to face his father.

"It has nothin' to do with you," Vince snapped.

"It does if I can help."

"I don't want your help."

"Vince had to borrow from the bank last year to—" the cook started.

"Shut your yap, Charlie," Vince snarled. "If you want to keep workin' for me."

"It don't much matter if I got no one to cook for, does it?" Charlie shot back at his friend.

"Will the seventeen thousand help?" Quade asked.

"What good is it when I don't have it?"

"I'll get it for you."

"I don't need your help."

"You are a stubborn old man," Mary snapped. "Your own son wants to help you, probably the only person who can, and you throw his offer back at him. If I was a man, I would hit you myself."

Quade and Vince both stared at Mary. Charlie Brown stifled a smile. "Seems I've seen that temper somewhere before."

Then something strange happened. Vince smiled. "She's every inch her mother's daughter. Do somethin' useful, girl. Get your brother cleaned up and then we'll talk. Charlie, get some coffee on. You other men get back to work."

CHAPTER 7

Twenty minutes later, Mary had Quade's cuts and abrasions patched up and they met their father and Charlie inside the house. Quade sipped his coffee: black and strong and good. It reminded him of the stuff made by an old Mexican woman along the border who'd looked after him while he was recovering from a bullet wound. That was back in the young days of using his gun to make a living. He'd chased the stage robbers south and caught up with them in a small one-burro village. During the ensuing shootout, he'd been unfortunate to pick up a bullet.

It wouldn't be the last time he'd get shot.

Vince was the first to speak. "So, son, what is it you propose?"

"How much do you need to repay the loan?"

"Five thousand."

"I won't ask what it was for. That's your business, but I'll talk to the railroad man and see if we can get a deposit on what they're prepared to pay."

"You think they'll do that?" Vince asked.

"They'll do it. Now, about that fence…"

"Can't do nothin' about it, Jack," Vince said. "The papers are legal."

"The papers might be legal, but I doubt what was done to get them is. Did you contest them?" Quade asked.

"What for?"

"Tomorrow, go to town and start proceedin's to contest the boundary in a court before the judge."

"It won't do no good."

"It might shake somethin' loose, Pa. Meanwhile, I'll go to the land office and see what I can find out."

"I thought you were here tryin' to find a killer?" Vince asked.

"I can do both."

"Jimmy is one of my pupils, Jack," Mary said. "I can arrange for you to talk to him in the morning."

"Do you think he'd willingly return with me to the murder site?"

"I don't know. You could ask him."

"I'll do that."

"You want to stay for supper, Jack?" Vince asked his son.

The Faraday man shook his head. "Not this time, Pa. There are a couple of things I need to do."

Vince nodded. "All right, son. Be careful."

"Just go to town tomorrow and do what I said."

* * *

"Are you feeling all right, big brother?" Mary asked Quade on the ride back to Sagebrush Creek.

He smiled. It seemed like an age since she'd called him that. "I'm fine, Little Freckles."

"In case you haven't noticed, I don't have freckles anymore."

"I did. I guess all that scrubbin' you did as a kid worked." Quade referred to an incident when Mary was seven or eight. He'd come outside and found her standing at the water trough with his mother's scrubbing brush, tears in her eyes as she did her best to remove them.

"You are mean," she replied and poked out her tongue.

They both laughed. It was funny now, but at the time, Quade had wrapped his big arms around her and held her tight, watching the sun rise, until she'd finished sobbing.

"I'm sorry I left you, Mary."

"It's in the past—"

Mary's words were interrupted by the whiplash of a rifle from an outcrop of rocks up ahead and the crack of the bullet as it cut between them.

"Get down," Quade snarled, dropping from the saddle. He reached out and pulled Mary down with him.

They hit the ground hard just as a second bullet hammered through the dry afternoon. Quade palmed up his Colt and heaved himself upright. He slapped the roan on its rump. It lurched forward out of the firing line. Then he grabbed Mary by the arm and dragged her to her feet. "Move."

He put her horse between them and the shooter before ushering her toward some substantial rocks beside the trail. Taking cover behind them, Quade sent the mare to safety, then peered around a rock just as the rifle whiplashed again. The bullet hammered into their sanctuary, spraying a shower of sharp projectiles through the air.

Quade ducked back and looked at his sister. Surprised at Mary's composure, he'd somehow expected her to be flustered.

She said, "Someone really wants you gone."

"They're usin' a rifle," Quade said grimly. He held up his Colt. "Too far for this. Stay here."

"What are you doing, Jack?" Mary asked, grabbing his arm.

"I need to get closer."

"You don't need to get shot."

"Who said anythin' about gettin' shot?" Quade asked with a grin and was up and running.

The shooter fired again, creating small eruptions of dirt at Quade's heels. Running hard, his direction was forward and to the left across the trail.

The rifle fired twice more in quick succession, but to no avail. Quade dropped to relative safety behind a clump of brush. Noticing the rising gun smoke from the rocks where the shooter was hidden, he raised his .45 and fired twice. Then Quade was running again.

This time, the rifle failed to bark. The Faraday man dropped behind a rock and waited. Still, there was no more gunfire. Then came the distant sound of retreating hoofbeats. Quade stood, knowing the immediate threat was over. He walked up to the rocks where the bushwhacker had been. There were spent casings scattered on the ground and two cigarette butts. Whoever it was had waited patiently to take the shot.

Quade leaned down and picked up a casing. It was a .44-40. As common as grass on the plains. What wasn't common, though, was the strike. There was a deviation off to the side. Not dead center. He put it into his pocket.

The Faraday man walked through the rocks to where a lone tree stood. That was where the shooter had left his horse. The fresh horse droppings and the hoofprints attested to that.

Movement behind him made him turn to see Mary approaching. "I told you to stay."

Her eyes narrowed. "One, I am not a dog, and two, I watched you walk up here and not get shot, so I assumed that it was safe."

There she was, scolding him again. He ignored it and pointed to the distant hills where the tracks of the horse had retreated. "Is that Rockin' R range?"

"Yes."

Quade nodded. "Let's get back to town."

* * *

When they reached Sagebrush Creek, Quade's first point of call was the gunsmith. He left his sister, whose last words were, "Have dinner with me tonight."

Quade had nodded. "See you at seven."

In the gunsmith's, the man behind the counter wore a leather apron and had dark hair and a waxed mustache. "Can I help you?"

Quade removed the casing and placed it on the counter. "You ever see a pin strike like this before?"

The man picked it up. He frowned and then shook his head. "No, can't say that I have."

"Are you sure?"

The gunsmith turned the casing in his fingers before placing it back in front of Quade. "No."

Quade picked the casing up and nodded. "Thanks."

Leaving the store, he walked across the street and down the sidewalk toward the jail. Pushing the door open, he stepped inside to find Carter and Tobin talking while they drank coffee. "What can I do for you, Quade?" Carter asked.

"Someone took a shot at me and my sister out on the road to Double Q," Quade replied.

"They obviously missed," Tobin said. "Must have been poor shots."

Carter glared at his deputy. "Go and find somethin' to do, Chuck."

"But—"

"Now."

Tobin nodded. "I'll take a walk around the town."

"You do that."

Once Tobin was gone, Carter said, "Tell me what happened."

Quade related the details of the ambush. The sheriff listened quietly and then pointed at Quade's face. "Looks like you've been fightin'."

"Holiday. Rafferty came out to the Double Q and tried to throw his weight around."

"You think it was Holiday who took a shot at you?"

"It would make sense, but I can't prove anythin'." The Faraday man reached into his pocket. "Ever seen a pin strike like this before?"

Carter picked it up. "No. Did you try the gunsmith? Seems if anyone would know, it would be him."

"He knew nothin' either."

"Leave it with me, I'll go and have a look around tomorrow mornin'."

Quade nodded.

Carter said, "You mentioned Rafferty bein' out at Double Q. Why?"

"He came to gloat. He bought Pa's debt from the bank, and in a week, if Pa can't pay, he says he'll start pushin' him off."

Carter stared at Quade. "I'm guessin' that you're goin' to have somethin' to say about that."

"If I have to."

"I won't have any range war," Carter said sternly. "I already warned you about that."

"If it comes, I won't be the one who starts it, Carter. But I won't run from it, either. If Rafferty calls the ball, I'll take the first dance."

Carter stared at him. "You've been warned, Quade."

"Yes, sir."

Taking his leave from the sheriff's office, Quade walked along the street to the land office. A rat-faced man wearing spectacles was just locking the door. He turned and saw Quade standing on the boardwalk. He squinted at the Faraday man through narrowed eyes. "Come back tomorrow. I'm closing up for the day."

"Are you Amos Dent?"

The man nodded. "That's right."

"Then open up, we have business."

"I beg your pardon." There was shock on the man's face.

"I said open the door."

"Who are you?"

"Jack Quade," Quade replied. "Open the door or I'll kick it in."

Dent's mouth opened and closed like a fish out of water, gasping for breath. He thought about protesting but decided against it and instead put the key back in the lock. The lock rattled and the land agent opened the door.

Once inside, Dent closed and locked the door. "What is it you want, Mr. Quade?"

"Why was the boundary between Double Q and Rockin' R moved?"

Dent shook his head. "It wasn't moved. It's where it has always been."

"The boundary is the creek. Always was so both ranches could have access to a permanent water source in tough times."

"I'm afraid you're wrong."

"Show me," Quade said.

"I beg your pardon?"

"Show me the map."

"I don't see why I should," Dent said defiantly.

"If I have to look for it, you rat-faced son of a bitch, I won't leave a thing standin' in this office. Includin' you."

"I shall go to Sheriff Carter about this," Dent bleated. "He will put you in jail."

"You do that."

In spite of the protests, Dent found the map and laid it out upon his scarred desktop. He ran a finger hastily over the map and said, "There is the creek and there is the boundary. See?"

Quade did see but didn't like what he saw. "Light the lamp."

"What?"

"Do you have a hearin' problem, Dent? I said light the lamp."

The land agent did as ordered, striking a match and holding it to the cotton wick. Quade leaned over the map and was able to see better. He traced the line to the Double Q side of the creek that marked the boundary. With a nod, he added, "That's all I wanted to see."

Dent inclined his head nervously. "I told you. Are you satisfied now?"

"Maybe."

But Quade was far from satisfied. He'd seen the faint smudges along the creek line as though something had been rubbed away. Then there was the new boundary mark. It seemed cleaner than the others. Newer.

Quade stared at the land agent. "Be sein' you, Dent."

Dent swallowed hard. The comment sounded almost like a threat.

* * *

Once Quade was gone, Dent locked up and hurried away from his office to the livery stable. He found Silas feeding the horses. "Well, lordy be. If'n it ain't Amos Dent. What can I do for you?"

"I need use of a buggy," Dent said hurriedly.

"Doc took the buggy. Gone to deliver a baby out by Ross Creek."

"Then I'll hire a horse," Dent said.

"Sure you will." Silas looked him up and down. "Old Ned will do you."

"I don't care about the name of the damn horse," Dent growled. "Just as long as it goes."

"All right, all right, hold on to your bloomers. Give me a few minutes."

Silas walked to a stall near the end of the stable and opened the door. Inside was a tall gray. He had a quiet nature and was old. He was kept specifically for those who seldom rode but knew which direction to point the horse. He threw a saddle on him and led him to Dent. "You sure you can ride him?"

"Of course I can." There was more than a hint of indignation in his voice.

A few minutes later, Dent was riding the big gray out of town under a pair of watchful eyes.

* * *

Since his return to Sagebrush Creek, Quade had been busy but still wasn't done. He knocked on the door of the room that Franks and Grimshaw were sharing and waited for them to let him in.

"Everythin' is set up for tomorrow," he told Franks.

"Great. I have received confirmation that the price has been agreed upon."

"Yeah, about that," Quade said.

Franks frowned. "I don't think I like what comes next."

"We need a deposit. An upfront payment."

"What? It doesn't work like that, Jack," Grimshaw blustered, giving his fellow agent a dark look.

Quade explained what was happening. "If he gets pushed off his land, or a range war begins, the railway won't get on it. In the end, it will cost them far more when one man owns the lot."

The surveyor shook his head. "How much?"

"Five thousand."

"It'll have to be brought in."

"I'm sure the Chicago, Rock Island and Pacific Railroad can manage it. I'll meet you at the ranch tomorrow."

* * *

Quade met Mary at seven that evening as promised. The dining room was quiet, and as luck would have it, Lucy Carter was working. She saw Quade and gave him a shy smile as she collected plates from another table. Mary saw it and said, "I think you have an admirer, Jack."

"Lucy?"

"Uh, huh. I tried to warn her about you, but it looks like her sights are set."

"What about Tobin?"

"That's complicated—no, he's complicated. He's no good for her, and I think she knows it. You are too."

"Complicated or no good for her?"

"Maybe both," Mary replied. "No matter how you break it down, you still live by your gun, Jack."

A moth fluttered around a wall lamp over Mary's shoulder. Quade stared at it. Then he nodded slowly. He understood what she was getting at. "A man can change, Mary."

"Can you really, Jack?"

"I'd like to think so."

"Can I take your order?" Lucy asked, interrupting.

"What's the special?" Quade asked.

"Roast chicken with vegetables and gravy," she replied.

Quade felt his stomach growl. "Sounds good to me. Ain't a war party of Apache could stop me eatin' it."

Lucy turned. "Mary?"

"I'll have the same, please, Lucy."

"Coming up."

* * *

The big gray horse galloped into the Rocking R ranch yard, lathered in sweat, while its rider wore a thorough coating of trail dust. Dent fell out of the saddle and started toward the ranch house, letting the sweating horse wander off. Before he could set foot on the steps, his path was blocked by Harry Crosby. "What do you want, Dent?"

"I need to talk to Rafferty," he gasped.

"Mr. Rafferty is busy entertainin' his new bride-to-be and said he was not to be disturbed."

"Then you need to disturb him," Dent panted. "What I have to say to him is important."

"Important enough to half-kill a bronc ridin' out here?"

"Yes."

"Then tell me and I'll decide."

"I had a visit at the office by Jack Quade," Dent explained.

"What did he want?" Crosby asked with a frown.

"To look at the boundary map and Divide Creek. Damn it, he knows. I should never have listened to Rafferty in the first place."

Crosby grabbed his collar. "Calm down, Dent. What do you mean he knows? Knows what?"

"That I moved the boundary, damn it. Rafferty asked me to do it. Paid me to do it. Once the line was moved, then he could fence it."

"How do you know he knows?" Crosby asked.

"Why else would he want to look?" Dent's voice was becoming more anxious. It went up in pitch to almost a shout.

"Keep it down, damn it."

Suddenly, Rafferty appeared. "What the hell is going on here?"

Dent started to crumble now. The pressure of keeping the secret was overwhelming him. "He knows, Rafferty. The man knows."

"Who knows what?"

"Quade. He—"

"Shut up," Rafferty hissed and grabbed Dent by the arm. He dragged him into the ranch yard away from the house. "Now, start from the beginning."

"Quade, he came to the land office to look at a boundary map."

"Which one—don't worry, it was a stupid question."

"He knows, Tom. I tell you, he knows the line was moved."

Rafferty waved a dismissive hand. "How could he know, you fool. Did you tell him?"

"No, but—"

"Get on that damn horse, Dent, and get back to town. If I were you, I'd ride slow so you don't kill the poor animal."

"What about Quade?"

"What about him?"

"He—"

"He nothing. Now get."

The two men watched Dent ride out of the ranch yard. Crosby turned to Rafferty. "You want somethin' done about him?" the gunman asked.

Rafferty shook his head. "Not yet. I still need him."

CHAPTER 8

"Am I to have the pleasure of an escort home this evening, Jack?" Lucy asked coyly as she collected their plates.

Quade glanced at his sister, who was dabbing at her mouth with a napkin, her face deadpan. He nodded at Lucy. "It would be my pleasure."

Lucy gave him a broad smile. "I'll be finished soon."

Once she was gone, Mary placed the napkin down and leaned closer to the table. "Didn't anything I said get through to you?"

"It did."

"Well then?"

"Why don't you walk with us?" Quade said.

"I can see myself home, thank you." Mary got to her feet, her irritation evident.

"I'll see you in the mornin'."

Lucy reappeared a few minutes later, wrapped in a shawl. "Mary gone home?"

"Yes, she has."

"Then I'm all yours—oh, no."

Quade turned to see what Lucy was looking at. In the doorway stood Tobin. His demeanor was calm right up to the moment that he saw Quade. Then it changed.

Stepping forward, he said, "Lucy, I was just doin' rounds and thought I'd offer to walk you home."

"I'm sorry, Chuck, but Jack is doing the honors."

"Him." The deputy's top lip curled.

"That's right."

"So be it," Tobin said abruptly before spinning on his heel and leaving.

Lucy looked at Jack. "Shall we?"

* * *

The night was cool, which made the shawl a good choice. The sky was dark and clear, and millions of silvery eyes winked down upon the couple as they strolled arm in arm.

"It is a beautiful evening," Lucy said.

"Yes, ma'am."

"There you go again, calling me ma'am."

"Sorry."

"Will your pa be home when we get there?" Quade asked.

"Why? Is he more interesting than present company?" Lucy asked.

"I didn't say that," Quade replied.

Lucy chuckled. "He might be. Although you never can tell. I went to see him today at his office and he wasn't there. Chuck said he was out doing something."

When they reached Lucy's home, she turned to face Quade. "There is something about you, Jack. Something that I find intriguing."

"How do you mean?" he asked.

"You're a gunfighter, but not like any I've encountered before. Yet also, you seem to be holding something back."

"Really?"

"Yes, like a secret. Are you keeping a secret from me, Jack?"

Her words took him aback. He'd been careful to keep his cover. The only ones who knew were family or Franks and Grimshaw.

Lucy reached out and touched his arm, looking up into his eyes. "You aren't married, are you, Jack?"

He laughed out loud, relief washing over him. He was about to say something when Lucy surprised him again. This time, she stood on tiptoes and kissed him on the lips. It lingered longer than was proprietary, and Quade found himself responding to her. Suddenly, he grabbed her arms and forced her back. "Lucy, I—"

Then everything went black.

* * *

Quade came to in a cell. He could hear voices in the distance. One was high-pitched, the other two were deeper. All three were angry. Quade sat up, moaned, and held a hand to the back of his head. There was a lump there for sure, and it felt sticky to touch. He pulled his hand away and looked down at the red patch on his palm.

"Jack, you're awake," Lucy said, hurrying over to the cell bars. "Are you all right?"

"I'll live, I guess. What fell on me?"

"That would be Chuck Tobin," she growled.

"He was molestin' you," Tobin snarled.

"We were kissing, you darn dunderhead," she snarled at him.

"All right, that'll do," Carter snapped. "Chuck, go home."

"But—"

"Darn it, Chuck, must you argue all the blamed time?"

The deputy stormed out of the office, slamming the door behind him. Thin walls rattled with the force, making the whole office shudder. Carter shook his head. "Damn that boy."

"Can you let me out now?" Quade asked.

The sheriff's eyes narrowed. "That depends. Were you kissin' my daughter?"

"Pa!" Lucy exclaimed.

"Quiet, girl."

"I'm a grown woman."

"And you're my daughter," Carter snapped back. "And he is a—"

"A gunfighter?" Lucy cut him off. "Just say it, Pa."

"All right then. He's a gunfighter."

"He's different."

"None of them are different."

Quade cleared his throat. "Maybe you would like to continue this in private."

"Good idea," Carter growled, reaching for the cell keys. He let Quade out and gave him back his Colt. Then he said, "Stay away from my daughter."

"I wasn't lookin' to cause trouble."

"Well, you managed to."

Quade looked at Lucy. He touched his hat brim. "Ma'am."

Then he left.

If Quade thought his troubles were over that night

after leaving the sheriff's office, he was wrong. He'd not gone far when Chuck Tobin stepped out of the shadows. Quade's hand dropped to his holstered .45. "Good way to get yourself shot, Deputy."

"You'd like that, wouldn't you? It would clear everythin' out of the way, and you could have Lucy to yourself."

"If you keep stompin' around Sagebrush Creek like a bear with a sore head, I won't have to do a thing," Quade assured him. "You'll take care of that on your lonesome."

The Faraday man went to step around and Tobin blocked his passage. "I'm not done warnin' you yet."

"Yes, you are," Quade assured him quietly. "I'll give you some advice for free. Stop crowdin' me, mister. It'll end bad for one of us. And I'm guessin' it won't be me."

"Are you threatenin' a duly sworn peace officer, Quade?"

"Go home, Tobin. Just go home."

This time, when Quade stepped around him, Tobin didn't move. He just watched him go, his anger stirring inside.

* * *

Quade was about to go to bed when his attention was drawn to the door by a soft knock. He grabbed the Colt from his holster and moved silently to the door. The knock came again, this time more urgent. "Jack, it's me."

Lucy.

He opened the door and let her in. "What are you doin' here?"

Lucy grabbed his arms. "I had to make sure you were all right."

"I'm fine. You should go. If your father finds out, he'll be madder than a prodded hornets' nest."

"I don't care," Lucy said stubbornly.

"I do," he replied, grabbing her arm and guiding her toward the door.

Lucy shook him loose. "Don't you just brush me away, Jack Quade. You kissed me too, remember."

"I remember," he replied. "And it was a mistake."

"Don't you dare say that. You felt it too. I know you did."

The Faraday man shook his head. "It doesn't matter, Lucy. It was a mistake, and you should go."

Tears came to her eyes, and he felt bad for hurting her. Lucy slapped his chest. It was a stinging blow in more ways than one. Her eyes blazed. "I was wrong about you, Jack Quade. You are just like the rest of them. Maybe even worse."

Without waiting for Quade to reply, Lucy spun around and stormed out, sobbing, slamming the door behind her.

Shaking his head and feeling bad, Quade knew it was for the best. Maybe later, after she knew the truth, Lucy would forgive him, but until then, he had a task to complete.

* * *

"I warned you, didn't I?" Mary blazed the following morning out the back of the schoolhouse. She shoved her brother in the chest. "Damn you, Jack."

"Good news travels fast I see," Quade replied grimly.

"Lucy came to me crying last night and kept me up until all hours, and it was your fault."

"Did she tell you what else happened?"

Mary's face softened. "She did. Are you okay?"

"I'll live."

"What happened?"

Quade told her and then explained about his shift toward Lucy. "I can't have her in the way. I don't want her gettin' hurt."

"Did you tell her that?"

"No. There is only a few who know the real reason that I am here. I'd like to keep it that way."

"Fine, but you've really hurt her, Jack. Don't be surprised if she isn't there when this is over."

"I'll have to risk it. There is one other thing."

"What?" Mary asked.

"Rafferty's new bride-to-be," Quade said.

"Abigail?"

"We have a past."

"Oh, great. Does she know you're a detective?"

Quade shook his head. "No, just the other side of things."

"By golly, big brother, you sure know how to attract trouble. Wait here, I'll go and get Jimmy."

While he waited, Quade caught sight of Franks and Grimshaw riding out of town trailing a pack mule. Grimshaw nodded when he saw him.

Mary reappeared with Jimmy. "This is Jimmy, Jack. Jimmy, this is my brother Jack."

"Oh, cool, a real-life gunfighter." There was awe in the boy's voice.

"Don't get too excited, Jimmy," Quade said. "I bleed just like you."

"How many men have you killed?"

"Jimmy," Mary admonished him.

"Sorry, miss. But wow."

Quade said, "Jimmy, I'm goin' to ask you some questions and I want you to forget you ever talked to me. Can you do that?"

"Sure, but Miss said—"

"I think it is better if you stay here."

The boy's head hung in disappointment, and he kicked the dirt. "Sure."

"Tell me about the day you were out with Sam Roberts."

Jimmy suddenly looked scared. "I don't want to talk about it."

"It's okay, Jimmy. I just need to know what happened," Quade said.

"But what if he finds out I talked and comes after me?" Jimmy asked.

"He? Who is he?"

"The rider I saw."

"What rider?"

The boy's jaw dropped as he realized he'd said too much. "No, no more. Tell him, miss. I don't want to talk anymore."

"I think that will do, Jack," Mary said.

Quade ignored her. "Jimmy, Mr. Roberts was a friend of mine. You'd want me to find the man who did it, wouldn't you?"

He nodded.

"Jack," Mary protested.

"I'm almost done, Mary." He looked back at the kid. "I won't ask you about him anymore, Jimmy. But I do need to know where you were so I can look for myself."

"We were out in the valley where the free range borders the Rockin' R. It was over the next ridge."

"Okay. Thank you. I'll take it from here."

"He—" Jimmy stopped.

"Yes, Jimmy?" Mary asked.

"He was near the trees on the ridge."

Quade nodded. "Thanks, Jimmy."

Jimmy said, "Mr. Roberts was good to me. He was a good man."

"I'm sure he was."

Mary squeezed Jimmy's shoulder. "Go back inside, Jimmy. I'll be right along."

"Yes, miss."

"Remember, Jimmy," Jack said. "Not a word. Our secret."

"Yes, sir."

Jimmy ran inside and Quade put his hand on his sister's shoulder. "Keep an eye out for Pa."

"You just be careful."

"Always."

Quade climbed aboard the roan and pointed him toward the trail out of town. However, his discussion with the boy hadn't gone unnoticed.

* * *

"All right, children, time for recess. Be back—" the scrape of chairs and shouts of joy drowned out the rest of Mary's words.

Jimmy jumped from the top step and ran around behind the schoolhouse, where he planned to sit and think about the meeting earlier with a famous gunslinger. When he was out of sight, he made a gun with his thumb and forefinger and practiced his fast draw.

"BANG! BANG! Take that, you backshootin' varmint."

"Did you get him, son?"

Jimmy whirled about, alarm on his face. Then he saw who it was and smiled nervously. "Sure did."

"Good work. Listen, I saw you talking with Jack Quade earlier. You care to tell me what he wanted?"

"I—" Jimmy stopped.

"What is it, son?"

"I promised I wouldn't tell."

"But you can tell me," the man said. "It's okay."

Jimmy thought for a moment.

"He—he wanted to know about the day Mr. Roberts was shot. What I saw."

"What did you tell him?"

"Nothin'. Just where it happened," Jimmy explained.

"But you didn't see anythin', did you, Jimmy?"

The kid looked guilty.

"Did you, Jimmy?"

"I—"

A knife appeared in the man's hand. "Tell me what you saw, Jimmy."

* * *

"Jimmy, where are you?" Mary called out as she walked along the side of the schoolhouse. The boy had not returned after recess.

When he wasn't there, Mary asked the other pupils, "Has anyone seen Jimmy?"

"No, miss," came the reply from almost all of the pupils. Except for Holly Jackson. "Miss, I saw him walking to the back."

Mary nodded. "Thank you, Holly. Everyone get their slates and copy what I've written on the board. I'll be right back."

Mary left the schoolhouse and walked along beside it. When she reached the rear, her face changed, and her expression became one of horror. What followed was the anguished cry of someone who'd just discovered something terrible.

CHAPTER 9

Charlie Brown saw them coming while he swept the rough boards of the ranch house veranda. "Riders. Wonder who they could be."

Then he remembered, the surveyor was coming out to the ranch. Turning, he carried his broom inside. He found Vince in the kitchen, pouring a cup of coffee.

"Riders comin' in. Be that surveyor feller, I expect. You know, the one Jack told you about."

"I remember, damn it," Vince growled.

"I'm glad you remember somethin'," Charlie replied. "'Cause you seem to have trouble rememberin' where the darn coffeepot goes."

The cook grabbed it from the table and placed it back on the stove.

"There you go, complainin' again."

Both men went outside and stood on the veranda just as the riders came into the yard. They eased up in front of the ranch house and waited for one of the men in front of them to speak.

"Help you gents?" Vince asked.

Franks removed his hat. "My name is Dennis Franks. I'm a surveyor for the Chicago, Rock Island and Pacific Railroad. This is Hamish Grimshaw. He's my hired help. We are meant to meet Jack Quade out here. I take it you are his father?"

"You would take it right," Vince replied. "Step down, gentlemen, come through to the kitchen. The coffee pot is still hot."

"Wouldn't be if'n it had been left on the table," Charlie Brown growled quietly.

Vince glared at him but said nothing. The two new arrivals tied their horses to the hitchrail out front and followed Vince and his cook inside.

Charlie poured the coffee while the others talked. "Jack told us to start on your land, Mr. Quade," Franks said. "Probably until he can figure out what happened to the last surveyor."

Vince nodded. "Call me Vince. How long do you figure to be out here?"

"Valley this size, depending on the weather, could be a month."

Vince's eyebrows shot up. "That long?"

"Surveying can be a slow process."

The front door opened, and they heard footsteps coming toward the kitchen. Quade filled the doorway. "Sorry I'm late."

"Not at all," Franks said. "We were just getting acquainted."

"How did you get on with the thing we discussed?" Quade asked.

"It'll be on the stage tomorrow," Franks said.

"Thanks."

"I have a question before you all leave," Vince said. "Will I need to fence the right of way?"

"That is up to you," Franks replied. "It isn't necessary, but accidents do happen."

Vince nodded. He looked at Grimshaw. "Your friend don't say much, does he?"

"He's a very quiet man," Franks agreed.

"Can he use that gun he's got hidden away?"

"If he needs to."

"Well, gentlemen, I need to go to town. I'll bid you good day."

Franks and Grimshaw finished their coffee then walked back to their horses, escorted by Charlie. Quade remained with his father. "Pa, on that stage tomorrow, there will be a box with five thousand cash on it. The down payment for the rail line."

Vince was stunned. "How, boy? How did you do that?"

"I wasn't goin' to stand by and watch you lose this ranch, Pa. Not now, not ever."

Vince patted him on the shoulder. "It's good to have you home, Jack."

* * *

The three men drew rein in the middle of the valley where a small creek ran along beside a stand of trees. Like the rest of the ranch, the grass was brown. In the shade of the trees lay some cows, not far away from the water source. They looked skinny, their ribs starting to show. Rain was badly needed to put feed on the ground.

"Start here," Quade said. "Work your way northeast toward the town. You'll come across Lazy S eventually. Back over this low ridge is Rockin' R."

"Yes, the Rafferty spread," Franks said. "Will we get any trouble from him?"

"I shouldn't imagine so. He wants it just as much as anyone. His issue is the other ranchers. He wants their land."

"So he has nothin' to do with the murder of Sam?" Grimshaw asked.

"I don't think so."

"So then, who?"

"That is the big question. I'm ridin' over to where it happened to have a look around now. Just keep your eyes open."

"You do the same."

Quade left them to get started. He traversed the ridge until reaching the fence to Rocking R range. Lined along it were about thirty cows, looking at the creek on the other side. A creek that they had once used. He muttered a curse and climbed down after he was sure no one was watching. He reached into his saddlebags and took out some wire cutters he'd taken from the ranch before they had left.

The fence was three-strand barbed wire. It was relatively new to the West, having been developed over a few years. It was cheap and easy to install. It also contained stock with great efficiency. But keeping another man's cows from a water source that was used by the ranches bordering it was not one of them.

Once the wires were cut, Quade grabbed his rope and hooked it to the nearest post. Then he wound it around the saddle horn and put the roan to work. Within minutes, Quade had a couple hundred yards of fence pulled down.

The thirsty cows bellowed almost in delight as they walked through the opening and made their way toward the creek.

Satisfied, Quade kept riding.

* * *

Quade leaned down and rubbed the roan's neck. "This looks to be about it."

He climbed down, taking the Winchester from the scabbard. He left the horse ground hitched and started to walk around. Below him was the valley where Roberts had been shot.

Quade walked through the trees and then around some rocks. From where he was, the shooter would have had a perfect line down to the valley floor.

The first thing he found was the hoofprints from a horse. Lack of rain had not washed them away, and they were as clear in the dirt as though they were done yesterday.

The Faraday man walked back to the rocks and studied the ground closer. Then he found it. A casing. Quade picked it up and ran a thorough gaze over it.

He stopped when he got to the firing cap. "Well, hello."

The pin strike was off-center, the same as the one he'd found when he and Mary were bushwhacked. Quade put it into his pocket.

Suddenly, the roan whickered. It was an alarm. Quade spun and brought the Winchester up to his shoulder.

On a hill to his west sat a figure on a horse. There was no way of telling what he looked like, but the Faraday man knew what he was doing. He was watching him.

The rifle lowered and the two men remained staring across the divide at each other. Then the man turned his horse and disappeared behind the hill, leaving Quade wondering if he was the killer.

Quade walked back to the roan then put his rifle in the scabbard. He glanced back in the direction of the hill and found it still clear. "Who do you suppose he was, horse?"

The roan snorted.

"Yeah, I got no idea either."

* * *

When Vince Quade rode into town, there was a hell of a racket all along the main street. The old man seemed confused. He'd never seen the normally lazy street like this before. There was a crowd gathered outside the sheriff's office. Vince could hear yelling and see fists being shaken in the air. Then one of the crowd turned and saw him riding along the street. "There he is!"

Heads turned, and all of a sudden, the angry mob was coming toward him. "What on earth?"

Vince reined his horse in, and his hand dropped to his old .44. As the mob grew closer, he contemplated drawing the weapon, but he saw Carter following along behind them. He wouldn't let anything get out of hand.

The angry crowd stopped a few feet from the bay Vince was riding. Every man among them wore an expression of pure hatred. Jerry Price, the Sagebrush Creek Mayor, stepped forward. "Where is he, Vince?"

"Where is who, Jerry?"

"That murderin' son of a bitch you call a son, that's who," the mayor snarled.

The crowd behind him became rowdy once more.

"What the hell are you talkin' about?" Vince demanded.

"The cold-blooded killin' of Jimmy Lewis, that's what I'm talkin' about."

"Jimmy Lewis? He's just a kid. Who would want to murder him?"

"Your son, that's who," Price shouted.

"It wasn't Jack," a new voice joined the noise. Vince looked and saw Mary. "He talked to Jimmy and rode out of town. I was with him."

"He could have doubled back and done it," someone else shouted.

"What reason would he have?"

"Yeah," said Vince. "What reason?"

"That's what I need to ask him?" Carter said.

"You too, Lyle?"

"I just need to talk to him. That's all," Carter replied. "Where is he, Vince?"

"I have no idea," Vince replied.

"Liar!" snarled Price. "Come on, let's get him down. I'll make the old coot talk."

The old .44 slid free of leather and a gnarled thumb eased the hammer back. "I may be old, and I may be a little slower, but my eyes are fine, and my aim is good. Take one more step, Price, and I'll gut shoot you like a dog."

The surging crowd stopped dead. No one was willing to test the old man. Vince spat on the street in disgust. "Just as I thought. Not one of you man enough to be the first to die."

"Put the gun up, Vince," Carter said as he pushed through the crowd. "All of you go about your business."

The mob looked to Price for guidance. Instead, he offered them nothing as he stared down the barrel of Vince Quade's gun. The Double Q owner's lip curled. "What's it goin' to be, Mayor?"

Price pressed his lips together and turned away,

shoving his way through the crowd. Carter lifted his head and said out loud, "The rest of you go too."

Slowly, they all dispersed until it was only Carter, Vince, Mary, and Chuck Tobin. The deputy stepped forward, "So where is your murderin' son?"

Vince's face set like granite. You may be younger'n me boy, but I could still whip you to a damn stand still."

"I asked you a question, old man."

"I'll handle this, Chuck," Carter said. "Go and let Swampy out of his cell. Tell him he owes me for a meal."

Tobin nodded. "Anythin' you say, Sheriff."

Vince climbed down from his horse. "Care to tell me what the hell is goin' on, Lyle?"

"Jimmy was killed. Someone took a knife to him. Mary found him. Your son was the last person the kid talked to."

"I was with him," Mary said. "He didn't do it."

"Like was said before. He could have doubled back."

"But Jimmy was inside until recess. It couldn't have been Jack."

"I guess the inquest will bring that out," Carter said. "He'll get his chance to tell the truth there."

"You can't be serious," Vince said, astonished.

"I'm as serious as that dead boy. What did he want with him anyway?"

"How should I know?" Vince snapped.

"Jimmy saw him and wanted to talk to a real-life gunslinger," Mary lied.

"Is that all?" Carter asked.

"Yes."

"So, where is he?"

Vince shook his head. "I told you, I don't know."

"Be better if I bring him in, Vince," Carter said. "The others will lynch him without a trial."

"What about proof?" Mary asked. "Where is your proof?"

Carter reached up and touched his hat brim. "Be seein' you."

"What are we going to do, Pa?" Mary asked.

"Ride out to the ranch and warn Jack. I'll go and see the judge. I need to get these papers investigated. I'll be out after I'm done."

"Okay, Pa."

"Be careful, girl."

"Aren't I always?"

Judge Elmer Hamilton was sitting behind his desk in the back room of the Sagebrush Creek courthouse. And he wasn't alone. He was playing checkers with an old friend. Seamus Grimsby ran the feed and grain store along with his son. When Vince found them, Judge Hamilton was cussing up a storm after Grimsby had just wiped him off the board. "Son of a bitch, how the hell did you manage to do that?"

"You need new glasses, Elmer," Grimsby replied.

"If I find that you cheated, I'll give you thirty days."

There was a knock at the door to his office. The judge looked up and called out, "Go away, I'm busy with important legal matters."

Once, Hamilton had been a circuit judge. Always on the road, traveling from town to town. With advancing age, he'd determined it was time to slow down and needed to stay put somewhere. Sagebrush Creek was it.

The door opened and Vince walked in. "It's me, Judge."

"Vince. I'm certainly surprised to see you. Especially after the ruckus that's goin' on out there."

"I wouldn't be here if it wasn't important," Vince replied.

Grimsby got to his feet. "I'll leave you to it, Elmer."

"Same time tomorrow?"

"I'll be here."

"Right, Vince, what is this about?" Hamilton asked.

"I need an investigation done."

"You need to see the sheriff, Vince, he does the investigatin' around here."

"Jack said to see you," Vince said. "It's about the boundary bein' moved."

Hamilton nodded. "You mean you want to contest it?"

"If that's the correct way of sayin' it, yeah."

"Why?" Hamilton asked.

Vince shrugged. "Judge?"

"For there to be a hearin', I need to know why, what doubts you have. Then I make my decision on what to do next."

"I see. Well, on the grounds that the creek was always the border between the Broken J and the Double Q. Then when Rockin' R took over, the line suddenly changed and a fence was put up to stop my cattle from gettin' water."

"Did you go to Amos Dent?" Hamilton asked.

"Useless as a range without water," Vince replied.

"Did he show you the map?" Hamilton asked.

"Not the same one as I saw when I first came here."

"How do you mean?"

"The darn boundary line had moved."

"Any of the other lines?" Hamilton asked.

Vince shook his head. "No, just the creek."

"Okay, we'll hold an inquest in two weeks. Is that good enough for you?"

"Thank you, Elmer."

* * *

Monte Cable had watched the excitement concerning Vince Quade from across the street as he leaned against the awning post of the barber shop and smiled. It looked like the son of a bitch was going to get what was coming to him. And, if it came down to a lynching, he'd be out front with the rope.

The word about Jimmy had spread like wildfire through the town. Then came the news that Jack Quade was the prime suspect, and that put a smile on the gunfighter's face. The news would also put one on Rafferty's face as well. But first, he had something else to do.

Cable walked along the street to the telegraph office. Once inside, Cable flipped the sign around to *CLOSED* and focused his stare on the telegrapher. "Mr. Rafferty hasn't heard from you in almost a week, Vern. He wants to know why?"

Vern Moss started to sweat. "Nothin' to report is why. Up until now at least."

"Why, what's important about now?"

"There's a shipment of money comin' in on the stage tomorrow."

"So, we ain't stage robbers, Vern."

"I haven't told you what the money is for yet," Vern replied.

"All right, Vern, what's it for?"

"Vince Quade."

That got his attention, and Vern suddenly felt smug. "How much?"

"Five thousand."

Cable nodded. Rafferty would want to know that. "Anythin' else?"

Vern thought about the news that concerned Quade and how he worked for the Faraday Security Service. Then he remembered the warning and made his decision. "No, nothin'."

"Good, now the boss wants you to send a message for him."

When it was done, Cable turned the sign back around and left the office.

CHAPTER 10

Quade was riding back across Rocking R range when he saw her. She was riding a bay along the creek where the boundary fence was. At first, Quade wasn't sure it was her, but when he drew nearer, there was no doubt that it was indeed Abigail Davis.

He drew the roan to a halt near a tree so she could be in the shade. The expression on her face was one of confusion. "I wasn't sure if it was you when I got off the stage or not. Then I heard Tom and his men talking. Now I see you in the flesh."

Quade stared at her. If anything, she seemed even prettier. It made his breath catch in his throat and wonder why he'd left her sobbing in the middle of the street all those years ago. "Hello, Abbey."

Her expression changed. There was disdain there now. "Still selling your gun, I see."

"A man finds it hard to change," Quade replied.

"Now you are fighting my husband-to-be."

"Is that what he said?"

"I overheard them talking," Abigail said.

"Don't believe everythin' you hear, Abbey."

"I don't, Jack. Especially when it comes from you."

There was bitterness in her voice and her words cut deep. "Yeah, I'm sorry about that."

"Wow! Big Jack Quade apologizes for leaving me crying in the street. After all these years. I was young and loved you, damn your hide."

The roan under Quade shifted as though it wanted to be anywhere else but there. He stroked its neck. "Are you done, Abbey?"

"Not by a long sight," she spat at him.

"Just so you know, it is your husband-to-be who is behind the trouble in the valley," Quade said. "He wants all the land for himself."

"Why shouldn't he?" she snapped. "What's wrong with being ambitious?"

Quade shook his head. "Nothin' at all. But it's how you go about it that counts."

"What is that supposed to mean?"

"Ask Rafferty."

The sound of hoofbeats broke through their conversation. Quade looked up and saw two riders coming toward them on broad-chested mounts. When they were close enough, Quade recognized them both. Crosby and the other gun, Jones. They drew up in front of the couple and Crosby said, "Been lookin' for you, Miss Abigail. Quade givin' you any trouble?"

Abigail stared at him. "No, no trouble."

Crosby noted the fence across the creek. The cows had moved back to their side. The gunfighter said, "That your doin'?"

"Would you believe a big wind came up and blew it down?" Quade asked.

The hired gun smiled. "Still the same Quade."

"Not you, though. Was a time you'd hire out on the side of right. Now it's all about the money."

"I say we take him back to the ranch house for Mr. Rafferty to deal with," Jones said.

Quade stared at Crosby. "Best tell your friend to slow his roll, Harry. I don't much feel like killin' anyone today."

"Leave it be, Tobe," Crosby said.

"What if I don't want to?" the young gun asked. "Summers was a friend of mine. Maybe it's time someone stood up for him seein' as you won't."

Crosby shook his head slowly and eased his horse over to where the woman watched the exchange.

"What are you doing?" she asked.

"Just movin' you over a safe distance, ma'am," Crosby replied. "I'd hate for you to catch a stray bullet."

That left just Quade and Jones facing each other, both men mounted. Quade said, "You can stop this. Just say the word."

Jones shook his head. "Nope. Come too far."

Then he drew.

Hands flashed down and came up with roaring .45s in them. Jones was quick, Quade had to give him that, but he wasn't in the same league as the Faraday man. The bullet from Quade's gun punched into Jones's chest and knocked him back over the animal's rump.

Jones didn't even get his weapon up, so when he squeezed the trigger, the bullet plowed into the dirt near his horse's hoofs, making the animal buck wildly.

Quade eased back the hammer once more as Jones somehow managed to stagger to his feet. The Colt in his hand started to rise. Quade snapped, "Don't!"

The gunman either didn't hear or didn't want to listen. The gun kept coming up, and Quade fired again.

This time, Jones stayed down.

The Faraday man turned to face Crosby. The killer hadn't moved. Quade said, "I gave him a chance. He might have lived."

"He was on a runaway train to Boot Hill. I warned him, he didn't listen. All that's left to do is bury him."

"He's your trash. I'll leave him to you."

A disgusted sound escaped Abigail's lips. "Is that how you treat life? With such disdain?"

"He lived the life," Quade said.

Crosby nodded. "He who lives by the sword."

"Very philosophical of you, Harry."

"I thought so. Now, get out of here, Quade. You—" Crosby stopped, looking at a distant ridge.

Quade followed his gaze. The rider was back. "Know him, Harry?"

"Not one of ours."

"Second time today I saw him."

"Where was the other?" Crosby asked.

Quade grinned at him. "I forget."

He turned the roan. "Be seein' you, Harry."

"You too, Jack."

"You're just going to let him ride out of here after he killed your friend?" Abigail said heatedly.

"Jones weren't my friend, Miss Abbey," Crosby said flatly. "Quade, on the other hand, would be the closest thing I ever had to a friend."

"What happens when you have to fight him?"

Crosby's face hardened. "I kill him."

* * *

Cable's horse was blowing hard when he rode into the ranch yard. It skidded to a stop and Cable came clear of the saddle in one smooth motion. He strode purposefully toward the ranch house and moments later was inside Rafferty's den, where the rancher was seated at a large hardwood desk.

"Boss, I got somethin' to tell you," he said to Rafferty.

"What is it that is so important?" Rafferty asked, annoyed at the intrusion.

"There is a shipment of money comin' in on the stage tomorrow for Vince Quade."

Rafferty stopped writing and stared at the gun hand. "How much?"

"Five thousand."

This was troubling. "Where would he get that much money from?"

"The railroad. It's a down payment for the right of way."

"If he gets that money, then he can pay off the bank loan that I bought. We can't have that. Tomorrow, you get a few hands together and you rob that damn stage."

"I'll take care of it, Mr. Rafferty."

"See that you do. We'll talk about it in the morning. Was there anything else?"

"Somethin' that you might call interestin'."

"Go on."

"It seems that Quade is wanted for questionin' about the murder of a kid," Cable explained.

"Did he do it?" Rafferty asked.

"Don't matter much if he did or not. He'll be locked up until Carter works it out. The way the town is wound up, they'll probably lynch him before the sheriff finds out."

"That would be a shame. Did you send that message?"

"Yes, sir. Right where you said to."

"*Tom! Tom!*" the voice came across as high-pitched and distressed.

"Abbey? I'm in my office."

She rushed in and threw herself into his arms. "It was terrible, Tom. Absolutely terrible."

"What was, my dear?"

"The murder of your man by Jack Quade."

He held her out at arm's length. "Murder? Did you witness it, Abbey?"

"Yes, it was shocking. He never stood a chance."

"It wasn't quite that bad," Crosby said from the doorway.

"You were there too?" Rafferty asked.

"Saw it all."

"Then why didn't you stop it?"

"I tried," Crosby explained. "Jones wouldn't be swayed. He poked the bear and got bit."

"It was murder," Abigail persisted.

Crosby stared at her, wondering what her game was. "It was a fair fight."

"Wait," Rafferty said. "Just wait a minute. If my fiancée says it was murder, then I'm apt to believe her. Would you swear to that in a court of law?"

"Of course." She looked at Crosby, a mischievous glint in her eye. "Anything to uphold the law."

"Good. We'll go to town this afternoon and file the complaint with the sheriff. While you are here, Harry, I've sent for Hunk Dawson."

"That is not a wise thing to do, Mr. Rafferty," Crosby cautioned. "Him and his boys are pure evil. Besides, there is nothin' I can't do."

"The decision has been made. I want the Lazy S and Double Q as soon as possible." Rafferty suddenly realized that Abigail was still there. He looked at her.

"Don't worry about me, Tom, I can be just as ambitious as you."

He smiled. "I knew I was marrying you for a reason."

* * *

Mary was at the ranch house when Quade rode into the yard. "Oh, Jack, thank goodness."

"What is the problem?" he asked.

"Jimmy is dead," she replied. "Someone murdered him out the back of the school."

"Hell and damnation. Are you okay?"

Her head bobbed frantically. "Someone told the sheriff that you were talking to him and now they have it in their heads that you killed him."

"Who?"

"The mayor, the town, everyone."

"But you were there."

"I know, and I said that, but they say you could have doubled back and done it. They were going to hurt Pa and make him tell where you were."

"Is he okay?"

Mary nodded. "Yes. He's fine. Oh, Jack, what are you going to do?"

"I have to go to town," Jack said.

"No, you can't."

"It's the only way I can clear my name."

"There was talk of lynching, Jack. It was so scary."

He touched her shoulder. "No one is gettin' lynched. Carter will see to that."

They were still talking when Vince arrived back at the ranch. Mary hurried over to him while he was still astride his horse. "Oh, Pa, tell him not to go."

Concern came to the old man's face. "Go where?"

"To town."

"Now, why would you do that?" Vince asked, bewildered. "There is a necktie social with your name all over it when you get there. The whole town is madder'n a butt slapped grizz."

"It's the only way to clear my name, Pa."

"Get your damn neck stretched, you mean," Vince growled.

"I'm goin' and that's it."

"It's your decision, but don't come cryin' to me when you're dancin' at the end of a rope."

"I won't."

* * *

One hundred miles to the west in a small town called Hope, a band of four gun-toughs were drinking and, as they would put it, having fun. In the middle of the Hope Springs Eternal Saloon, a gun roared, and the leg of a chair lost an inch from its base. The man standing on top of it wavered and almost fell, but he retained his balance and, more importantly, that of the chair.

Beads of sweat rolled down his face and caught at the hemp noose around his neck. The other end of it was tied to a saloon rafter. Hunk Dawson shook his head. "Damn, Sheriff, you done look like one of them ballerina women I saw once."

Hunk Dawson, mid-thirties, was a hired gun, callous killer, and wanted outlaw. He dressed clean and was always clean-shaven, apart from the black mustache that matched his hair. His *segundo*, Jesse Crow, was a stark contrast. Wiry, unshaven, dirty and worn clothes, same age.

"Hell, Hunk, why don't we shoot another son of a

bitch out and see how he goes?" Crow took a slug of the whiskey bottle and brought up his Colt to fire.

The gun crashed, and splinters flew out of the wood floor near the leg. He fired again for the same result. "Darn it, a man's too drunk to shoot straight."

"I got it, Jesse," a high-pitched voice said. It belonged to the youngest of the gang, Joe Trent, a nineteen-year-old wannabe. "I'll show you how it's done."

Sober, they were all fast and shot straight. But every one of them was drunk, except for Dawson. He was under the weather, but not like the others.

The .44 in Trent's hand roared and the mirror behind the bar shattered, falling like a waterfall in a thousand pieces onto the floor behind the bar. "Aw, shoot. Did you see that?"

"Get out of the way, Kid," called Utah.

He was a fast gun from Kansas. Early forties, and the oldest of the group, he had nothing to do with Utah. Trent turned to face him. "How you goin' to see from that far, old man?"

The fast gun released the painted woman he'd had his arm around and drew and fired in one smooth motion. A hole appeared in the sheriff's chest next to the badge he wore. The man slumped, and the rope became taut.

"How's that?" Utah crowed.

"Did you have to damn well kill him?" Dawson growled.

Utah spun his Colt on his forefinger and dropped it into his holster. "Right good shootin' if you ask me."

"No one asked you, old man," Trent sneered.

Dawson looked across the room at the deputy marshal seated in the corner of the saloon. He pointed his Colt at him and said, "Looks like you're up."

The marshal had ridden into Hope that morning,

teaming up with the sheriff with the intention of ridding the town of the scourge called the Dawson bunch.

The group of bandits had arrived in the usually peaceful town two weeks earlier and had spent each day since fleecing the town of everything. In desperation, the sheriff had sent a wire to the marshals.

Trent and Utah grabbed him while Crow got rid of the sheriff. The deputy fought as best he could, but his efforts were futile. The barkeep watched on, wishing he was brave enough to do something. But he wasn't. The percentage girls were gripped by a fascinated horror.

"What are you doin'?" Dawson asked.

"What's the problem?" Crow asked.

"Get a new chair."

"Good point."

The batwings opened and a timid-looking man entered. In his hand, he held a piece of paper. "Mr. Dawson."

Dawson turned his head to look at the man. "What do you want?"

"I have a wire for you."

"Who would be sendin' us a wire, Hunk?" Crow asked.

"Only one man knows where we are," Dawson replied. "Same man who hired us last time he wanted somethin' done."

"You mean the stampede?"

"Yeah." Dawson urged the man forward. "Give me what you got."

The telegrapher passed the paper over and beat a hasty retreat. Meanwhile, Dawson read the message. "Well, well. Time to go, boys. We've got a job to do."

"What about the deputy?" Trent asked.

Dawson drew his gun and shot the deputy marshal in the chest. "Problem solved."

* * *

As Quade rode into town, the looks he was getting from the townsfolk, some of them whom he knew, showed their evil intentions. He figured that every one of them was contemplating lynching him right at that moment.

"Murderer!" someone called out.

Quade needed to keep an eye on the gathering crowd. By the time he reached the jail, the townsfolk were thick on the ground. As he stepped down, Chuck Tobin appeared. In his hands, he carried a shotgun. "Get up here, killer, or I'll blow your guts through your spine."

"Let us have him, Chuck. It'll save the trouble of a trial," a voice called from the crowd.

"You know, that is a temptin' proposition."

Quade saw the look in the deputy's eyes and knew he was considering it. "You got it all wrong, Deputy," Quade said.

"Shut your mouth, killer," the deputy snarled. "Lord knows I should let them have you. Now, get inside where I can lock you up."

Quade stared at the shotgun. There was no arguing with it, so he did as ordered.

Once inside the sheriff's office, Tobin snapped, "Stop there. Keep your hands in the air."

Tobin stepped forward and Quade felt the familiar weight of the .45 leave its holster. The deputy tossed it on the sheriff's desk and then grabbed the cell keys. "In the cell. You'll find the door open."

The Faraday man walked through the door and Tobin

closed and locked it behind him. Quade turned and said, "You're makin' a big mistake."

"We'll see," Tobin replied with a sneer.

"Where is the sheriff?"

"He'll be here shortly."

The door to the office opened and Lucy Carter entered. Tobin turned and said to her, "You shouldn't be here, Lucy."

"I had to see for myself, Chuck."

The deputy pointed at the cell. "There he is. The killer himself."

Lucy walked toward the cell. "Was it you, Jack? Did you kill Jimmy?"

Quade shook his head. "No. You have to believe me, Lucy. I don't even know how I got roped into this mess."

"Because you were seen talkin' to the kid," Tobin snapped.

"Just because I was talkin' to him, doesn't mean I killed him." Quade looked at Lucy again. "You must believe me."

"I want to, Jack, but..." her voice trailed away.

The door opened again, and Carter appeared. "I see you've got him locked up, Chuck. Lucy, go home."

"But, Pa."

"Now, girl."

She gave one last pitiful look at Quade and left.

"Right," Carter said. "Convince me that you didn't kill that poor kid."

"I didn't kill him," Quade said. "When I left, he had already gone back inside. Ask Mary."

"That's what she said."

"She would though. She's your sister. You could have doubled back and waited then killed him with a knife," Tobin stated.

"Why would I do that?" Quade asked. "Tell me. Why would I kill a kid for no reason?"

"We'll find out why," the deputy sneered.

The door opened once more, this time admitting the mayor. Jerry Price took one look at Quade behind the bars and asked, "Well, has he confessed yet?"

"Not yet," said Carter. "We don't have any proof either. Only a witness who saw him talkin' to the kid."

"Who?" Quade asked. "Who is the damn witness?"

"I am," Carter said.

The Faraday man shook his head. "Sheriff, can you get everyone out of here? I need to talk to you in private."

Carter looked at the others in the jail. Both stood there defiantly, unwilling to leave. Carter nodded. "Okay, everyone out. That means you too, Chuck."

"Damn it, Lyle."

"Out."

"You don't talk to me like that, Sheriff," Price blustered. "Not if you want to keep your badge."

"Then find someone else who wants it," Carter said. "Especially with a range war hoverin' over the town."

Price hesitated and turned to follow Tobin out.

Now alone, Carter faced the cell. "Speak and make it good."

Quade took out his identification and passed it through the bars. The sheriff frowned as he took it. "What is this?"

"My credentials."

Carter stared at what he'd been given. "Faraday— you're a Faraday detective?"

"That's right," Quade replied. "Have been for some years. I was sent here for the Chicago, Rock Island and

Pacific Railroad. I'm investigatin' the murder of Sam Roberts. Among other things."

"What other things?"

"The fact that Tom Rafferty is tryin' to force everyone off their land before the railroad maps the right of way."

"Is that what he's doin'?"

"Of course he is. That was why he came here. He knew what was happenin' before anyone else did. But that isn't why I'm in jail. I didn't kill the kid. He told me what I needed to know."

"And what was that?" Carter asked.

Quade related the kid's story.

"Is that where you were today?"

"Yes. And I found another casin' the same as the one I found after Mary and me were bushwacked on the way to town."

"You're sayin' that it was the same person?" Carter asked, raising an eyebrow.

"I am. And it's the only lead I have."

The office door opened again. Carter's temper came to the surface. "Damn it, what now?"

Standing in the doorway were Rafferty and Abigail.

"I'm busy, Rafferty," Carter said. "Whatever it is will have to wait."

Quade looked at the woman. She glanced sheepishly at him in return, and the Faraday man knew instantly what was about to happen. Rafferty said, "Good, you have the murderer locked up already."

"I'm not convinced he killed the kid," Carter said.

"Not the kid. One of my men," Rafferty replied. "He shot down Toby Jones in cold blood."

"That's a mighty tall allegation. Do you have a witness?"

139

"The witness is here with me. Miss Davis. She was out riding when the incident occurred."

"Is that right, miss?" Carter asked.

Abigail's head bobbed. "Yes, it is."

"What do you have to say, Quade?"

"The woman is a liar," the Faraday man said.

"By God, sir," Rafferty exploded. "If you weren't locked away, I'd beat the truth out of you."

"Be thankful I am," Quade replied. His voice was ice cold, and death sat deep in his eyes. "Sheriff, talk to Harry Crosby. He was there. He'll tell you. The fight was fair. Jones drew first."

Carter looked at Abigail again. "Ma'am, would you like to tell me what happened?"

"I was out riding and came across Mr. Quade near the creek boundary. He'd just finished pulling down a section of fence. Mr. Crosby and Mr.—" she hesitated and dabbed at the corner of her eyes.

Quade shook his head. There were no tears. Carter said, "Go on, ma'am."

"That was when the other two men appeared, and Mr. Quade shot down Mr. Jones."

"What did Crosby do?"

"There was nothing he could do."

"I'll need to talk to Crosby, Rafferty," Carter said.

"I'll have him come in tomorrow morning."

"You do that. In the meantime, Quade, you go nowhere until this mess is sorted out or you go before the judge."

"It's all a load of horse sh—"

"I guess we'll find out. One way or the other. And if it's the other, you'll hang."

* * *

Once outside the jail, Rafferty placed Abigail in the buggy and waved Monte Cable over. "What's up, boss?"

"The sheriff has Quade locked away for now. But I want to make sure he doesn't get the chance to face a jury. Understand?"

"I guess I do."

Rafferty nodded. "I'll see Abbey home then I'll return. Start laying the groundwork in the saloon. By the time I return, I want even the stiffest of trees starting to bend."

"That might take a bit, sir."

Rafferty reached inside his coat and took out a fistful of money. "That should help to get things started."

CHAPTER 11

"I have some food for you," Carter said as he unlocked the cell door. "Just step back against the wall for a moment."

Quade did as requested. He was hungry, having not eaten since early that morning. Once the door was closed, he crossed the cell to pick up the tin plate and spoon. The meal was beef stew with some vegetables thrown in to bulk it out. Quade sat down on the bunk and started eating. "Lucy cook this?"

"She did," Carter confirmed. "What's wrong with it?"

"Nothin'. It's quite good."

"Yeah, she takes after her mama that way."

Quade kept eating. It was around eight in the evening, and although the temperature outside was dropping, elsewhere in town it was rising. There was a knock at the door and Carter walked over to it. "Who is it?"

"Franks and Grimshaw. We work for the railroad," came the voice from the other side.

The sheriff opened the door and let them in before locking it behind them. "What can I do for you gents?"

"It's what we can do for you. The saloon has a mob inside it fit to bust," Grimshaw said. "There's talk of lynch law, Sheriff, and Jack is invited to the party."

"Jack? You know Quade?"

"Should do. We work for the same man."

"Faraday?" Carter asked.

"Yes."

"This just gets better and better," Carter growled. He looked at Franks. "What about you?"

The surveyor shook his head. "Not me, Sheriff. I'm strictly railroad."

"What is goin' on here?" Carter demanded.

"I'm surveying for the railroad, Grimshaw is my help and my protector if you would," Franks said. "Quade is investigating the murder of my colleague. Although at the minute you have him locked up and a sitting duck for the lynch mob that is getting warmed up."

"Nobody is lynchin' anyone," Carter growled.

"Then I suggest you tell them at the saloon because they're being plied with enough liquor to float a Mississippi river boat."

"I'll deal with it when the time comes," Carter said.

This time, the knock on the door was a thumping sound. Carter opened it and let Tobin in. "Lyle, things are startin' to get out of hand in—"

The sound of gunshots shattered the night. Carter hurried to the wall gunrack and took down a shotgun. "No need to guess where that came from."

He started for the door. Tobin followed. "You stay here. No one gets in or out. Anyone tries to break in that isn't me, blast them."

"What about these two?" Tobin asked, indicating Grimshaw and Franks.

Carter looked at them. "Go back to your rooms and stay there."

Then he was gone.

* * *

The soft knock at Mary's door drew her away from the window where she'd been staring anxiously out at the street. "Who is it?"

"It's Lucy."

"Just a minute." She crossed the room, unlocked the door with the key, and opened it. "Come in."

Mary closed the door behind Lucy and turned hurriedly. "Are you okay?"

Lucy shook her head. "Oh, Mary, it's terrible. The mob that is gathered in the saloon."

"It's a lynch mob, isn't it?"

Lucy nodded. "I've seen things like it before. It only ends badly."

"What about your father?"

"He'll stand. That's why I'm so scared. He won't give your brother up without a fight."

Mary took her by the hand. "It will be fine, you'll see. Stay with me for as long as you like."

"I'm scared, Mary."

"So am I. But—"

"I love him."

"Oh no, Lucy," Mary gasped.

"I—I can't help it. Even though he rejected me. And I hate him for it. Hate him!" She collapsed into Mary's arms.

Mary thought long and hard before she said, "I need to tell you something."

Lucy stepped back and stared at her through tear-filled eyes. "What?"

"Jack isn't who you think he is. He's a Faraday detective."

"A detective?" Lucy was confused. "But he never said."

"No, he's working undercover. He's investigating the murder of the surveyor," Mary explained.

"He didn't say. Why didn't he say?" Lucy was shocked by the news.

"He couldn't. He was using his name as a gunfighter to be his cover. People thinking he'd come back to help Pa was his cover."

"But didn't he?"

"In a way, I guess he did," Mary acceded.

"Now he's in jail for murder."

"He didn't kill Jimmy," Mary said firmly. "I know he didn't, and I'll swear to that in a court of law."

"I know that, but what about that hired gun for Rafferty he killed? He's the one behind all of this."

"I know, Lucy. We just have to trust in the law."

"But which law?" Lucy asked.

"The right one."

* * *

Carter entered the saloon amid a raucous uproar. Carrying the shotgun in one hand, he didn't want to appear threatening. Not just yet. He wanted to reason with them if he could. In situations like this, he found that a shotgun deterred most people, but if action was needed, you always took out the leader. Cut the head off the snake.

Still keeping the shotgun in his hand, Carter drew his six-gun and fired a round into the ceiling. The bar went quiet immediately. "Now that I've got your attention, the bar is closed and you are to all go home."

"You can't do that, Sheriff," a cowboy bleated.

"I can do whatever I want," Carter stated. He looked at the barkeep. "The Tall Grass is now closed for business. Jasper, get them out."

"You're doin' me out of business, Lyle," Jasper whined.

"All you're doin' is feedin' a lynch mob courage," the sheriff snarled. "Well, I'm puttin' a stop to it."

Rafferty squeezed his way through the crowd. "All that's going on, Sheriff, is a friendly drink."

"The hell it is."

"You could make it easy and hand the murderer over."

"He gets a fair trial, Rafferty. In front of a judge and a jury."

"We already had us a trial, Sheriff," Cable said. "He's as guilty as sin."

"Yeah!" the bar erupted.

Carter was about to speak when a cowhand stepped up behind him and swung a chair. The chair splintered as it crashed down upon the sheriff's head. Carter staggered and fell, unable to rise. "Tie him up," Cable snapped.

It took only a minute for the sheriff to be secured. Then Rafferty stepped forward, "Let's go and have ourselves a lynching."

* * *

Tobin watched out the window as the mob left the saloon carrying lanterns and a rope. Out front were

Rafferty and Cable. "Here they come, killer. Looks like they're all liquored up and howlin' at the moon."

"Can you see the sheriff?" Quade asked.

"Nope, not a hair."

Quade glanced around the cell. It was a useless gesture because there was nowhere to go. "Let me out of here, Tobin. Before they get in."

"You ain't goin' anywhere," the deputy growled and opened the door to the jail.

"What are you doin'?"

"Goin' to stop this mob."

Tobin closed the door behind himself and stood on the boardwalk outside the jail. "That's far enough, Rafferty."

The mob kept coming. "Step aside, Deputy."

Tobin fired the shotgun into the air, stopping the mob mid street. "I said stop there. I still got one barrel left."

"You don't get paid enough, Deputy," Rafferty said. "Just step aside like I said. You may get one of us, but you won't be able to reload before someone gets you."

Tobin scanned the mob before him and started to get nervous. It was the first time he'd faced anything like it, and he was on his own. "Where is the sheriff?"

"He's a little tied up right now." Cable grinned. "Sleepin' too."

Now he was nervous. His eyes darted left and right as he looked for help. He was all tough on the outside, but when push came to shove, he wasn't so sure.

"What's it goin' to be, Deputy?"

Once the shotgun started lowering there was no stopping it. Then he stepped aside, leaving the way clear for the mob. Rafferty nodded. "That's it, boys, go and get him."

Five men charged past Tobin and inside the jail. There came the sound of a scuffle from within and shouts and cussing. Then they appeared with Quade struggling to get away from them. The Faraday man stared at Rafferty. "You son of a bitch. You know that he drew first."

"Get him over to the tree," the rancher snarled.

The mob dragged Quade along the street to where a lone oak stood. Cable snapped, "Get the rope over that branch."

The rope was tossed over a strong branch and the noose at the other end was dropped over Quade's head. There was to be no drop from a horse. They were just going to string him up like a side of beef.

"Right," called Rafferty. "Get the bastard up."

"Stop!"

Heads turned toward the authoritative voice. Sitting atop his horse was Harry Crosby. Both his hands were filled with his Colts. "First man that pulls on that rope, I kill."

"What are you doing, Crosby?" Rafferty growled.

"It was a fair fight, and you know it, Rafferty," Crosby said stoically. He pointed a gun at the nearest man to Quade. "Untie his hands."

"No," Cable snapped, stepping in front of the Faraday man. "He killed Summers and Jones."

"Now, Monte, don't make me shoot you."

"I'm not movin', Harry. And he ain't bein' set free."

The Colt in Crosby's hand barked and Cable staggered with a bullet in his left shoulder. Crosby said, "If you want, Monte, I can bring the next one across a few inches and kill you dead."

Cable stepped aside and the man Crosby had ordered

to untie Quade completed his task. Rafferty, by now, was beyond angry. "You're done, Crosby."

"I guess so," the gunfighter replied. "Jack, your horse is outside the gunsmith."

"Thanks, Harry."

"Don't thank me yet, we still have to get out of here."

Using his knees, Crosby backed his horse up. Quade reached the roan and climbed aboard. "I'm ready, Harry."

"Then let's go," the gunfighter said and fired some shots over the mob before turning his mount and kicking it into a dead run. Behind them, the crowd gathered itself quickly and started firing at the retreating riders. Shouts filled the night, the loudest voice of all belonged to Rafferty. "Get after them! Get your horses! Five hundred dollars to whoever gets the killer."

As the mob scattered, none of them saw the lone figure standing in the shadows watching on.

* * *

Two miles from Sagebrush Creek, things took a dramatic turn. "We need to pull up. I don't feel so good," Crosby called out.

They eased down and stopped in the middle of the road. "What is it?"

"I stopped a bullet on the way—" Crosby slumped in the saddle.

Quade moved in before he could fall to the ground. "Darn it."

Quade eased the horses off the road and into some trees. He climbed down and checked Crosby over.

"Yes, you sure stopped a bullet," the Faraday man said as he felt the blood-soaked material on the man's back. "We need to get you somewhere."

Suddenly, the rumble of distant hoofbeats reached out of the darkness. Quade knew his roan would be fine, but he was unfamiliar with Crosby's horse. He reached up and placed a hand on the horse's muzzle to calm it. The rumble grew louder, and he could start to hear the riders urging their mounts on.

Then out of the gloom thundered the makeshift posse. They rode as they had stood in the street. An uncontrolled mob. Then they were gone.

What he needed now was somewhere safe to hide Crosby so he could be looked after. An idea came to him. He didn't like it, but there was no doubt in his mind that the gunman wouldn't get far in his condition. "Ah, hell."

* * *

Quade snuck into Mrs. Hamblin's Boarding House the back way up the stairs. Surprised to find the door at the top open at night, he let himself in. Walking as silently as he could along the hallway until he reached Mary's door, he knocked softly.

"Who is it?" he heard in response.

"It's me," he whispered. "Let me in."

Urgent footsteps crossed to the door. The key turned in the lock, and the door opened. "Good Lord, Jack, quick, come in." He slipped through the opening, and Mary closed the door.

"Jack, what are you doing here?" It was Lucy.

"What are you doin' here?" he asked.

"I was here when the mob took over."

"They were about to hang me when Crosby took a hand. We got out of town and then had to come back. Tobin, the useless vulture, stood there and watched them drag me out and put a damn rope around my neck."

"What about Pa?" Lucy asked.

"I don't know. They did somethin' to him."

There was concern on her face. "I must go and find him."

Quade blocked her path. "Be careful, Lucy. The streets are dangerous."

"I'll be fine."

"Don't tell him you've seen me."

"Okay."

She disappeared and Quade turned to his sister. "I need your help."

Mary nodded. "To hide?"

"Yes, but not me."

She frowned. "Who?"

"Crosby took a bullet on the way out of town. He needs doctorin' and somewhere to rest."

"Here?" Mary asked, shocked by her brother's request. "You want him to stay here?"

"He won't make it to the ranch, Mary. It's here or nowhere."

Mary shook her head and shrugged her shoulders. "Sure, why not?"

Quade took several minutes to get back down and return with the half-conscious Crosby. When they made it to her room, Quade laid the wounded man on his stomach and began removing the clothes. He looked at the bullet hole and saw that it was close to the gunfighter's spine. "He's goin' to need Doc Cleaver."

Mary gave him a funny look. "Doc Cleaver has been dead for six years, Jack. We have a new one now."

"Then get him, Mary."

"I'll take care of this, Jack. You need to get out of town. Head out to the ranch."

Quade shook his head. "No, I'll head over to the line

shack under Coogan's Bluff and lay low there for a time. Once Crosby is well enough, fetch the sheriff and have him tell Carter the truth."

"What are you going to do?" Mary asked.

Quade strapped on Crosby's guns. "Wait until I'm in the clear. Once I am, come and find me."

* * *

It was Tobin who found Carter trussed up like a Christmas turkey on the floor of the saloon. The sheriff was conscious, but no one would go near him to set him free. "What is wrong with you people?" Tobin snarled, his pride still wounded from being made to back down.

He set Carter free, and the lawman sat up, rubbing his head where he'd been hit. "What happened, Chuck?"

"The mob broke Quade out of jail and tried to lynch him," Tobin explained.

"Damn it. You say, tried?"

"Yes, Harry Crosby managed to stop it, and they rode out of town. Rafferty formed a posse to go after them."

Carter climbed to his feet. He wobbled a little and then straightened. "How did they get him out?"

"Well, I—"

"Pa!" Lucy exclaimed as she entered the saloon. "You're okay?"

"Stop fussin', girl," the sheriff growled. "I been hit harder by your mother."

Lucy hugged her father and then focused her built-up rage on Tobin. "You. You're a low-down skunk."

"Whoa, girl. What are you sayin'?" her father asked.

"Chuck stood by and let them take Jack from the jail to be hung. All because he doesn't like him."

"That's not true," Tobin snapped at her. "I tried to stop them, but there was too many."

"You didn't try too hard!" Lucy exclaimed.

"Let's get back to the jail," Carter said. He turned and pointed a finger at Jasper Foley. "I'll talk to you later. If you have any sense, you'd damn well leave town."

"I never hit you."

"You never did anythin' to stop it, either. Damn son of a bitch. I'll be back."

* * *

Once they reached the jail, Carter asked, "What happened to the mob?"

"Like I said, they rode out after Crosby and Quade with Rafferty bayin' for blood," Tobin explained.

"Damn it, that's all I need. A trigger-happy posse gallopin' all over the county shootin' at anythin' that moves."

"There is somethin' else you should know," Tobin said.

"What?"

"I heard Crosby say that he was there when the gunfight happened and said it was a fair fight."

"That means Jack is innocent," Lucy said positively.

"Maybe so, girl, but Crosby needs to say it in a court of law."

"You mean Jack still needs to go on trial?" There was more than a hint of disbelief in Lucy's voice.

"The accusation still stands, girl. He needs to be cleared legal-like. It's the law."

"Damn the law."

Carter nodded. "In the mornin' I'll ride out and see if

I can find them." He looked at Tobin. "Do you think you can manage to stay out of damn trouble while I'm gone?"

"You mean I still have a job?"

"There ain't no one else to replace you. If there was, I'd rip that star right off your damn chest. Are you comin' home, girl?"

"I'll be there soon, Pa. I just want to check on Mary."

"All right. Just don't be too late."

Lucy left the jail and hurried across the street and along to the boarding house. When she arrived outside Mary's door, she knocked softly, waiting for Mary to answer. "Lucy, you're back."

"Yes, I came to see you before I go home." Mary nodded but didn't invite her in. "Is everything okay, Mary?"

"Yes, just fine. I was getting ready for bed."

"With your clothes on?"

"Yes. I haven't changed yet," she replied nervously.

"What's going on? Is Jack still here?"

"No."

There came a moan. Soft, pained. "Who is that, then?"

She pushed her way in. Mary staggered back. "Lucy, wait."

But there was no waiting. The sheriff's daughter took one look at the form on the bed and realized that it wasn't Jack Quade. "Harry Crosby."

"Yes, he was shot when they ran out of town. He's got a bullet in his back, and it needs to come out."

"Why haven't you gone for the doctor?"

"Because I'm not sure I can trust him," Mary replied.

"I'll go. I'll be back soon."

"You don't mind, Lucy?"

She shook her head. "He saved Jack. It's the least I can do."

CHAPTER 12

Dr. Julius Ferdinand was reading a medical journal by lamplight when the hurried knock came at his door. His wife was asleep in bed due to the sedative he'd given her earlier in the evening to calm her nerves.

He and his wife had moved to Sagebrush Creek soon after his predecessor had died of a heart attack. After seeing an advertisement for a doctor in his local paper at Halliday Falls, he'd held a discussion with his wife, Mabel, and the pair had decided a change was in order.

With the sound of the barrage on the door, he frowned and removed his glasses. Placing the journal on the arm of his chair, he rose to his feet. It took a few steps to get his legs working properly, and by then he was completely mobile. Damn getting old.

He opened the door and found himself staring at Lucy Carter. "Good Lord, young lady. Do you know what time it is?"

"I'm sorry, Doctor. But I have an emergency. Gunshot wound to the back."

"Oh, dear, I'll just grab my bag."

Ferdinand disappeared and returned a short time later with his medical bag. "Lead the way, girl."

Following Lucy to the boarding house, Ferdinand became suspicious when she led him in the back way. But by the time they reached Mary's room, he was certain something was going on. Then he saw Crosby. "Good Lord. What do we have here?"

"It's Harry Crosby," Mary said.

Ferdinand looked at her. "I can see that, Mary. The question is, what is he doing here?"

"He was shot helping Jack not to be lynched. Now he needs your help. Please, Dr. Ferdinand."

"I never said I wasn't going to help him. Get me some water and I'll have a look."

"Thank you."

* * *

The posse drew to a halt five miles from town on jaded horses. They had been ridden hard and needed a spell. There was no sign of the two fugitives, and even after this short distance, the grumbling had already set in.

"We'll never find them in the dark," growled a cowhand.

"You heard Crosby. He said it was a fair fight," said another.

"Might as well leave it until the mornin'," said another.

"What is wrong with you people?" Rafferty demanded. "You let a damn murderer ride free?"

"It was legal," the second man said.

"And I tell you Crosby lied. My fiancée was there, she saw it all."

Slowly at first, riders started to turn their mounts

back toward town. "Come back, damn you!" Rafferty snarled.

"In the mornin' Rafferty," the first man said.

"But he could be anywhere by then."

"If he has any sense, he will be."

* * *

"There," Ferdinand said. "I think that'll make him feel better."

"Will he be all right?" Mary asked.

"Give him a few days and he'll be fine."

A noise from the street outside drew Lucy to the window. She looked down and saw the horsemen riding slowly along it. "The posse is back."

Mary joined her. "They look all done in."

"They just needed to run their drunk off," Ferdinand said.

Mary turned to face the doctor. "You can't tell anyone he's here."

Ferdinand closed his medical bag. "Your secret is safe with me."

The doctor slipped out the way he'd come in, leaving the two women to watch over the patient. Mary said, "I don't know what I'll do tomorrow. I have school."

"I'll come and watch him while you're there," Lucy said. "Then you can take over while I'm working in the dining room."

"Oh, Lucy, you don't have to do that."

"I want to."

"Fine. You'd better go home then."

She gave Mary a hug and left. Mary looked down at Crosby and said a silent prayer over the gunfighter.

* * *

It was two hours before dawn when Quade reached the line shack beneath the bluff. All the way there, he couldn't help but think that someone was following him. At one point, Quade stopped and checked his backtrail. Satisfied that it was nothing more than his imagination, he moved on.

Upon reaching the shack, Quade lit the stove and piled on the wood. The roan was secured in the side corral. In the morning, after the sun came up, he'd get some meat. He should be able to find a deer.

Spoiled for choice with two bunks, he opted for the one with the least lumpy mattress. That was where he lay and was asleep within minutes.

Bright sun woke Quade the following morning. It streamed through one of the shack's windows and tried to blind him. The Faraday man climbed out of bed and walked over to the window to look out. Observing nothing of any danger, he went to one of the cupboards to see what was inside. There was a sack of coffee left for the rider unlucky enough to be sent to the bluff. Quade filled the coffee pot with water from the nearby stream. Then he relit the stove and started it to boil.

It was the roan that sounded the alarm. Quade had been sitting at the small table with his steaming mug, thinking about the times when he and Mary were small, how their father used to bring them to the bluff. Sometimes their mother would come. Better days.

The high-pitched whistle from the animal was a warning Quade had heard before. He dropped a hand to a holstered Colt and drew it on his way to the window.

He peered out and saw the rider about a hundred yards out, just sitting there unmoving. Quade watched him while he watched the shack. Quade found himself wondering if it was the same rider he'd seen the other day.

"Let's see what your intentions are."

Quade went outside and stood under the awning. The rider remained where he was, unmoved. Watching the shack and now the man. Quade was about to go back inside when the rider turned his horse. Not away from the shack, but toward it.

They approached slowly, rider and animal moving as one. Then, when the rider was close enough, he stopped and thumbed back his hat to reveal his face. "Howdy."

"Howdy yourself," Quade replied.

"Just passin' by, smelled your coffee," the stranger said.

"Has a strong smell to it," Quade said.

"Spare a cup?"

The Faraday man nodded. "Sure. Step on down."

The man climbed down and tied his horse to the corral. "You from this ranch?"

"You could say that."

The stranger nodded. "Figured as much."

"Didn't catch your name," Quade said.

"Didn't give it," came the reply.

"What do they call you?"

"Some folks call me some things, some others. Most call me Pike Miller."

Quade nodded. Miller was a killer. No, more than that, he was a hired assassin. If he was here in the valley, he was here for a reason. The two men went inside, and Quade poured the coffee into two tin cups.

"Just passin' through, Miller?" Quade asked.

"Figured I might hang around for a while. Seems like a pretty valley."

"Been here a while?"

The killer shook his head. "Nope. Not long at all. Few days."

The Faraday man put two and two together. It had been him whom he'd seen on the ridge. Quade drank his coffee, keeping a careful eye on Miller. The killer finished his and placed the cup on the table. "I guess I'll be goin' now. Thanks for the coffee."

Miller started to stand and suddenly found himself facing the serious end of a Colt which rested on the edge of the table. Quade had drawn it silently and kept it beneath the table just in case. Now, as Miller stood, he showed the killer he had it as a warning.

Miller nodded. "Never can be too careful, Quade."

That was why he'd not asked his name, he already knew it.

"Why are you here, Miller?" Quade asked.

"Got a job. Be seein' you, Quade. Count on it."

Quade watched Miller leave and contemplated killing him while he had the chance.

* * *

Scratch Morton and Windy Wills had been working the stage to Sagebrush Creek for the past eight years, and after the first few, Scratch, the driver, always said that he could get there in his sleep while dreaming about Miss Fanny's dance hall girls. Every time he said it though, he was full up on red-eye.

Windy was the shotgun guard and Scratch's good friend. The two were inseparable. Before hiring on to the stage line, they had driven freight wagons into Indian country. It took a hard man to do it, and these two had once been the hardest. Now, they were getting on in years. Hair starting to gray, waistlines expanding, the pair had a penchant for reliving the good old days.

Scratch cracked the lines across the backs of the six-up team and let out a wild yell. "Get up there, you rascally varmints! Put some back into it."

"You ain't talkin' to mine workers, you know, Scratch," Windy called over to his friend. "They're darn horses."

"Cow Creek Crossin' comin' up, Windy," his friend shouted.

"Damn it, I know that, you fool."

The trail snaked around a hill and a line of cottonwoods came into view. The trail seemed to get swallowed by them as if they were hungry animals. Running along their base was Cow Creek as it cut across the landscape. Here, the trail dipped, and the driver had to slow his team to a crawl. If ever there was an ideal place for a holdup, this was it. It made Windy nervous, even after years of never experiencing any trouble.

As the creek and cottonwoods loomed closer, Scratch eased the team down. He figured to give them a drink before moving on. They still had five miles to go until the next change and then five miles into Sagebrush Creek.

By the time they reached the creek bank, the team was down to a walk. Then it stopped, and in the partial silence that followed, the hammers on the shotgun could be heard going back.

The reason? There was a rider unmoving in the middle of Cow Creek. He seemed to be watering his horse. However, when he looked up, the two men atop the stage could see the bandana around the lower half of his face.

"Ah, horse sheeit!" Windy exclaimed and started to

bring the shotgun around, but failed to bring it into line in time.

Two rifles hidden in the trees, one on either side of the trail, roared to life.

The driver and guard were punched from the seat. They tumbled to the ground and landed with dull thuds. The horse team snorted with surprise but stood their ground. Two men emerged from the trees and approached the stage. The rider came out of the shallow creek and climbed down, drawing his sidearm. "Everyone out of the stage," he barked.

The door opened and a man, a whiskey drummer, climbed down. The three killers waited for the rest, but no one else emerged. The leader of the three indicated for one of the others to look inside. The closest man poked his head in the open door and then leaned back. "There's no one else."

The boss of the gang nodded, shifted his aim, and shot the whiskey drummer cold in the chest.

"Right, get the strongbox down, Yost."

Climbing onto the roof, Yost found the strongbox and threw it to the ground. Cable came alongside and, with his sidearm, shot the lock off. The box was opened, and there within was the money. Cable removed the cash and stuffed it into his saddlebags. "Make sure everyone is dead, and we'll get gone."

Yost checked the driver and the guard, while Frost, the third man, checked the drummer. All three were dead and they had the money. Mission accomplished. Rafferty would be happy.

* * *

"Where do you think they are?" Abigail asked Rafferty.

"They could be anywhere," he replied. "But I can't worry about that at the moment. I have other issues."

"Can I help?" she asked.

He was about to tell her no when Cable arrived back. In his hand, he carried his saddlebags, which he tossed onto Rafferty's desk. He said, "Present for you."

The rancher opened the bags and took out the money. "Any trouble?"

Cable shook his head. "Not now and not in the future."

"Well done."

Rafferty took the money and locked it in his safe. "Take Yost and Frost and head up to Celtic Ridge. It'll give you an alibi."

"Yes, sir."

Rafferty took out a piece of paper and a pencil stub. He started writing, and when he was finished, he gave the paper to Cable. "When you get there, give this to the town marshal. He owes me a favor. Just in case. Understand?"

"Understood."

"Good, go."

* * *

Leaving Sagebrush Creek shortly after the sun had poked its head over the eastern horizon, Sheriff Carter had a headache, which did nothing to improve his mood. He'd heard tell of a line shack at Coogan's Bluff and had an inkling that that may be where Quade and Crosby headed to hole up. He'd go there and check it out.

The mayor had already chewed his ear that morning, wanting to know what he was going to do about the escape of the murderer and the man who had helped him. Carter had stared at him and replied, "I'll get them back, and when I do, I'm goin' to start lookin' into that lynch mob from last night. Then I'm goin' to start arrestin' people for attempted murder. No matter who they are."

That had brought about an immediate silence.

It was about mid-morning when the line shack came into view. Carter stopped and sat watching it to see if there was any sign of life. He waited and caught the faint wisp of smoke coming from the shack's chimney.

Carter drew his six-gun and kneed the horse forward. He figured that if Quade was truly innocent, he wouldn't fire. And right at that point in time, he had doubts about the man's guilt.

As rider and horse closed the distance to the shack, nothing happened. No movement, and more importantly, no shot. When he reached the corral, Carter cautiously dismounted and tied the horse to the middle rail.

Approaching the door slowly, he stopped first to peer through the window. The shack appeared to be empty. The sheriff stepped up to the door, taking a breath before opening it, then stepped to the side to prevent himself from being framed in the doorway.

Nothing happened. The shack was empty.

He entered and looked around. There were two cups on the small table. He figured they had both been here. But now they were gone.

CHAPTER 13

Quade figured he'd be better off at the Double Q ranch house. His father would hide him and feed him while he was there. That way, Quade could get a better feel of what was happening in town.

When he rode into the ranch yard, his father was at the corral. He stared at his son. "Damn it, boy, you're takin' a chance comin' here."

"I got nowhere else to go, Pa. Especially now."

"What do you mean?"

"The law wants me, and there is a killer ridin' the range and I think he wants my hide."

"Who, boy?"

"A hired gun called Pike Miller."

Vince spat in the dirt. "Never heard of him."

"You're not supposed to. That's the point," Quade explained.

"He the one who killed that surveyor feller?"

"I don't think so. I think he's here for me."

"Then you'd better stick close until it's all figured out," Vince said, turning to head for the tack shed.

"Thanks, Pa."

"I'll get one of the men to take care of your horse. Get inside out of sight. Have Charlie cook you somethin' to eat. I've got to go to town and meet the stage."

"Can you do me a favor while you're there?"

"What is it?" Vince asked.

"Ask Mary how Harry Crosby is?"

"Why would I do that?"

"Because he saved me from a rope and took a bullet while he was doin' it."

"All right, I'll ask her."

"Be careful, Pa."

"We'll see."

Quade went inside and found Charlie in the kitchen. "Well, well, if it ain't the most wanted man in the territory."

"Not funny, Charlie," Quade replied.

"Don't expect it is, son. Now, what can this old chowhound do for you?"

"Coffee would be good," Quade replied.

"Comin' up, Jack. Take a seat."

* * *

Carter rode into the Double Q ranch yard an hour later. Vince had already left for town to meet the stage. Lucas Howard met the sheriff before he could climb down from his horse. "Help you, Sheriff?"

"Vince here?" Carter asked.

"No, he's gone to town to meet the stage," Howard explained.

"You in charge?"

"Me and Charlie," Howard answered with a nod.

"The cook?" There was surprise in the sheriff's voice.

"That cook has been with Vince since this place was settled. Now, Sheriff, what is it you want?"

"You have a line shack out at the bluff." It was a statement, not a question.

"We do. No one there at the moment. We're not runnin' enough beef."

"I tracked Jack Quade and Harry Crosby there this mornin'," Carter explained. "They were gone when I got there. Haven't seen them by any chance?"

Howard shook his head. "Nope."

Carter didn't believe him. "In case you do happen to see Jack, tell him I need to see them both to get this mess cleared up. If I believe what I'm hearin', then there will be no need for a trial."

"I'll make sure to do that."

With a nod, Carter turned his horse and rode out of the yard. The moment he was gone, Quade appeared.

"You hear all that?" the foreman asked.

"Yeah. Thanks."

* * *

Vince rode into town and over to the stage depot. He tied his horse to the hitch rail and stepped up onto the boardwalk before going inside the office. A young woman was behind the desk. Bethany Roper looked up and smiled. "Morning, Mr. Quade. Here for business?"

"Just here to meet the stage, Beth," Vince replied.

"Visitor coming in, sir?"

Vince shook his head. "No, Beth, no. Somethin' better. What time is the stage due?"

"About ten, but you can always add an hour to that. Scratch and Windy might be the best team on the stage line, but being on time is not their strong point."

"That's fine, I'll go along and see Mary."

"Any news about Jack?"

Vince shook his head. "Nothin' new I heard."

"Ghastly thing, a lynch mob. I'm glad he got away."

Vince nodded. "Thanks, Beth. Me too, I guess."

The old rancher left the stage office and walked along the street. As he approached the schoolhouse, he saw a group of kids run out. Mary was close behind them and stood on the steps watching them go. She spotted her father and waved.

Vince waved back and waited as she bounced down the steps and hurried toward him. "Hello, Pa."

"Hi, Mary, girl. Them kids keepin' you on your toes?"

She smiled. "When don't they?"

"You and your brother were like that. I don't know how your ma kept up with you."

"Oh, Pa, it's terrible," Mary finally burst out. "They tried to lynch Jack last night. If it hadn't been for Harry Crosby, they would have succeeded."

"So I heard."

"The sheriff is out looking for them. Have you seen Jack?"

Vince gave a slight nod. "He's fine, Mary. Just fine. Can't say I've seen Crosby though."

Mary gave him a sheepish look. One he'd seen all too often as she was growing up. "Where is he, Mary?"

"In my room." Before her father could explode, she went on. "He's been shot. The doctor took out the bullet and says he'll be fine. Lucy is with him at the moment."

"Lucy Carter?" Vince asked.

"Yes, Pa."

"Jumpin' Jehoshaphat. If her pa finds out, he'll lock both of you up."

"He saved Jack, Pa. I couldn't let him die. Besides, it was Jack who brought him to me."

Vince shook his head. "That boy ought to have more sense."

"You raised him, Pa."

"You'd better take me over there before—"

Suddenly, the cacophony of iron-rimmed wheels and galloping hoofs assaulted the steady hum of the main street. Both Vince and Mary turned and saw the stage-coach thundering into Sagebrush Creek, a horse tied behind. There was only a single man up top. "This isn't good," Vince muttered.

"Hold up!" the driver shouted. "The stage has been held up!"

Vince glanced at Mary. A look of horror appeared on her face. "Pa?"

The rancher nodded. "I know, Mary. I think I've wasted my time comin' to town."

The man atop the stage managed to get the team stopped outside the jail. "Someone better get the under-taker, I got three bodies inside."

The driver jumped down and opened the door as a crowd began to gather. Tobin emerged from inside the jail and demanded, "What's all the yowlin' about?"

"The stage has been held up and everyone killed," the man stated.

"Held up, you say?"

"Yeah. The strongbox was empty on the ground. I found the stage at Cow Creek."

Vince turned to Mary. "Go and tell your brother what's happened. He's out at the ranch."

Filled with questions, Mary knew that now wasn't the time. "I'll send the children home and go then."

Jerry Price stepped forward. "You'd better get a posse together, Chuck. You might be able to track the killers."

Tobin nodded. "Who's comin'?"

No one moved.

"Come on, someone has to come, that's the meanin' of a posse."

Still, no one moved.

"I see. You were all big and brave last night goin' after an unarmed prisoner with a rope. But when it comes to somethin' like this, you all have a streak of yeller runnin' down your backs."

"No worse than you last night," someone called from the crowd.

Tobin ran his gaze over the gathering and then turned and walked back into the jail. Crossing to the gun rack, he took down a Winchester. Then he grabbed a box of .44-40s. Vince entered the jail and stopped in the middle of the room. Tobin glanced at the rancher. "I don't have time for whatever it is, Vince."

"I'm comin' with you, Chuck," Vince told him.

"Why would you do that?"

"Because in that strongbox was five thousand dollars meant for me. If I don't get it back, I lose my ranch."

Tobin nodded. "You got a rifle?"

"Just my six-shooter."

Tobin grabbed another Winchester from the rack and passed it to Vince. "Thanks, Vince."

"I ain't doin' it for you, Chuck. Just so we're clear."

Ten minutes later, they rode out of town together.

* * *

Meanwhile, as Tobin and Vince left town, Carter was staking out the Double Q from a stand of trees overlooking the ranch house. He watched on with interest as Mary rode into the yard, her horse lathered and blowing hard. Lucas Howard saw her coming and met her in the yard. He grabbed the horse's bridle and looked up at Mary. "What are you doin', girl? You tryin' to kill this animal?"

"I need to see Jack. It's important."

"I don't know what you're talkin' about."

"I know he's here. Pa told me."

The Double Q foreman nodded. "You'll find him in the ranch house. Most likely in the kitchen."

Mary hurried toward the house and dashed up the steps and inside. Like Howard had told her, Quade was in the kitchen talking to Charlie. He took one look at her and asked, "What is it, Mary?"

"The stage was robbed out at Cow Creek. They took the money meant for Pa."

"Damn it," Quade growled. "Where is he now?"

"He went with Chuck Tobin. No one would join his posse. Pa needs that money, Jack, otherwise he will lose this place."

Quade nodded. "Charlie, get Howard to settle my horse."

"You can't go out there, Jack," Mary pleaded.

"I have to. We need to find that money, otherwise this place will be gone within the week."

"Your old man would never let that happen," Charlie told him.

"I know. That would mean one thing. A full-blown range war."

Charlie hurried out of the kitchen to go and see Howard. Mary stepped closer to her brother. "I'm scared, Jack. If Pa loses that money, he's not going to give this place away. I'm worried that Rafferty will kill him."

"Not while I'm here, he won't."

Quade picked up the gun belt that had been Crosby's. He buckled it on and adjusted it. He had an afterthought. "Did you pass Carter on the way into town?"

Mary frowned. She shook her head and said, "I didn't pass anyone."

"That means he's out here somewhere. Possibly watching the house."

"Then you can't go, Jack."

He patted her on the arm. "I'll be fine."

* * *

Now what is going on here? Carter wondered to himself. He'd caught sight of Mary coming up the trail, flat out on the horse. The animal was tired and its gait weary. There was obviously something important that she needed to get to the ranch for. But not to see her father. Her father wasn't there.

He watched her dismount and talked to Howard. He pointed toward the ranch house and Mary ran toward it and disappeared inside. The sheriff's suspicions grew.

A few minutes later, Charlie Brown, the cook, appeared. He ran to the barn, and then after a few more minutes, he emerged with a saddled horse. Carter knew the roan anywhere. So Quade was there.

It wasn't long before the man himself appeared, running toward the horse and then climbing into the saddle. Charlie Brown patted Quade on the leg to wish him luck, and then the gunfighter was gone.

Coming to his feet, Carter ran toward his own mount tied to a tree. He couldn't let Quade get too far away. Climbing into the saddle, he began following the wanted man.

* * *

When Vince Quade and Chuck Tobin arrived at the scene of the holdup, they climbed down from their horses and started to look around for any sign of who they might be after. There were plenty of tracks to be found along with numerous bullet casings where the two bushwhackers had fired their weapons from the trees.

After twenty minutes of looking, Tobin looked at Vince. "What do you figure happened?"

"How about you tell me, Deputy?"

"I think there was someone blockin' the trail in the middle of the creek. The stage stopped up there on the bank, and then the two men who were in the trees opened fire."

"That is the way I read it. But you're forgettin' somethin'."

"The third man who was shot?"

Vince nodded. "He would have still been in the stage when the shootin' started. What they've done, they've ordered him out and then they've shot him down cold so there was no witness."

"How do you figure that?"

"Because that's the only thing that makes sense."

Tobin kicked the empty strong box that had been left behind. "Once they cleaned the strong box out, they left."

Vince pointed toward a low hill. "They went that way."

"There's nothin' over there except for..."

"Rockin' R range," Vince finished.

The sound of a galloping horse turned both men around. Tobin frowned. "Is that who I think it is?"

"Damn fool," Vince muttered.

"It is him."

"Of course it's him, you lame brained idiot," Vince exploded.

Quade drew the roan to a halt on the creek bank, not far from where his father and Tobin stood. The deputy now had his handgun out and pointed in Quade's direction. "Get down nice and easy, Quade."

"Put the gun up, Chuck," the Faraday man said. "You don't need it. I'm here to help."

"The hell you are. You are goin' nowhere but back to jail."

"You must be the dumbest son of a bitch God ever gave breath to," Vince said. "If we have to go on Rafferty land, we're goin' to need every gun we can get."

"He goes back to jail." Tobin was adamant.

"Then you can argue it with him," Vince said, nodding toward another rider coming toward the creek.

Carter drew rein and stared at the three men before him. "What in the hell is goin' on here?"

"Sheriff, I caught Quade."

"I can see that, Chuck, but why is everyone here?" Carter asked.

"The stage was robbed. I wouldn't be surprised if Quade had somethin' to do with it."

Carter shook his head. "Sometimes, Chuck, you can be such a dunderhead."

"What did I do now?"

"I just followed him from the Double Q."

"And why would I steal from a stage that carried money that would save the ranch?" Quade growled.

Tobin poked at the ground with his boot like a scolded child. Carter said, "Tell me what happened."

Tobin ran through what he and Vince had deduced. When he was finished, he said, "The three outlaws rode toward the Rockin' R."

"Then we'd better get goin' then," Carter said. "Lest Windy and Scratch will get no justice, and Vince will lose his ranch."

"Don't you want me to take Quade back to town?" Tobin asked.

"No, I don't want you to take Quade back to town. He's comin' with us."

"You want I should take his guns then?"

"We're about to ride into a nest of rattlers, Chuck. What do you think?"

* * *

Following the trail, it didn't take long for the four riders to make it to Rockin' R land. Quade rode up front with Carter. "I come across two sets of tracks at the line shack and two empty cups. But you're on your own. Has Crosby left the county?"

"He's holed up with a gunshot wound," Quade said.

"I suppose you don't want to say where?" Carter asked.

"Not likely."

"The second cup?" Carter asked curiously.

"Hired killer goes by the name of Pike Miller. Seems he's interested in me too."

"You upset someone else?"

"I thought it might be Rafferty who hired him, but now I'm not sure."

"Look, I know what happened, and I know what Crosby said. I just need to confirm it with him. If I can, there's a chance there won't need to be a trial."

"You get me in a cell and Rafferty will try to hang me again. I'm not forgettin' what that son of a bitch tried to do. But right now, I have more important things to do."

175

"Like gettin' your pa's money back?"

"That and findin' out who murdered Sam Roberts."

"I keep forgettin' you're workin' on that for Faraday," Carter replied.

"You've heard of us?" Quade asked.

"I have. I met a detective once in Hurstville while I was the sheriff there. Someone had derailed a train and killed some passengers. It turned out it was a freighter who didn't want the competition. Figured if he put the line out of commission for a time, he could earn extra money to stop his business goin' under."

"Progress," Quade muttered.

"Say, do you have any leads on that killin'?"

"Only that shell casin'."

"Why would anyone want to shoot a railway surveyor?" Carter asked. "What do they gain from it?"

Quade shrugged. "I have no idea. When I work it out, I'll let you know."

They kept riding until the Rocking R ranch house came into view.

"Well, the trail leads right into the snake pit," Carter said.

"Now we just need to be careful not to get bit," Quade said and took his Winchester from the saddle scabbard.

"Now, don't go startin' anythin', Quade. Just because the trail leads to the front door, we still need proof that Rafferty was responsible."

Vince leaned in the saddle and spat on the ground. "I got all the proof I need."

"Just keep a check on that temper of yours, Vince," Carter cautioned him. "All right, let's go."

They moved out single file toward the Rocking R ranch house.

176

CHAPTER 14

Mary went back to town after she'd seen her brother. She returned the horse to the livery and left it with Silas. He took one look at the animal and said, "Be surprised if'n this animal don't fall down when I take the saddle off it."

Mary ignored the comment and hurried away. Reaching the boarding house stairs, she was stopped by Mrs. Hamblin.

"Mary." She seemed surprised. "I was just upstairs, and I thought I heard you in your room."

"No, Mrs. Hamblin. I left my window open, so it might have been a voice or noise from outside."

The woman looked at her doubtfully. "I suppose it could have been."

Relieved to have diverted the inquiry, Mary hurried upstairs to her room. She opened the door and found Lucy talking to Harry Crosby, who was now awake. Lucy's eyes widened. "Where have you been?"

Mary held a finger to her lips. "Keep it down. Mrs. Hamblin heard you."

"Where have you been?" Lucy asked again.

"The stage was held up. Whoever did it killed the driver and guard and a passenger out at Cow Creek Crossing."

"Damn it, I think I remember somethin' about that, but it's all fuzzy," Crosby said.

"How are you feeling?" Mary asked him.

"I don't feel too bad."

"Good, because tomorrow night, we need to get you out of here."

Lucy gasped. "Mary, no."

"He can't stay here. If I can get a buckboard or something else, then I can take him to the ranch. Jack is out there."

"What about the surveyors?"

"What about them?" Mary asked.

"Isn't he meant to be watching over them?"

She stared at Lucy. "Darn it, Lucy."

"Hold on," Crosby said. "Are you sayin' that Jack is a Faraday detective?"

Mary gave her a *see-what-you've-done-now* look. "Yes, he is."

"So he wasn't here to buck Rafferty?"

"Not in so many words."

Crosby started to chuckle. "Well, I'll be. He's here lookin' into the death of that surveyor feller, isn't he?"

"Yes, he is."

"Tell him I have information that he might like to know about."

Mary frowned. "What do you mean? What information?"

"I seen somethin' that might help."

"Why didn't you say something about it before?" Mary demanded.

"Because he was on the other side," Crosby replied. "And railroad business don't concern me."

"I have to go," Lucy said. "I need to get ready for work."

Mary looked at her friend and took her hand. "Thank you, Lucy. I'm sorry I was late."

"That's okay. I'll see you tomorrow."

Mary turned back to Crosby. "Tell me, what was it—"

Her interrogation would have to wait. Crosby was asleep.

* * *

The quartet rode into the Rocking R ranch yard and received the reception they had anticipated. Staring down the muzzles of a dozen rifles.

Rafferty pushed between his men and stood before them. He indicated Quade and said, "I see you've caught the killer, Sheriff."

"He kind of caught himself," Carter said. "But that's not why we're here."

"Really?"

"The stage was held up over at Cow Creek Crossin'," the sheriff explained. "We followed the trail of the robbers right back here."

"You'd better explain what you're saying."

"He's sayin' that you or some of your men robbed the damn stage," Vince growled.

Rafferty's voice turned to ice. "You'd best take that back, old man, I don't take kindly to accusations."

"I'll take nothin' back."

Rafferty glared at him. "Where is your proof, Sheriff? Other than some tracks that supposedly lead here?"

"That's all I'm workin' with at the moment."

Quade looked around and saw Abigail on the veranda. She had a smug look on her face. The Faraday man shifted his stare back to Rafferty and asked, "Where is Cable?"

"I sent him to Celtic Ridge on some business for me. He left this morning."

"Kind of convenient, isn't it?"

"I don't have to answer to you," Rafferty growled.

"But you do to me," Carter stated.

"Sheriff," Tobin said.

"What is it, Chuck?"

"I don't see Yost or Frost either."

"What about it, Rafferty?" Carter asked.

"They went with Cable," the rancher replied.

"Must have been important business to take three men away from the ranch?" Carter said.

"All my business is important. But while you're here, Sheriff, I have something I need for you to witness."

"What would that be?"

"I'll be right back."

Quade glanced at Carter as Rafferty disappeared back through his men and went inside. He returned moments later holding a piece of paper. Holding it up, he announced, "This is an eviction notice I am serving to Vince Quade for outstanding loan payments."

"Why, you dirty rotten son of a bitch!" Vince exploded.

The rancher made to grab his gun, but Quade reached out and grabbed him by the wrist. "Cool it, Pa."

Carter held out his hand and Rafferty passed it to him. He looked the paper over and then passed it to Quade, who handed it to his father. "I had until the end of the week, you skunk."

"Will you be able to pay it by then?" Rafferty sneered.

Vince said nothing.

"Then the eviction still stands."

"What about the inquest?" Vince asked.

"What inquest?"

"The one that I organized with the judge to inquire about the movement of the boundary."

Rafferty was taken off guard by this news. His eyes narrowed as his mind ticked over. "I have heard nothing about any inquest."

"It's in two weeks. Once it's over, we should have all these lies sorted out once and for all."

Rafferty said, "The inquest will be too late. You won't need it by then because I will already have your land."

"The hell you will."

"He's got until the end of the week," Quade said. "A lot can happen by then. If I see you or any of your cattle on that land, there will be hell to pay."

Rafferty smiled. "You will be in jail."

"We'll see about that."

Carter straightened in the saddle. "All right, that'll do. Time to leave."

"What about my money?" Vince asked.

"We have no proof."

One by one, they fell into line behind the sheriff. Quade was last. Rafferty kept smiling. "Be seeing you at the end of a rope, Quade."

"Be seein' you over a smokin' gun, Rafferty," Quade countered, turning his horse and riding away.

A mile from the ranch. The four came to a halt. Carter said, "The only way we get the money back is to find the robbers."

"That's what I aim to do," Quade said.

"You seem to forget I have a prior claim," the sheriff reminded him.

"You know just like I do that it was a fair fight, Carter. The only way you stop me is to shoot me. I'll be back the day after tomorrow."

The three men sat in their saddles and watched Quade ride away.

* * *

It was dark when Carter and Tobin arrived back in Sagebrush Creek. Carter took his horse to the livery and then went to the saloon dining room for his evening meal. Lucy was working and saw her father come in.

"You look all done in, Pa. Did you find Jack?"

"I'll tell you all about it when I get home later," her father said. "Meantime, I'll have steak and potatoes and a bucket of coffee."

"Coffee first?"

"That would be great."

Carter managed two cups before his meal arrived. He took his time eating it and had another cup of coffee to wash it all down. Lucy came out and joined him. When she sat down, he stared at her.

"What?" she asked.

"I know that look. You used to get it when you were a little girl and had done somethin' wrong."

"Really?"

"What is it?"

"There is a problem."

Carter took a sip of his coffee and nodded. "I figured there was. You'd better tell me and don't leave anything out."

The truth about Harry Crosby's condition and whereabouts came out, revealing the fact that she and

Mary had been caring for him. The sheriff nodded. "So that's where he is."

"He says he has information about the dead surveyor. Says he saw something. He wants to see Jack."

"I'd better go and see him now then," Carter said.

"You won't get in, Pa. Best leave it until the morning."

"Then that's what I'll do," Carter said with a reassuring smile. "After all, he's not goin' anywhere, is he?"

* * *

The door to Mary's room snicked open without a sound. It swung open just enough to admit the intruder. Then it closed.

The intruder crept silently across the room toward the bed where the sleeping gunfighter lay. Mary was asleep in the chair where she'd been ever since Crosby's arrival. Her breathing was quiet, nearly inaudible. Crosby's was almost the same.

The intruder stepped quietly over to the bed. They stood there for a moment, then reached out. The moonlight coming through the window glinted on something metal. Then, with a swift movement, the figure drew their weapon across the sleeping man's throat.

Crosby lurched weakly under the motion, and the sickening wet sound was followed by a quiet gurgle and then nothing.

Then, just as silently as the figure had entered, it left.

* * *

Quade spent the night in a stand of trees beside a sweetwater creek. He had killed a cottontail rabbit and cooked it over a small fire that he'd built to keep the chill away. While he ate, Quade had the strange feeling that he was being watched.

That night, when he turned in, he moved away from the fire into the shadows, leaving his bedroll looking as though he was asleep in it. Once Quade bedded down, he placed his rifle close by and waited.

An hour later, a figure emerged from the darkness. Quade picked up his rifle and waited to see what would happen. The first figure was joined by another. This one was a few yards away from his companion.

Quade eased the hammer back on the Winchester and waited to see what they did next. Both men came closer, and once they were almost on top of the bedroll, they raised their weapons.

Quade gave them a chance to realize what they were doing—intended to do—was wrong. But once they opened fire, they had crossed that line.

The Winchester roared and the first bushwhacker was punched back by the heavy round. He hit the ground hard and never moved. The second would-be killer got the shock of his life and turned in the direction the shot had come from. Quade had already levered another round into the breech and dropped the hammer again.

The second killer died just as violently.

Quade walked out of the shadows and checked the two dead men. He went through their pockets and found two pouches of fifty dollars in coins. He put them in his pocket, figuring he'd earned them.

Then he dragged the bodies away from the fire and went to sleep.

The following morning, after another look, Quade recognized one of the shooters as a man he'd seen at the Rocking R. He guessed the other was too because it all made sense. The Faraday man found their horses and put them over the saddle, tying them down. Then he continued to Celtic Ridge.

* * *

It was the sun filtering through the slightly open curtain, striking her in the face, that woke Mary. She cracked an eye before closing it again with a wince. "Darn it," she growled.

She hesitated before moving. Knowing what awaited her after yet another night in the uncomfortable chair. There was a chill in the air, and she pulled the blanket up higher around her neck.

After a couple of minutes, she suddenly realized how quiet it was in her room. Crosby was such a heavy breather that she could normally hear him. And what was that smell? It was a sharp smell that reminded her of rusted iron she smelled on her father's ranch as a child.

Mary opened her eyes properly this time. She brought a hand from beneath the blanket to block the sun's assault. Then Mary got to her feet, walked over to the window, and opened the curtain and the window to let the smell out.

She did it quietly so she did not wake Crosby. He was obviously sleeping better now. Maybe on the mend.

Mary had a wash and decided that she would go downstairs for breakfast. Glancing at Crosby, she hesitated. He was facing away from her and the sun fell across his still form. She became curious as to why he hadn't moved.

"Harry, are you awake?"

There was no answer.

185

She walked over to the bed to check on him and froze when she saw the sheets. Mary staggered back, her hand coming to her chest. "Oh, good Lord, not again."

CHAPTER 15

Mary hurried out the back of the boarding house and ran to the jail. It was locked, but after banging on the door furiously, Lyle Carter opened it. "Mary! What are you doin' here at this hour, girl?"

"He's dead. You have to come."

"Who's dead?"

"Crosby. He's in my bed. So much blood."

Carter closed the door behind him. "You'd better show me, girl."

They hurried back to the boarding house, using the front door this time. Mrs. Hamblin was in the reception area and was stunned by the pair barging through the door. "What on earth is going on?"

"I'll tell you in a moment," Carter replied.

He and Mary hurried up the stairs. Mrs. Hamblin was close behind. When they entered the room, Mary stepped aside to let the sheriff have access to the body. All Mrs. Hamblin saw was the man in the bed. "What is he doing here?"

Even though it was a cursory glance, Carter turned

and said, "He's dead all right. Someone has cut his throat."

"Oh, my goodness," Mrs. Hamblin gasped, a hand fluttering to her chest.

"What's happening?" Lucy asked from the doorway, having seen her father and Mary rush to the boarding-house. Then she saw what they were looking at. "Oh, no! What happened?"

Mary shook her head. "I don't know. I—I was asleep all night, and when I woke up, he—he was dead."

Lucy put an arm around her. "Come on, let's find you a drink."

"Good thinking," Mrs. Hamblin said. "I could use one myself."

* * *

Celtic Ridge was a town that was growing with every passing day. Its two main qualities were a crooked main street and a crooked town marshal. As Quade rode along the aforementioned crooked street, a loaded wagon complete with a family rolled past.

He'd been in a hundred towns just like this one over the years. The street was dry, the roan's hoofs kicking up dust with every step.

As usual, his first port of call was the livery. If Cable and the others were in town, then he figured the hostler would know. Outside a big, newly built long barn/stable, he pulled up and dismounted, looping the reins over a hitch rail beside the main doors.

Quade walked inside. The stables smelled like straw and horses. "Hello?"

"Out the back, stranger!" a voice called.

Quade looked toward the rear of the building, where

there was another set of double doors. He walked to the other end and found the liveryman outside near a corral. He was admiring an Appaloosa stallion moving around in it. "Now ain't that the purtiest sight you ever saw?"

"He's a fine lookin' animal," Quade allowed.

"The town marshal owns him."

"He's a lucky man."

The liveryman spat on the ground. "Lucky, hell. He killed the previous owner."

Quade eyed the man cautiously. "Not so lucky for him."

"Thought he could outdraw the marshal. Mind you, Quincy pushed him into it."

"Marv Quincy?" the Faraday man asked.

"That's right. You heard of him?"

Quade had. Quincy had been a hired gun who rode the wrong side of the line more often than not. Having a badge seemed odd. "How long has he been here?"

"About a year."

This changed things. Quincy was a killer, and now he had a badge to back him. "What fool gave Quincy the badge?"

"He took it off the body of the last one."

There was no need for an explanation. Finally, the liveryman turned and looked at Quade. "You lookin' for a stall?"

"Information."

The man stared at Quade warily. "Not sure I'll be able to help."

"Three men would have ridden in over the past day or so." Quade described Cable.

"Might have seen him," the hostler said, lifting a hand to his head and scratching his neck.

Quade dug into his pocket for a coin. He tossed it in

the air for the liveryman to catch. But Quade was quicker, and he caught it himself. The hostler screwed up his face. "I might have seen him with two other fellers. Could be they came here lookin' to put up their horses."

The liveryman waited impatiently for the coin. Quade said, "Where are they now?"

"Where does anyone go when they have money?" the man replied. "The saloon or Miss Jackie's."

"Miss Jackie's?"

"Uh, huh. They be there sowin' oats."

Quade flicked the coin again. This time, the liveryman caught it. The Faraday man turned and walked away.

"Do you want me to take care of your horse?"

"Only if I don't come back."

Quade walked along a street laden with horseshit. It looked like the town council either didn't care about it or the town didn't have a town council.

Ahead, Quade could see the marshal's office. He figured he'd get the formalities out of the way.

The Faraday man stepped up onto the boardwalk and walked up to the jail door. Turning the knob, he went inside. Quincy was seated at a desk, his boots on top, and a coffee in his hand. The marshal's eyes narrowed as he stared at the visitor. "I know you."

"You should," Quade said. "We faced each other in the Pleasant Valley fight."

Pleasant Valley had been a range war in Kansas. The owner of the Bar Y was trying to push off nesters. The homesteaders had pooled their resources to hire protection against the Bar Y hired guns. Quade had been that gun. Quincy had been on the other side. He'd killed a homesteader who had been accused of drawing first. It had been murder, plain and simple.

Quincy nodded. "Yeah, hell of a fight. What can I do for you?"

"I'm lookin' for three men who robbed a stage, killed the driver and guard."

"What makes you think they're here?" the killer asked.

"Because I followed them here."

The boots came down off the desk. Quincy leaned forward and said, "I'll have no trouble in *my* town." There was a lot of emphasis on *my*.

"I don't plan on makin' trouble. Just want the three and then I'll be gone."

"I see," Quincy said slowly. "I guess I'd better come with you to make the arrest."

Quade was suspicious and watched Quincy walk over to the gun rack and take down a shotgun. "Never can be too careful," he said.

Quade started toward the door when he heard the hammers on the shotgun go back. The Faraday man stiffened. Then Quincy said, "Nope, never can be too careful. Drop the gun right there, Quade."

Quade reached down and unbuckled the gun belt with Crosby's twin six-guns in it. They fell to the floor with a dull thud.

"Right, turn around."

Quade did as ordered. "Long time to hold a grudge since Pleasant Valley."

Quincy shook his head. "I was told you'd be comin'."

"Rafferty?"

"Yeah."

"So what happens now?" Quade asked.

"I'm goin' to lock you up and then in a week or so, hang you."

"What for? Why not just shoot me now and get it over with?"

"The spectacle of it, Quade. Every now and then, these folks need to learn who is in charge. And what better way than hangin' a known gunfighter."

Quade just stared at him.

Quincy motioned with the shotgun. "Right, into the first cell with you. The door is open."

Once Quade was inside, the door slammed shut, and it was locked behind him. He peered through the rows of bars at the grinning Quincy. "You just made your first mistake, Quincy."

"Really?"

"Yeah, you should have killed me while you had the chance."

"I can still accommodate you, Quade," he sneered. "My word, I can."

* * *

The whore's incessant giggling was starting to get on Cable's nerves. Here he was trying to enjoy himself in a squeaking bed with a lumpy mattress and all she could do was giggle like a girl.

He untangled himself from her and got out of bed, all thoughts of fun gone. "Where are you goin', sweetness?"

"For a drink," Cable growled as he pulled his pants on.

"But you haven't finished."

"Not damn likely to either with all that racket."

"What racket?" the prostitute asked. "I can't hear nothin'."

"I don't expect you would," he quipped and headed toward the door.

The saloon, a relatively new build, was one of the only decent buildings in the town. It had two floors, with the bar and gambling on the lower level and the rooms for the girls and other accommodation up top.

Cable stood at the top of the stairs and cast an eye over the bar. Seeing nothing of concern, he started walking down. By the time he reached the bottom, the batwings had parted to admit Quincy. Catching sight of Cable, the marshal walked over. "I have Quade in jail."

"Why didn't you kill him like the note said?" Cable asked.

"I'm goin' to hang him," Quincy replied.

"Hang Quade? Just shoot him,"

"I'll do my thing my way," Quincy stated. "Now, how about you boys get your horses and get the hell out of my town."

Cable and the others were gone within the hour. But the conversation between the two men hadn't gone unheard, and for once, the town of Celtic Ridge saw a light at the end of their outlaw run tunnel.

* * *

The former mayor of Celtic Ridge, Linus Potter, had held the position for more than three years upon Quincy's arrival in town. With the changing of the badge, the gunman had taken over and made Potter redundant.

He was in his early sixties with a mop of gray hair covering his bullet-shaped head. His face was deeply lined, and his brown eyes tired.

Since being out of a job, he spent his days in the saloon trying to avoid his nagging wife and drink himself into oblivion. Upon overhearing the dialogue between Quincy and Cable, he identified an opportunity for the town to extricate itself from the influence of the corrupt town marshal.

He watched both men leave and then shifted from his table to another in the corner, where Ralph Honner was playing solitaire. "What do you want, Linus?" he asked without looking up from his game.

"I just overheard something that may solve all our problems," Potter said.

"What could possibly do that?" Honner asked.

"Not what, who."

"Who?"

"I just overheard Quincy talking to one of the strangers who arrived in town. Guess who he's got locked up in his jail?"

"Damn it, Linus, who?"

"Jack Quade."

"Who?"

"You know, the gunfighter," Potter urged as though it would trigger a memory.

"Never heard of him."

The former mayor stared at Honner. "What rock have you been living under?"

"I'm sorry, Linus, I've got more things to worry about than some gunfighter locked away in Quincy's jail."

"Like twenty percent that you're paying him?"

"Exactly."

"We need to call a meeting for tonight," Potter said.

Honner looked up from his cards. "Absolutely not. The last time we did that, Quincy found out, and Lucius died."

Lucius had been the security for Honner's saloon, the Tired Wrangler. "That was because someone talked."

"Who is this Quade anyway?"

"He's one of the best."

Honner snorted. "Can't be if Quincy has him locked away."

"Then we bust him out," Potter told Honner.

The saloon owner paled to almost white.

"Are you serious?" he hissed. "Just go to the cemetery now and dig yourself a hole. Don't forget to climb in and cover yourself up. Darn fool."

"Then I'll find someone else to help me," Potter said.

Potter rose from the table and hurried out of the saloon. Honner watched him go, already feeling like he'd let the town down.

* * *

Potter hurried along the boardwalk, oblivious to those around him. His destination was the gunsmith, Gert Wilders, a big Dutchman who'd been in town for five years.

As he strode past the jail, a voice said, "In a hurry, Mayor?"

Potter jumped. The voice sent a chill up his spine. He stopped and looked at Quincy. "What?"

"Sorry, you're not mayor anymore." Quincy smiled and then said, "Just sayin' you look like you're in a hurry."

"Yes, yes."

"Any reason in particular?"

Potter's head dropped and he turned away. As he started walking again, he said, "No."

"Have a nice day," Quincy called after him and went inside.

Fear and trembling ripped through Potter's body as he hurried off. He prayed that the killer wouldn't call him back, and with each step, the fear began to ease.

When he reached the gunsmith, he rushed inside, slamming the door behind him and leaning on the wooden barrier as though barring the way.

Looking up at the odd spectacle, Wilders asked, "Are you all right, Linus?"

"Me? I'm fine," the former mayor said, adjusting himself before stepping away from the door as though that was the way he normally entered the premises.

"What can I do for you?"

"I need your help," Potter replied.

"What with?"

The former mayor laid out his loosely formed plan and watched the expression on the gunsmith's face change markedly. "No."

"Come on, Gert, this is our only hope. From what I've heard, Quade is good. Very good. If we can break him out, I'm sure he'll help us."

"And if he isn't, Quincy will kill us."

"Do you want to keep living under his heel? Giving him ten percent of everything you make?" Potter asked.

"You know the answer to that," Wilders said with a shake of his head.

"Then help me."

"What about Ralph?"

Potter shook his head. "He won't help. You're the only one left."

"I don't know, Linus. This is very risky."

"All we have to do is wait for Quincy to leave the office and we can get Quade out."

"What about keys?"

"What about them?" Potter asked.

"Quincy takes them everywhere he goes. Why not pass a gun through the window?"

"Because it might not work. If we can get him out, then he's free to do what he needs to do."

"Again, what about the keys?"

"You know the jail?" Potter asked.

"Yes."

"Can you lever the door off?"

"If I have to," Wilders replied.

"Then we'll do that. We'll have to wait until after dark when Quincy is out prowling around the town."

"I still don't like it," the gunsmith said.

"Will you help me or not?" Potter asked, placing his hands on his hips.

Wilders thought about how much money he was losing and the hold Quincy had over the town. "All right. Tonight?"

"Yes, tonight."

* * *

Lying on his bunk, trying to formulate a plan to extricate himself from his current predicament, Quade was determined that he was not going to hang. But after observing the crooked marshal's movements and his penchant for caution, Quade realized his chances of escape were nonexistent.

There was a noise at the window of his cell leading onto the alley behind the jail. At first, Quade thought he was dreaming. But no, the sound was there.

Sitting up on the side of the bunk, he rose to his feet and crossed the cold flagstone floor to the window. Although he knew that Quincy was out on rounds, he turned, nonetheless, to ensure that the marshal hadn't returned without him noticing.

Quade put his face up to the bars and looked out. He saw a gray-haired man staring straight at the window.

"What do you want?" Quade asked.

"We're going to get you out. Tonight," Potter whispered noisily.

"Why?" Quade asked.

"Because we need you, Quade."

"What for?"

"To get rid of Quincy."

"Why can't you do it?" Quade shot back.

"Do you want to hang or get out?" the man demanded.

"Fine."

Quade watched as the man hurried away.

"What are you doin' at the window?" Quincy demanded. Quade had not heard him return.

The Faraday man turned and said, "I'm tryin' to escape."

"Ha! Not out there you won't. Accept it, Quade, you're a dead man waitin' for a rope."

Quade left the window and sat back on the bunk. Quincy was closer to the bars now and stood there, gloating. "I must say, the news of your death will spread around the state like a damn brush fire."

Quade ignored him.

"Nothin' to say?"

Still silence.

Quincy shrugged. "I tell you what. I'll pick out a good spot for you to be buried when the time comes. Get you a gravestone too. Least I can do."

The killer started to laugh and walked away from the bars. Quade's gaze burned into his back, and deep down, he knew that after tonight, it would be Quincy who would need the gravestone.

CHAPTER 16

Night cast its dark shroud over Sagebrush Creek. Mary Quade had moved out of her boarding house room and back to the ranch. School would be closed for a week until she gathered herself sufficiently to return.

She sat in front of the fire, watching the flames and enjoying the heat radiating from it, wrapping around her like a comforting blanket. Her father sat in a chair to her left. Mary looked over at him. "Do you figure he's all right, Pa?"

Vince looked up. "Hmm?"

"Jack. Do you figure he's all right?"

"He's been all right this long, girl. I figure he can take care of himself."

"But what if—"

"Leave it lie," Vince said.

Mary stared at her father. "What about the ranch, Pa? What are you going to do?"

"I'll be damned if that son of a—that man will get one blade of grass of this ranch."

"So what will you do?"

"I'll fight like hell to hang on to it," he replied. "With the help of your brother."

They sat there in silence for a little longer before her father asked, "How are you doin'?"

Mary shrugged. "I still can't believe someone got into my room and killed him while I was there. Why didn't I wake up?"

"Don't blame yourself, girl. It's not your fault. If you had come awake, you might be dead as well. If I had a choice, I'd rather him be dead than you."

"Does the judge think you have any chance?" Mary asked.

"If he does, he never said. We just have to wait the two weeks for the inquest."

"But you only have a few days before they run you off."

"Try to run me off, Mary, try to run me off."

"Please, Pa, don't do anything silly."

"Don't you worry, girl. I'll be fine."

But Mary was worried. As she had right to be.

* * *

Quincy fed Quade that evening. He brought him over a plate of food from the cafeteria on Main Street. It was a good, hearty meal of meat and potatoes with gravy and a few vegetables on the side. He washed it down with a cup of almost-cold coffee. Provided a spoon to eat with, once he was finished, Quade placed everything on the floor just inside the door of the jail cell.

The killer saw him do it and came over to the cell door. Addressing his prisoner, he said, "Go and sit on your bunk."

The Faraday man complied and watched on as

Quincy opened the cell door. He bent down and retrieved the plate, spoon, and cup. The iron door then crashed closed, and the key rattled in the lock as Quincy secured it.

Quincy sighed. "Time to go out and see if everyone is in order. I'll be back, Quade. When I do, maybe you can tell me about the time you took down Red Rivers in Denver."

"Not much to tell," Quade replied. "He was too slow."

Quincy grinned. "Not what I heard. He got off a shot and put some lead into you. Some say he outdrew you."

"Don't believe what everyone says, Quincy," Quade replied.

"I'm faster than Rivers. That means I'm faster than you. Shame I'll never get to prove it." With that, Quincy left.

* * *

"There, he's leaving now," Potter whispered to Wilders. "Come on."

The gunsmith hesitated.

"Well?" the former mayor said. "We need to do it now."

Wilders followed Potter out of the alley and along the boardwalk to the jail. Before going in, they looked around to see if anyone was watching.

Once they were satisfied no one was, Potter tried the door and found it unlocked. They slipped inside and closed the door.

"Look for the keys," Potter said.

"Waste of time," Quade said from the bunk. "He took them with him."

Potter looked at Wilders. "Now we find out if you can lever it off."

Wilders walked over to the door. Quade got off the bunk and moved to the door. The Dutchman looked at it and nodded confidently. He reached out and took a good grip on the bars. Then his muscles flexed as he lifted straight up. At first, there was no movement, then metal screeched. The door hinges slid apart, and the door came free.

Quade shook his head. "If I'd known that, I'd have been out of here long ago. Thanks, gents."

The Faraday man strode over to a cabinet and opened the door. Inside, he found the double-gun rig that belonged to Crosby. He buckled it on and tied the thongs. Then he checked the loads and adjusted the weapons and looked at the two men. "Feels good."

"Are you going to keep your word?" Potter asked.

"I didn't give my word for anythin'," came the reply.

"But—"

"I never said I wasn't goin' to do it. Fact is, Quincy and me have a reckonin' comin'. Might as well get it over and done with. Where will I find him?"

"He would have gone straight to the saloon," Wilders said. "He always goes there first. Has a drink before he goes elsewhere."

"Then that's where I'll go."

Quade left the jail, followed at a distance by Potter and the gunsmith. Trailing him along the street, they stopped and watched on as he walked up onto the sidewalk outside the saloon. The Faraday man paused at the batwings and looked around. Quincey was at the bar with his back to the entrance.

Pushing the batwings wide, Quade stepped inside.

Behind him, Wilders and Potter hurried forward not to miss what would transpire.

All eyes turned to stare at the newcomer. Except for Quincy, who looked into the mirror behind the bar and frowned. "Now how the hell did you get out?"

"The door lifts off its hinges," Quade said.

The killer turned slowly, a shot glass filled with rotgut in his hand. He threw it back and placed the glass upside down on the hardwood bartop. Stepping away from the counter, he let his hands hang at his sides. "I already told you I was faster. I guess now you find out."

Quade remained silent while patrons made a mad scramble to clear out of the way in case of a stray bullet. The air was thick with anticipation and an overriding sense of hope. Was it really possible that this man could finally rid the town of their nemesis?

Quincy's eyes narrowed just before he went for his gun. It was his tell. Quade pounced upon it.

Hands flashed and guns came up. Hammers went back, followed by the crash of gunfire.

One shot.

It wasn't Quincy's.

The bullet from the gun in Quade's fist hit the killer like a hammer blow. Quincy staggered and looked down at the blood on his chest. His gaze came up and he stared uncomprehendingly at Quade. "Damn, maybe you are as fast as they say."

Those were the last words spoken before the killer fell to the floor and never moved.

A heavy silence descended over the saloon. Disbelieving eyes stared at the dead man. They were all in shock. Not because Quincy was dead, but because they had thought no one could fix their problem.

"Gosh darn," Honner said in a low voice.

The batwings flew open, and Potter rushed in. He stopped, stared to make sure that the killer was dead. Then he slapped Quade on the back and said, "You did it. Sure as shootin' you did it."

Quade holstered the six-gun and turned to leave. He took two steps before Potter asked, "Where are you going?"

"Home," Quade replied and disappeared outside.

* * *

The three Rocking R men arrived back at their home ranch the following morning. While the others took care of the horses, Cable went over to the house. He let himself in and walked into the living room.

Abigail was seated on a long sofa, reading a book. She looked up and saw Cable. "What are you doing here?"

Without answering, Cable crossed to a sideboard and picked up a bottle of whiskey. He grabbed a glass and poured a drink.

"No reason to stay away, now." He tossed the liquid back and felt the burn in his throat. "Damn, Rafferty sure has good liquor."

"You shouldn't be in here while Tom is out," Abigail said.

Cable poured another drink. He turned and said, "Look at Miss High-an'-Mighty playin' lady of the house."

"I beg your pardon?" she asked indignantly.

"Beg my pardon all you want," Cable sneered.

Taking another drink, he then replaced the glass. Crossing the floor rug to stand in front of her, he grabbed her arm before dragging her upright.

"Ow, what are you doing?" Her eyes were filled with fear and pain.

"What does it look like?"

"Stop. I'll tell Tom and he'll kill you."

Cable smiled wickedly. "All the fancy clothes, proper speak, and livin' under the roof of the Rockin' R ranch house won't wash away what you really are, Abbey. You'll always be a whore."

She slapped him with her free hand, the crack resounding throughout the living room. Cable's smile never diminished. He dragged her close and forced his lips against hers. After a few moments, Abigail managed to push him away. The result was another slap. "You bastard," she hissed.

Cable cackled almost maniacally. He said, "I'll be in the barn tonight if you want to continue what we started."

"Get out," Abigail snapped. "Get out!"

The hired gun gave her one last grin and left the house. Once he had gone, Abigail touched a trembling hand to her lips. Then her mind started to work.

* * *

Rafferty appeared as Cable was crossing the yard. "What are you doing back here?"

"It's all taken care of," Cable replied. "Quincy has Quade locked up and is goin' to hang him right soon."

"That's good news, but what about the sheriff and Vince Quade?"

"I'll deal with it if I have to," Cable said.

"Fine, get yourself a fresh mount. You can accompany me up to Ironwood Creek."

Cable selected a fresh horse from the remuda and

carried his saddle over to it. Once he was ready, he led the animal out and waited for Rafferty, who'd gone into the house. When the ranch boss reappeared minutes later, he said, "Are you ready?"

"As I'll ever be."

"Good. Let's go."

* * *

"Over to your right," Franks said to Grimshaw. "Another couple of feet."

Grimshaw moved. "Here?"

Franks looked up from his theodolite. "Yes, that's fine."

The surveyor made several notations in his book and then said, "Go back another twenty feet."

The agent turned and stepped out the required distance. He stopped and turned. They went through the processes again.

A cow lowed somewhere to the west of where they were working. Grimshaw looked in that direction and noticed a rider on the ridge. "Franks."

"Hmm?"

"We're bein' watched."

Franks looked up. He turned his head in the direction Grimshaw was staring. His eyes narrowed against the glare of the sun. "One of the Double Q hands?"

"Could be."

As they continued staring at the ridge, the rider remained unmoved. Grimshaw walked over to where he'd left his rifle leaning against a rock. He picked it up and moved back to Franks.

The surveyor said, "Surely you won't need that. We're miles from where Sam was killed."

"You never can be too careful."

The horse and rider moved, but not away or behind the ridge. Instead, whoever it was turned his mount toward the pair and began riding down.

Grimshaw thumbed the hammer back on his Winchester and held it in full view across his body. The rider kept coming and eventually was close enough to make out a face.

Franks sighed. "It's the sheriff."

Carter reined in and tipped his hat back on his head. "You gents had any trouble?"

"Not one bit," Franks replied. "Did you find the killer?"

"Not yet."

"Any idea who it was?"

"No." Carter looked along the valley. "So this is where the railroad is goin' to come through."

"It looks to be the right land," Franks replied. "Once the trains start coming, the whole town will grow and change."

"That's what I'm worried about," Carter replied.

Franks stared at him quizzically, but the sheriff didn't elaborate. Instead, he said, "Guess I'll be movin' along."

He kneed his horse forward and the two men watched the sheriff ride away, thinking nothing more of it.

* * *

Quade had traveled most of the night to get back to the valley. His path took him close to the border of the Rocking R range. He was about to change his path when he heard an explosion to the west. The Faraday man reined in and listened.

Another explosion followed, perhaps a mile away. "Think we should go have a look?" he asked the roan.

The horse looked back at him and Quade said, "You're probably right. But let's go anyway."

He turned the roan and headed west, the direction the sound had emanated from . He kept to the low ground so he wouldn't skyline himself. A stand of trees loomed ahead, and Quade pointed the horse toward it. The trees climbed a ridge, and the roan picked his way through them. Once the ridge was crested, the trees stopped. So did Quade.

Before him was a large expanse of water held back by a rock wall, which men seemed to be working on.

Another explosion drew Quade's attention, and he looked across the manmade lake toward a hill with a large cut in the side of it. This was where they were getting the rock for the dam.

The dam that had cut off the water from Ironwood Creek.

"So, that's what you're up to." Quade thought for a moment. "Why would you want so much water?"

"Hold it right there, stranger," a voice said from behind Quade.

The Faraday man remained still. The man circled him and came around to see his face. "Well, hell, you're meant to be in jail."

"You got it wrong."

The man shook his head. "Nope, you were there when we left."

So, he had been with Cable. "Yost or Frost?"

"What does it matter? If'n I shoot you, Rafferty will give me a hundred bucks for sure."

"You figure you can pull the trigger before I draw and plug you?"

"There ain't no one can beat the drop of a hammer," the man said.

"There are a few," Quade said. "I could be one of them."

For the first time since getting the drop on the Faraday man, the Rocking R hand looked uncertain. That was what Quade had wanted. Now he had the edge.

The man chuckled nervously. "You ain't that fast."

"Fast enough to kill Quincy before I left Celtic Ridge."

That unnerved the hand even more. He licked his lips, and Quade saw a change in his eyes. He was going to pull the trigger.

Quade's hand drove down and came up with a flaming Colt. The bullet punched into the man's chest and spun him around. He collapsed to the ground in a squirming heap.

Coming clear of the saddle, Quade knew he didn't have much time. He kneeled beside the fallen hand who was barely conscious. "The money you took from the stage. Where is it?"

The man coughed. "You kilt me."

"Where's the money you took from the stage? Where did you hide it?"

"Didn't hide it. Gave it to Rafferty."

"Rafferty has it?"

"Yeah."

"Where?"

The man coughed again, this time, blood flecked his lips. His mouth opened, and moments later, he was dead.

Quade could hear them coming. He knew the shot would have been heard, but they had gathered quicker than he expected. The Faraday man ran to his horse and leaped into the saddle. He heeled the roan forward and it lurched into a run.

There was a shout from somewhere behind him and then came gunfire. Bullets cracked as they passed close to horse and rider. Rounds hammered the trees, clipping small branches and leaves.

When Quade broke clear of the trees, he swung the roan back along the low ground following the path he'd come. Head down, he let the horse have his head. There was no horse around that could catch the roan, of that Quade was sure, and he'd soon put a lot of ground between himself and his pursuers. Seeing their plight was in vain, they gave up and turned back to the dam.

* * *

When Rafferty received word of what had happened at the dam, he was far from happy. It was late in the afternoon, and he was staring at the fire in his living room. He asked, "Who was this rider?"

"We don't know, sir."

"Don't know? Did anyone actually see his face?"

"Only Yost."

"And Yost is now dead."

"Yes."

"Damn it, if I didn't know any better, I would say it was Quade. But that isn't possible because he is in jail in Celtic Ridge." Rafferty turned to stare at Cable. "Isn't that right?"

"It is."

"Are you sure?"

Cable nodded. "He was locked up when we left."

Rafferty turned to the man who'd brought the news. "Go to town and send a wire to Celtic Ridge. Find out for sure."

The man nodded and turned on his heel. Cable was still skeptical. "It can't be him."

"Then I guess we'll find out one way or the other."

* * *

Quade arrived back at the Double Q around the same time that the rider from the Rocking R set out on the road to Sagebrush Creek. Lucas Howard met him in the yard. "I was wonderin' when you'd be back."

There was a tone in his voice. "What's happened?"

Howard told him about what had happened to Crosby.

"Damn it, is Mary all right?"

"A little shaken. She's inside the house with your pa." Howard took the reins of the roan. "Looks like he's been rode hard. I'll take care of him."

"Thanks."

Quade stomped the dust from his boots on the veranda before going inside. When Mary saw him, she leaped from her chair and rushed over to her brother. "Oh, Jack, I'm so glad you are here. Harry Crosby—"

"It's okay. Howard told me."

"It was awful."

Vince stared up at his son from his own chair. "Good to see you back, boy."

Quade nodded at his father. "Pa."

"Now, where is my money?"

Quade told them of the events that had occurred, including Celtic Ridge and Quincy.

"He was going to hang you?" Mary asked.

"That's what he said."

"On Rafferty's say so?"

"Yep."

"Oh dear."

"And Rafferty has got my money?" Vince asked.

"Yes."

"That son of a bitch. I ought to ride over there and—"

"Simmer down, old man," Quade said firmly. "Let me do this my way."

Vince glared at his son but remained silent. Mary asked, "What are you going to do, Jack?"

"Rafferty is goin' to find out soon that I'm not in Celtic Ridge and he won't like it. Before that, I need to find out what he's up to."

"We know what he's doin'," Vince blustered. "He's runnin' all the ranchers off the right of way for the money."

"What about the dam?" Quade asked.

"What do you mean? He's dammed the creek to force us off. No water means that we can't stock our range as we should. That means less money when we sell."

"Have you seen it?"

"No."

Quade shook his head. "Pa, Rafferty's dam has formed a small lake. There is way more water than what he needs. And he's still buildin' it."

"Why would he need so much water?"

"Only one thing I can think of. He's bringin' in more cows."

"But he's already stocked with more than his range can—son of a bitch. "It's not all about the money. It's the land. He stocks it and he doesn't have to drive to any railhead. It's all here for him. How do we find out?"

"I can send a wire, and I should get an answer."

"Good. That bastard."

"Where are Franks and Grimshaw workin'?"

"Out on Southline."

212

"I'll check on them tomorrow after I go to town."

"Are you sure that's wise?" Vince asked. "Once Rafferty finds out you're still alive, he'll come after you hard."

"Even harder now I killed another of his men," Quade pointed out. "I still need to go to town. I want to talk to Carter about Crosby."

"Just be careful, son," Vince said.

"Yes," agreed Mary. "Be careful."

* * *

It was after dark when the rider returned with the news. He entered the house and found Rafferty standing in front of the fire with a glass of whiskey. Bren Holiday was with him. The rider was worn out and looked about done in. He took a deep breath and said, "Quincy is dead, Mr. Rafferty."

The ranch owner nodded slowly. "Why am I not surprised? What happened?"

"Someone busted Quade out of jail, and he went lookin' for Quincy. Found him in the saloon and then Quade killed him."

"You want me to send some men to find him, Mr. Rafferty?" Holiday asked.

"No. Hunk Dawson should be here tomorrow or the next day. He can take care of Quade. I want everyone to concentrate on the task at hand. That being getting the dam finished."

"The herd?"

"Yes. Without the land and the water, the herd will fail. With it, I become the richest man in the damn state."

CHAPTER 17

Cable heard a soft rustling sound in the semi-darkness and shadows cast by the lantern. He emerged from a darkened corner and saw Abigail standing there looking around. "So, you came."

Her head whipped around so she could see him. Cable closed the distance between them and stood close. Abigail nodded. "Yes, I came."

The hired gun smiled. "I knew you would."

"Don't gloat, Monte. It's unbecoming."

"There you go again, usin' all them big words." He reached out and dragged her close. "Come here."

Abigail stared up into his face, her eyes searching his as the orange lantern light reflected off them. Cable forced his mouth onto Abigail's. This time, there was no resistance. She felt Cable's hand come up and roughly grab her breast. Then she heard herself gasp, "Please, Monte. Please."

A time later, as the pair lay together on a pile of straw talking, Abigail asked, "How did you know I would come?"

"I've known women like you all my life. One man isn't enough for you. I could see it in your eyes. It gives you excitement. That was why I kissed you in the house."

"What if you had been wrong?"

"I wasn't," Cable replied. "And I saw the way you looked at Quade when you first arrived. There was somethin' there."

"Used to be."

"I knew it. So why here?"

"All my life, I've had nothing. Even when I was married." She paused. "Yes, I was married before. But he was killed by Jack Quade."

"Quade killed your husband?" Cable chuckled. "This just gets better."

"I'm glad you find it funny," Abigail snapped, starting to rise.

Cable grabbed her arm and pulled her back down. "Tell me what happened."

So, she did.

"He left you cryin' in the street, huh? Now, here you are."

"Yes, here I am with something I could only dream about."

"I hate to tell you this, honey, but even after you are married, you will still have nothin'. Rafferty don't operate that way. All you'll be is a piece of Rockin' R. That's all."

"What if he's not around?"

Abigail heard him stop breathing for a moment before he spoke. "Are you sayin' what I think you are?"

"What if something happened to Tom and he wasn't around anymore?"

"That could well happen before you get married, woman. You know what he's up to, right?"

215

"Yes, he told me."

"Then there is a good chance that Quade will kill him before that happens."

"But he's in jail in Celtic Ridge."

"Word came tonight that he killed Quincy and got away."

"Then we need to make sure that it doesn't happen," Abigail said.

"Just how are we goin' to do that?"

"I'll tell you."

* * *

"Where have you been?" Rafferty asked when Abigail finally came inside.

"I was out wandering around the yard enjoying the evening," Abigail replied. "It's such a beautiful night. No clouds, the stars are everywhere. You should have been with me, Tom."

"I have better things to do than dream about stars," he said abruptly.

"Oh?"

Rafferty sighed. "I'm sorry, I've got a lot on."

"That's all right. I know you didn't mean it."

Rafferty nodded.

"Tom, should we talk about the wedding?" Abigail asked.

"What about it?" he asked.

"Shouldn't we start to get things organized? We haven't really got a firm date. We need to have invitations and a menu. I haven't even got a dress."

"I'm sorry, Abbey. You know I've been very busy with everything."

"Yes, I know, but—"

"I tell you what, go to town tomorrow and see Mrs. Highton. She owns the dress store in town. Find a wedding dress. If you have to order it in, that will take a couple of weeks. Everything should be wrapped up by then. After that, we can get married."

"You want me to go to town all on my own?"

"No, no. Take Cable with you."

Abigail nodded. "Thank you, Tom."

"Just put the dress on my account."

Abigail raised her eyebrows. "You have an account at the dress store?"

Rafferty grinned. "I will after tomorrow."

* * *

Quade was about to leave for town early the following morning when a rider appeared. He rode into the yard and stared at Quade. "You Jack Quade?"

"I am," Quade replied, tensing like a coiled spring.

"I have a message for you."

"What is it?"

Reaching into his breast pocket, the man retrieved a slip of paper. He handed it down to Quade, who unfolded it and read. Looking up, Quade asked, "Are you needin' an answer?"

"Never was told," the rider replied.

With that, he turned the horse and rode out of the yard. Meanwhile, Quade was left wondering what Abigail wanted.

"Who was that?" Mary asked from the porch.

Quade walked over to his sister and passed her the note. She read it and frowned. "What does she want?"

"To talk, I guess."

"Why you?"

Quade elaborated on their history. Mary said, "I don't like it, Jack."

"Neither do I."

"Are you going to meet her?"

"The meetin' is in town. Can't much go wrong there," Quade replied. "Besides, I still have to go. I need to send the wire to my boss."

"I'm coming with you."

"Mary, no."

"You need someone to watch your back."

"Mary—"

"I'm going. I either ride with you, or I follow, your choice."

Quade shook his head. At least if she rode with him, he could keep an eye on her. "Get ready. I'll saddle you a horse."

When Mary returned, she was carrying a Winchester. The Faraday man sighed at his sister. He reached out and took it from her. "You won't need that."

Mary snatched it back. "I can shoot just as good as you, remember? Pa taught us both. Just because I wear a dress—wait."

Mary turned and ran back into the house. A few minutes later, she returned wearing jeans and a long-sleeved shirt. "That's better. I'm ready to go."

"Lord, help us. An armed and dangerous schoolmarm."

"Call me that again and I'll use the damn Winchester on you," Mary snapped.

Quade laughed at his sister, and they mounted up for the ride into town.

* * *

By the time they reached Sagebrush Creek, Quade had time up his sleeve before meeting Abigail, so he utilized the time to head to the telegraph office. Vern Moss was seated behind his desk, and there was a look of panic when the Faraday man entered. "Can—can I help you, Mr. Quade?"

"I need to send a message."

"Will you be waitin' for an answer?"

"No, I'll check back before I leave town."

"Sure." Moss gave him a pencil and a piece of paper.

Quade wrote out the message. He handed it to the telegrapher. Moss started to read when Quade grabbed his shirt in a bunched fist. He said in a menacing voice, "Just so you know, if this gets out, like the money on the stage, I'll come back here and bury you."

Moss swallowed hard. "I—I don't know—"

"Just shut up and send the message, Moss."

Quade watched him work the key, and when he was finished, the Faraday man nodded. "I'll be back."

Mary had remained outside but had witnessed the incident through the window. "New friend, Jack?"

"Someone's friend. Come on, we'll go and see Carter."

They went over to the jail and found Carter standing at his window with a mug of coffee.

"I was wonderin' when you'd show," the sheriff said. "I heard a rumor you killed the town marshal of Celtic Ridge. Busted out of his jail."

"You know who he was?"

"I do," Carter said with a nod. "Couldn't happen to a better person. What happened?"

Quade told him. When he was done with the details, he went on to tell him about the incident at Ironwood Creek. "Before the man died, he told me about the robbery. Rafferty has the money."

"Who was he?"

"I don't know." Quade described him.

"That would be Yost." Carter shook his head. "Damn it, Quade, you just cause trouble wherever you go. Bodies just drop from the sky."

"There'll be more before we're done." The sheriff looked at Mary, who cradled her Winchester. "I see the tree sprouts the same fruit."

"Just in case, Sheriff," Mary said.

"Anythin' on Crosby's murder?" Quade asked.

"Could be any number of people. Rafferty's men, someone related to any number of people he killed."

"But how did they know where to find him?" Mary asked.

Carter shrugged. "I have no idea."

"You don't sound too enthused about finding his killer."

"No, ma'am, I don't think I am. One less killer like him in this world makes it just that little bit better."

"I can't believe you would think that way, Sheriff," Mary said.

"When you've seen as much as I have, girl, you might change your mind."

"The killer could have killed me."

"They weren't after you. That much is obvious."

"What are you goin' to do about Pa's money?" Quade asked.

"I need proof that Rafferty actually has it."

"Bring in Cable or Frost. You know they are the ones responsible."

"I will question them," Carter assured him. "Until then, stay out of trouble."

"Trouble is already comin', Carter, like storm clouds

across the prairie," Quade said. "And when it breaks, all it's goin' to do is rain lead."

* * *

Faraday looked over the wire from Sagebrush Creek. He looked up at the man who'd brought it in and asked, "What do we know?"

"I've got Roberts looking into it, sir."

"Was that all?"

"Yes, sir, Quade just wanted to know if there was a large herd coming into the area."

"There must be a reason," Faraday said.

"If there is, sir, he didn't say."

Faraday fingered the metal train on his desk. He thought for a moment and said, "Fine, let me know what is found out."

"Yes, sir."

* * *

Before leaving the jail, Carter gave Quade back his own Colt. The message that Abigail had sent told Quade to meet her behind the livery, where the corral and the barn were. That in itself should have been a warning. But maybe she knew where they were. Anyhow, Quade didn't think much of it at the time. He was more curious as to why the woman wanted to see him.

Heading for the scheduled meeting point, Quade reached the rear of the livery and walked past the corral and over to the barn. The doors were open on the large red building, so he stepped inside. "Abbey?"

"Over here," Abigail called back.

The voice emanated from the rear of the barn where

baled straw was stacked up. Quade walked in further and saw her standing near a partition. She said, "I'm glad you came, Jack."

"What is this about, Abbey?"

"I want you to leave town, Jack," she said.

"Why?"

"Before you get killed. Tom isn't going to give up until you are dead."

"Maybe I'll kill him," Quade replied.

"No, Jack, I'm going to marry him. I don't want that to happen."

"That's somethin' you can't control, Abbey," Quade told her. "If he keeps comin', one of us will die."

"I can't let that happen, Jack," Abigail said.

Quade frowned. "What do you mean, Abbey?"

"What she means, Quade, is that she can't let you kill her husband-to-be. Not before she's married to him, anyway."

Quade turned to face Cable. He had a handful of six-gun, and it was pointed at the Faraday man's stomach.

"What's this, Abbey?" Quade asked. "Couldn't rail-road me, so now you'll have Cable backshoot me instead?"

"This is me looking after myself," she replied bitterly. "Something you never did when you could have."

"I told you then it wouldn't have worked."

"Just like you killing Tom before we are married. I can't take that chance."

Now Quade understood. "I see. If I kill Rafferty before you're married, you'll get nothin'. But if I happen to do it after, then you stand to get it all. But what happens when you kill me now and then after—Ah, I get it, you've got Cable hooked around your little finger."

"I ain't hooked anywhere, Quade," the gunfighter sneered.

"Even if you kill me, you'll have Carter to deal with. He'll be all over this."

"Not if he's not around anymore," Cable said.

"What's that supposed to mean?"

"Rafferty has Hunk Dawson comin' in. He'll take care of Carter."

Hunk Dawson!

"Hunk Dawson will burn the town to the ground," Quade said. "Rafferty just messed up."

"If he has, you won't be around—"

"Hold it right there!" Mary's voice was loud in the confines of the barn. "Drop the gun."

Cable glanced at her. "You drop the gun, missy, or I'll plug your brother."

"I may be a woman, but I'm not dumb. As soon as I put the rifle down, you shoot Jack anyway. Now, drop the gun."

Cable smiled. It was cold and unfeeling. "I don't think you'll pull that trigger, Missy. I don't think you have it in you."

"Do you want to find out?" Mary asked bravely.

Cable nodded. "Yeah, let's find out."

The gunfighter spun, ignoring the fact that Quade was still armed. His Colt came around and Mary took a backward step.

A loud crash filled the barn and Cable staggered under the impact of a bullet. He looked questioningly at Mary and sank to his knees, turning his head to look at Quade. The Faraday man stood there with a Colt in his fist. Cable grunted. "Damn, I messed up."

The gunfighter crashed onto his face and never moved again. Quade turned his heated gaze to Abigail.

She backed away before letting out an alarmed cry, turning and running from the barn.

"She's getting away," Mary said.

"Let her go," Quade said.

"But—"

"It doesn't matter, Mary. There are more important things to deal with. I need to see Carter."

"I'm sure he will be here shortly."

And he was. He took one look at Cable and said, "You'd better explain yourself, Quade."

They told him what had happened, and the sheriff said, "You want I should go after her?"

Quade shook his head. "No, let her go. There are bigger problems afoot."

"Like what?"

"Hunk Dawson."

"Dawson?"

"Yeah, he's comin' here," Quade elaborated. "You need to be ready."

"I've dealt with men like Dawson before." Carter sounded confident. "It wouldn't be the first time."

"Dawson isn't like any other you've faced, Sheriff. Just remember that."

"I'll keep that in mind."

* * *

News reached the Rocking R of Cable's death when Abigail made it back. All the way home, she had time to work out a story that would suit her purpose. When Rafferty met her in the yard, she swooned slightly before saying, "He's dead."

"Who is dead?" Rafferty asked. "Where is Cable?"

"Dead. That's what I mean. Quade killed him."

"Damn it. What happened?"

"I thought I could talk to Quade, make him see sense."

"Why would you do that?" the rancher asked.

"Because I know him—knew him from another time. I thought if anything could sway him, it would be me."

"Why didn't you tell me this sooner?" Rafferty asked.

"I don't know," Abigail replied contritely.

"Tell me what happened."

"Cable thought he would end it then and there. But Quade's sister appeared and distracted him long enough for Quade to kill him."

"Damn it. Why couldn't you both leave it alone? Dawson and his boys will be here soon."

"What are they going to do?"

"Whatever I tell them to."

* * *

Faraday looked at the message he'd been given. He read it and frowned. Has a copy of this been sent to Quade?'

"Yes, sir, it was sent before I came here."

"And you're certain of it?"

"As certain as we can be."

The man read the message again. "All right, this is what I want you to do."

* * *

Moss found Quade at the dry goods store later in the day. Mary was making some purchases for school when it went back. Moss hurried up to him and said, "I been lookin' for you for the past thirty minutes."

He passed him the message. Quade read it and said, "Was that all?"

"Yes, sir."

"Okay, thanks."

Moss hesitated, expecting a tip. However, it wasn't forthcoming. Not then, not ever. The telegraphist turned and left.

Mary came over to her brother. "What was the note?"

"It was from my boss. Rafferty is bringin' in a big herd."

"How big?"

"Six thousand head. That's why he needs the water."

"His range isn't big enough for a herd like that," Mary said.

"Yes. We can expect him to move soon."

"It's going to be war, isn't it?"

Quade nodded grimly. "Yes."

CHAPTER 18

By now it was late in the day. Between waiting for the message and everything else, time had slipped away. Quade went to find Franks and Grimshaw at The Tall Grass. He'd meant to check on them out at Southline but...

He hurried upstairs and knocked on their door. There was no answer, so he went back downstairs and found Jasper Foley. "You want a beer?"

Quade shook his head. "Not at the moment. The two surveyors, not returned yet?"

"No. Didn't come back last night either. Figured they were stayin' at the Double Q."

"No, haven't seen them." Quade was becoming worried. "It's gettin' too late in the day to go lookin' for them now. Won't be able to see much at all. I'll set out early in the mornin' and see if I can find them."

"If they come back, I'll send a rider out to the ranch."

"Thanks."

* * *

Quade and his sister rode home and his prediction had been accurate. It was just on dark when they arrived. He took care of the horses while Mary went into the house. Once he was done, he went indoors too.

"Mary said you had some trouble," Vince said to his son.

"Nothin' I couldn't handle," Quade replied.

"Good thing your sister was along, if'n you ask me."

"You want some supper, Jack?" Charlie Brown asked.

"Don't go to any trouble, Charlie."

The old cook shook his head. "No trouble. I was fixin' somethin' for Miss Mary anyway."

Quade nodded. "That would be great, thanks."

"Mary mentioned somethin' about a herd comin' in," Vince pressed.

"That's right. Rafferty has a herd comin' into the valley. That's why he has all that water and wants all the grass. Without it, he can't move them."

"How long?"

"What?"

"How long until they get here?"

"Within the week," Quade replied.

"Then we can expect Rafferty to begin pressin' harder."

"You can."

"Damn it, man should just ride over there and put a bullet in his mangy hide."

"Easy, old man," Quade said. "Did any of the hands mention seein' the surveyors over at Southline?"

Vince shook his head. "No. The boys have been workin' Gray's Meadow. Why?"

"They didn't come in last night nor today," Quade replied.

"You worried about them, son?"

"Maybe. I'll ride over there in the mornin' and have a look."

"They could be in the winter shack over there."

"I guess I'll find out."

* * *

Four horses rode into the Rocking R ranch yard that evening. The riders climbed down, hitched their horses to the corral, and went over to the ranch house. The knock on the door was more of a crude thumping sound. Rafferty opened it with a scowl on his face. However, it disappeared when he saw who it was.

"Hunk, you made it."

Rafferty stepped aside and allowed the four men to enter. Once they were gathered in the living room, Dawson said, "You remember the boys."

"Been a while," Rafferty said, acknowledging them with a nod of his head. "Boys."

"Mr. Talbot."

"It's Rafferty now, remember? I changed it when I had you get rid of that rancher who owned this ranch."

"Our mistake."

"Just don't make it again."

"We came," Dawson said. "Now, what do you need us to do?"

Rafferty sighed. "I need some people moved off their land. I do not care how it's done."

"What about the law?" Dawson asked.

"He could be a problem. If he is, he'll need to be planted."

"I think we can manage that," the hired gun said with a wry smile.

"There is a fly in the ointment."

"Do tell."

"Jack Quade."

"Damn big fly," Dawson said. "Last I heard, he shot it out with Jim Kendall."

"The outlaw?"

"That's right."

"Why was he shooting it out with him?" asked Rafferty curiously.

Dawson was surprised. "You don't know?"

"I'm not exactly up on what gunfighters do every day, Hunk."

"Yeah, right. Quade ain't a gun for hire anymore. He's a Faraday man."

"Never heard of him."

With a shake of his head, Dawson said. "You been livin' under a rock. Faraday owns a security business. Detectives if you like. A railroad's Pinkerton."

Rafferty frowned. "Then what the hell is he doing here?"

"You tell me," Dawson commented.

"His father is one of the ones I want you to move, but there is something else. A while back, a railroad surveyor was murdered. The killer wasn't found."

"Quade and the sheriff. This will cost you, Tom."

"Doesn't it always? I'll pay five thousand if you can fix the problem within the week."

"Why so soon?" Dawson asked.

"I have a big herd coming in. I need that land."

"Nothin' to do with the railroad, huh?"

"That's just an added bonus," Rafferty acknowledged.

"Where do you want us to start?"

"Lazy S. Once I have that, I'll have the Double Q boxed in."

"We'll pay them a visit tomorrow," Dawson informed Rafferty.

The rancher nodded. "Good, I'll ride with you."

"Are you sure you want to do that?"

"If I'm going to ask you to do something, then I need to be there with you."

"Suit yourself."

* * *

"I heard Jack Quade was in town today," Lucy said, putting food in front of her father.

"He was," Carter replied.

"I heard there was some trouble."

"Seems to follow that boy wherever he goes."

"Have you got a lead on who killed Crosby?"

Carter shook his head. "No."

"To think that Mary was in the room at the same time, so abhorrent."

"She was lucky," Carter said and forked some stew into his mouth. "That's good food, Lucy. Just like your mama made it."

"Do you think he's closer to finding—"

"Let it go, Lucy," her father said curtly. "He's a man you can do without in your life. Wisp of smoke that one."

"Oh, Pa, I can't help it. There's something about him."

"Yeah, trouble. Somethin' you can do without."

Lucy went quiet then sat and ate her own meal. It stayed that way until they had finished. "I might go and visit Mary tomorrow," Lucy said.

"She was in town today," Carter said. "Totin' a Winchester like she knew how to use it. She was there when Quade shot Cable. I'm surprised she didn't come and see you."

Lucy frowned. "Me too. I guess I'll find out tomorrow."

"Just be careful."

"Yes, Pa."

* * *

"I know that look," Mary said as she came out onto the porch to sit in the light with her brother. "You used to get it whenever you were worried about something."

"Ma used to say the same thing," Quade said, putting his arm around her, pulling her close.

"Talk to me then. I'll listen."

"It's everythin', Mary. The ranch, the murder, Pike Miller—"

Mary sat up and looked at him. "Who is Pike Miller?"

"Pa didn't tell you?"

"No."

"He's a hired killer. He's skulkin' around out there somewhere. I think he's here for me."

"But why?" Mary asked.

"I have no shortage of enemies, Mary."

"But, Jack, surely he would have come for you before now."

"He did. The other night, he came to the shack."

"But nothing happened."

"Maybe he was just sizin' me up."

"Oh, Jack, what are you going to do?"

Jack shook his head. "I don't know, little sister, I don't know. But I'm startin' to get the feelin' that this could be beyond one man."

CHAPTER 19

Boone Coltrane sat looking at three queens, stroked his dark mustache, and hesitated before saying, "Raise you a hundred."

He threw the money into the pot and waited for the man opposite to figure out what he was going to do. Two other men sat at the table in the gambling hall and looked at each other with nervous gazes. Coltrane had drawn three cards, which had given him the extra queen. The man opposite had taken one card, which meant he either had four of a kind, two pair, or he might have got lucky with a flush or a straight. Whichever it was, the way he chewed his cigar, Coltrane figured he was confident.

Grady Tolliver glanced at the solidly built, dark-haired man across from him and chewed harder. "You sure you want to do that, Coltrane?"

"It's only money," Coltrane said evenly.

The smooth response was enough to make the man think twice. Tolliver had arrived in Battersby, Iowa, three days before Coltrane. Since his arrival, he'd been drinking and whoring. Spending up big.

To everyone in the saloon, Tolliver was a stranger. But not to Coltrane. To him, Tolliver was a murderer and thief. Part of a gang that had robbed an express box off a train in Kansas. The rest of the gang were either dead or locked away. Tolliver was the last.

Coltrane had been trailing him for a week. Sent on this sojourn by the Faraday Security Service. Now that he'd run him down and was certain of who he was, it was time to strike.

Tolliver pushed everything he had on the table into the middle. He grinned confidently at Coltrane. "All of it."

"How much is there?" Coltrane asked.

"Upward of two hundred. Why? Too rich for you, Coltrane?"

The Faraday man reached into his pocket. He took out a roll of notes and, without counting any off, threw it on the table. "That ought to cover it."

That wiped the smug look from the outlaw's face. He removed the cigar from his lips before it dropped on the floor, mouth agape. Then surprise turned to frustration. "You're bluffin', Coltrane."

"Let's find out, shall we?"

He dropped his cards on the table. "Three ladies."

At that moment, Coltrane knew he had the outlaw beat. The color drained from Tolliver's face, and for several heartbeats, he couldn't speak. Then the color rushed back and his voice became a snarl. "You cheatin' son of a bitch."

The killer lurched back and up, coming clear of his chair. His hand went for his holstered Colt in a final act of defiance.

But Coltrane was expecting him to do exactly that and already had his own gun's muzzle poking over the edge of the table and spewing flame.

Tolliver stiffened as the bullet punched into his chest. His face contorted, and he staggered back, falling over the chair behind him.

The killer hit the floor with a dull thud. Stunned onlookers watched as Coltrane rose from his seat and walked around the table. One look was enough to tell him that Tolliver was dead. He holstered the six-gun and kneeled beside the body, starting to go through his pockets.

"Wh—what are you doin'?" a man asked.

Coltrane ignored him. He found a roll of banknotes. They totaled sixty dollars. "I guess you spent most of your share," he muttered.

"All right, mister. Rise up, nice and easy," a firm voice ordered.

Coltrane came to his feet, keeping his hands out from his side, away from his gun. The man in front of him was pointing a Winchester at the Faraday man's middle. His face was set in a no-nonsense scowl, and Coltrane saw the badge pinned to his shirt. "Sheriff."

"You've got exactly one minute to tell me why I shouldn't throw you in jail for trial, mister."

"Do you mind if I just reach into my coat pocket?" Coltrane asked. "I have something there that will explain who I am."

"Do it nice and easy."

"Sure thing. Wouldn't want to get plugged before you find out." Coltrane reached into his pocket and took out his identification. He handed it over to the sheriff and said, "My name is Boone Coltrane. I work for Matt Faraday."

"Faraday, you say," the sheriff said, handing the ID back.

"That's right. The dead fella there is Grady Tolliver. Him and a few others robbed an express. He was the last of them."

The sheriff's eyes narrowed. "It didn't occur to you to let me know you were in town?"

"Didn't know if I could trust you or not. I guess now I know."

The sheriff grumbled under his breath. He turned to some men close by. "Get this corpse out of here. Before it starts stinkin' up the place."

They moved and grabbed Tolliver by the feet and dragged him toward the doors. But the sheriff wasn't done yet. He glared at Coltrane and growled, "You be gone in the mornin'."

"Yes, sir, Sheriff. Just like you say."

A small, meek man with glasses and a tick entered the saloon holding a piece of paper. He stepped aside as the body was dragged past him, turning pale as it disappeared. He pushed his wire-framed spectacles back further on his nose and hurried forward. The sheriff gave him a look of disdain. "What do you want, Elmer?"

"I have a message reply for a man named Coltrane. He's meant to be in town, but I wasn't in the office when it went out. Do you know the name?"

The sheriff glared at the Faraday man. "You might say that I do know him."

Elmer glanced at Coltrane. "Oh, you're him?"

Coltrane reached out and took the paper. "I'm him."

"Oh." He waited for a moment and then disappeared.

"Looks like I'll be leaving you a mite early, Sheriff," Coltrane said. "This is rather urgent."

"Can't say I'm sorry," the badge packer grunted. "The sooner the better."

* * *

"Darn it, Harlan, how the hell did you get yourself into this mess?"

A bullet ricocheted off a boulder near Harlan Baines's camp—behind which he had taken refuge—and screamed off into the brush. The Faraday agent had been woken by the crash of a rifle, and as luck would have it, the bullet had missed. He'd thrown himself free of his blanket and rolled his six-foot frame to the relative safety of the rock with only his six-gun, his rifle lying uselessly beside the smoldering fire.

The early Missouri morning was cold, but Baines wasn't feeling the effects of it. With adrenaline coursing through his bloodstream, his will to live was keeping him warm.

"You dead down there, Baines?" a gravelly voice called out.

"Not yet, Frenchy," Baines called back.

"Shame, I was hopin' this would be easy."

"Not hardly," Baines said as he reloaded his gun.

He heard Frenchy shout, "Chester, circle around and get behind him."

"Sure thing, Frenchy."

"Caleb, you still there?"

No answer.

"Caleb!"

Nothing. It looked like Baines had thinned them down from three to two.

Frenchy Lomas and his two friends had murdered a track boss in a trackside saloon outside of Dexter. The railroad had sent word to Matthew Faraday that a manhunter was required. Baines had been allocated the job. He'd picked up their trail two days earlier, after they'd killed the sheriff of Jericho. Baines thought he'd been careful trailing them, but obviously they had doubled back, creating the predicament in which Baines now found himself.

"Dumb son of a bitch," he muttered.

Baines finished reloading and thumbed back the hammer of his Colt. He turned to look behind him to see if there was any sign of Chester Glebe.

At first, there was nothing. Then he saw the flicker of cloth through brush. The Faraday agent snapped off two fast shots but immediately knew he'd missed. "Shoot."

Frenchy lifted his rifle and opened fire again, sending four rounds hammering into the boulder. Baines hunkered lower, his eyes scanning the brush for Chester. He knew he had to move. Should the outlaw get into position, he himself would be wide open.

On the far side of his campfire was another boulder. Bigger than the one he was currently behind, and would be safer than where he was. All he had to do was make it.

"You're a fool," he muttered and lurched from cover and started to run.

Baines had almost reached the campfire when he fell. Tripped over his own feet and fell flat on his front. Air whooshed from his lungs in a sudden gust. Suddenly, a storm of lead was sent his way as Frenchy worked the lever and trigger of his rifle with furious abandon.

Baines caught sight of his own rifle out of the corner of his eye. Reaching out, he snagged it, then rolled onto his back and started shooting in a similar fashion to the outlaw. Moments later, Baines came back to his feet and continued his race to the boulder.

Reaching it, he threw himself flat, crawling further around the granite beast. Baines pressed his back against the boulder and worked the lever of his Winchester. "You're still a damn fool, Harlan."

"Baines? Almost got you that time!"

"You talk too much, Frenchy," Baines threw back at him.

"Only a matter of time."

"Yeah, until I get you, you son of a bitch," Baines muttered.

Time to move.

With the boulder protecting his back, the Faraday man slipped into the dense brush out of sight of Frenchy. Slithering beneath the almost impenetrable vegetation, he was stopped twice due to snags. Once clear on the other side, he came up into a crouch and began circling around toward Chester.

He found him crouched behind a rock that overlooked Baines's last position. However, the Faraday man was no longer there.

"Drop the weapon," Baines whispered, pressing his rifle muzzle against the outlaw's head.

The weapon fell as though it was red hot. Chester swallowed and said, "D—don't shoot, Baines. I did what you asked."

"Do you see him, Chester?" Frenchy called out.

Chester looked pleadingly at Baines.

"Chester! Do you see the son of a bitch?"

"Answer him," the Faraday man said.

"No, I can't see him."

"Well, he has to be somewhere."

The Winchester arced and crashed into Chester's head. The outlaw slumped sideways and never moved.

"That'll keep you quiet until I'm finished," Baines muttered.

Now for Frenchy.

Baines set off again, circling around the outlaw using the brush for cover. He heard Frenchy call out again. "Baines. I know you're out there. You got no chance of gettin' away. I'm goin' to kill you, Baines."

Baines let him speak and continued creeping through the brush. When he was finally in position behind the killer, he crawled closer to Frenchy and then came out from behind a tree. "Drop the gun, Frenchy."

The outlaw froze. "Well, now. Looks like you got the drop on me, Baines."

Frenchy came erect and turned slowly. Baines indicated to the rifle that he was holding. "You still have that gun, Frenchy. I won't ask again. Maybe a lot of people won't care if I bring you in face down over a horse."

The rifle hit the ground and Frenchy's shoulders slumped in resignation. "Well, I guess you got me."

"The six killer."

The outlaw reached up and took off his hat with his left hand. He sleeved sweat away from his brow with his forearm. "Whew, for a cool mornin' it sure does feel hot. Don't you think?"

"The—"

With a flick of his wrist, Frenchy's hat cut through the air directly at Baines's face. His right hand dove for his holstered weapon.

Baines threw himself backward and to his left. He hit the ground hard as the .45 slug cut the air where he'd been standing.

With a cracking report of the rifle whiplashing through the thin morning air, the bullet punched into Frenchy's gut, tearing through everything it touched.

With a grunt, the killer staggered. He fought to get another shot off. Baines levered another round into the breach of the rifle and fired again. The bullet sped across the short distance, tearing through the killer's fleshy throat in a spray of blood.

This time, Frenchy flopped onto his back and began bleeding out while Baines reloaded his weapon.

Once sure the outlaw was dead, Baines went in search of the outlaws' horses. Loading the bodies up first, he then got Chester mounted and tied. It was a half-day's ride to the nearest town. He would leave them with the local law and wire Faraday that the job was done. Then he would have a break. Something he was looking forward to.

* * *

Quade had been in the saddle for an hour when he reached the place Franks and Grimshaw were meant to be. But they were nowhere to be found. The only sign he saw was some blood on the grass. Dry, maybe a day or so old. He walked around, reading the ground, looking for clues. At first sight of the blood, his heart clenched in an iron fist and his own blood ran cold. While he'd been concentrating on one thing, he'd let the other slip. Damn Faraday for sending him here.

At first inspection, the only things he found were scuff marks and the blood. Looking harder, he discovered something that the killer had obviously missed. All around the area, Quade had not found one bullet casing, which meant that whoever had done the shooting had used a six-gun or picked the casings up.

It was the latter. Glittering as the sun caught it at the right angle, the casing drew Quade's attention. He leaned down and picked it up. Closer inspection told him all he needed to know. The strike matched the other casings he'd found.

Looking around, he saw crows performing lazy circles above the trees to the north, about a mile distant. Quade walked back to his roan and climbed into the saddle. As he pointed his horse toward the trees, he knew what he would find.

The roan came to a halt just inside the tree line, and Quade stared down at the bodies. Both Franks and Grimshaw had been shot, the Faraday agent twice. Someone—presumably the killer—had dragged them into the trees. Their horses were tied to the trees and left. Quade frowned. Why would someone do that?

Before doing anything more, Quade searched the immediate area for a sign. He found nothing to tell him who had killed these men. Now he had to get their bodies loaded and take them into town. Then he had to tell Matthew Faraday the bad news.

"Damn it."

* * *

Barnabas Sampson was hanging on by the skin of his teeth. His ranch hands had been scared off by the Rocking R gun hands, the water had been cut off to a trickle from upstream, Bobcat Spring had been fenced, and his cattle were showing the effects of it. If he could hang on until the rains, the grass would have new growth, and just maybe he could get his cows to market to pull himself out of the mire. Then there was the railway. He'd been expecting someone to visit and make an offer for right of way, but he'd seen neither hide nor hair of anyone.

The sound of approaching horses came before he saw them. It was like the rumble of thunder from a far-off storm. His wife heard it from inside the house. She appeared in the doorway holding her husband's Winchester.

"Here, you might need this."

"Darn it, Emily, get back inside," Sampson growled.

"Don't you give me orders, Barnabas. Take the rifle."

Relieving her of the weapon, he said, "Go back inside, Emily, and stay there."

"Be careful."

"Always."

The riders appeared and Sampson immediately recognized Rafferty and Bren Holiday. The other four, he didn't know, but they looked like trouble. The riders stopped in the ranch yard. Sampson thumbed back the hammer on his Winchester.

"What do you want, Rafferty?" he asked.

"I came to make you a final offer, Sampson," Rafferty said.

"I already told you what you can do with your offer," the rancher snapped.

"Is that your last word?"

"Yes, it is."

Rafferty's voice grew harsh. "Then I must inform you that I have bought out your mortgage from the bank, and if you can't pay, you have two days to get off my land."

"The hell you did," Sampson said, astounded.

Rafferty reached inside his coat and took out a piece of paper. "See for yourself."

Taking the proffered paper, Sampson studied it, his expression changing the further he read. When he was done, he savagely screwed it into a ball and tossed it aside. "That's the biggest load of horse leavin's I ever read. Now get the hell off my land."

"My land," Rafferty corrected.

The rifle came around. "The hell it is."

The sound of a shot came, but it wasn't from the Winchester. Dawson held a smoking Colt in his fist. Sampson staggered and fell to his knees. Then he grunted and fell face down.

With a yelp of alarm, Emily Sampson appeared from the house and ran across the yard to where her husband lay. "Barnabas!"

She kneeled beside him and checked for any signs of life. The killer's bullet had done its work. She looked up, tears on her cheeks. "Murderer!"

"He made to shoot Mr. Rafferty, ma'am. It was self-defense."

A dark rage came over Emily Sampson, and she made a momentary decision that cost her life. With a guttural growl, she grabbed her husband's rifle and started to bring it up. Dawson fired again and the woman fell across her husband. The killer looked at Rafferty. "You just got yourself a ranch."

"Get the bodies on a buckboard. We'll take them into town. Make it all legal."

Dawson nodded. "You're the boss."

* * *

The wary eyes of Harrietville watched the macabre procession traversing the town's main street. Each person stopped and stared at the bodies draped over the trailing horses while a third man sat upright, tied to the one he was on. Out front was a bigger man, his clothes covered in trail dust.

A woman ushered her young son along the board-walk as he fought her guidance, wanting to watch the scene. Other ladies hurried away after seeing them.

Baines drew a halt outside the sheriff's office and climbed down. He walked back, untied Chester, and pulled him from the saddle.

"Take it easy, Baines," he yelped. "I'm stiffer than a dried-out board."

"Stop your yowlin'."

A man appeared on the sidewalk outside the jail. He took one look at the scene before him and said, "For cryin' out loud, Baines. What have you done now?"

Sheriff Lyle Venters shook his head. Baines indicated to Chester. "Chester Glebe. The other two are Frenchy Lomas and Caleb Morrison. Wanted for robbery and murder."

"Faraday sent you after them, huh?"

"He did."

"The man must have had some kind of vision or somethin'," Venters said. "A wire arrived yesterday for you. I have it inside."

Baines gave Chester a shove. "Get movin'."

By this time, a small crowd of bystanders had gathered. Venters picked out a thin man with spectacles. "Jimmy, go and get Gomer. Tell him he's got a couple of men to plant."

Once inside, Chester was locked away. He looked at the sheriff and asked, "When does a man eat around here?"

"Whenever I feel like feedin' you. Now shut up."

Venters threw the keys in the top drawer of his desk. Before closing it, he took out the message and handed it over to Baines, who unfolded it.

"Darn it."

"What's up?"

"I have to leave for Sagebrush Creek. Some trouble up there. I hate to do this—"

Venters shrugged. "Don't worry. He can hang just as good here as anywhere else."

"Thanks, Lyle."

Five minutes later, Baines was riding out of Harrietville.

CHAPTER 20

The scene in Sagebrush Creek was like the one from Harrietville. People stopped to watch the procession of the dead. Lucy Carter was one of those who witnessed the spectacle. She saw them pass and gasped. "Oh, no."

Shadowing them until they reached the jail, she then stood in the doorway of the dress store and watched from there. Rafferty and Holiday she knew, but the other four men were new. Each was unkempt with the look of killers written all over them.

Across the street, Rafferty didn't get a chance to dismount before Carter and Chuck Tobin appeared. The sheriff saw the bodies and asked, "What the hell happened?"

"We went to see Sampson and deliver the news he needed to vacate his ranch," Rafferty explained.

"Why would you do that?"

"Because I bought the mortgage on his ranch, and today was eviction day." Rafferty took out the scrunched-up paper and handed it down to Carter. "This will explain it."

The sheriff looked it over and shook his head. "This don't explain how Sampson and his wife wound up dead."

"Sampson tried to shoot me. Dawson here, saved my life."

Carter's eyes narrowed. "Hunk Dawson?"

"That's me, Sheriff," Dawson replied with a grin.

"What about Emily Sampson?"

"She tried to shoot me when she became over-whelmed with her grief."

"It was self-defense, Sheriff. Just thought we'd come in and report it. Now we'll be on our way."

Carter shook his head. "Nope."

"What do you mean?"

"Dawson is under arrest until we can have a hearin'."

"You don't want to do that, Sheriff. I'm not wanted in Iowa. None of us are."

"Doesn't mean I can't hold you for a marshal," Carter explained.

"You're makin' a mistake, Sheriff."

"Just get the hell off your horse," Tobin grated.

"You mind yourself, sonny," Dawson growled. "This don't concern you."

"The hell it don't. This badge says otherwise."

"Mighty purty it is too," Jesse Crow put in. "Look even better with a bullet hole in it."

"Like I said, you're makin' a mistake, Sheriff," Dawson spoke again.

"The only mistake was you ridin' into town, Dawson. Should have thought twice about it."

"Is that it?" Dawson asked.

"Yeah, that's it. Now, are you comin' quietly or not?"

Dawson stared at the sheriff. His visage was blank, emotionless. Carter narrowed his eyes, trying to read the killer's face. By the time he realized what was going to happen, it was too late.

"Not."

Dawson pulled his gun with blinding speed, taking Carter by surprise. The crash of gunfire sounded loud on the street. The sheriff staggered under the impact of the bullet. Dawson fired again, this time the bullet hit two inches to the left of the last. Both were gut shots. Carter sank to his knees and toppled forward.

Tobin broke free of the shock that suddenly engulfed him. He tried for his own weapon and was blasted by Crow. Three shots close together that seemed to roll along the street like thunder.

He was dead by the time he hit the boardwalk.

A cry of alarm sounded from across the street as Lucy watched on in horror. She jumped down from the boardwalk and ran across the street, pushing between the horses, and fell beside her father. "Papa? Papa?"

Carter moaned. Lucy looked up. "Someone fetch the doctor. Hurry, please."

"It was self-defense," Rafferty said out loud. "I saw it all."

"Liar," Lucy hissed. "I saw him shoot my pa down cold."

The rancher touched his hat. "Good luck getting a jury to convict on that, Miss Carter. Let's ride."

With that, the group wheeled their horses about and galloped out of town. All except one. Bren Holiday.

* * *

Carter moaned again. His face was a pasty gray color and his breathing ragged. Lucy looked up at the doctor who had just finished. "Well?"

Carter had been taken home. There had been hope in her voice, but Ferdinand gave her a solemn look. "He's dying, Lucy. There's nothing more I can do. He'll be lucky to last out the day."

"Surely there must be something you can do?"

"I'm sorry."

Lucy tried to stop her tears, but they started to roll down her cheeks no matter how hard she tried.

There was a knock at the door and Ferdinand said, "I'll get it."

"Tell whoever it is to go away."

The doctor nodded.

When he opened the door, he found Mary Quade standing on the porch. "Hello, Doctor."

"Miss Carter isn't up to seeing anyone right now, Mary."

With a nod, she asked, "How is her father?"

"He'll not last long."

"Oh dear. What about Lucy?"

"She needs a friend."

"Please ask if she'll see me."

"I'll try."

The doctor went back to Lucy. "It's Mary Quade, Lucy. Can I let her in? You could use a friend right now. Don't go through this alone."

Lucy nodded but never replied.

Back at the door, Ferdinand said, "Come in, Mary."

As Mary entered the room, Lucy took one look at her and then rushed over and threw her arms around her, sobbing uncontrollably. "Oh, Mary, look what they've done to my pa."

After a few minutes, Mary asked her, "What happened, Lucy?"

"Rafferty came to town with Holiday and some new

guns. Dawson, I think Pa said. He was the one that Jack warned us about."

Mary nodded.

"Pa tried to arrest him, and Dawson just shot him down. Chuck too."

"I'm sorry, Mary."

Lucy's expression changed. "None of this would have happened if Jack hadn't come back."

Mary saw the anger in her eyes. "That's not true, Lucy. This has been simmering for some time. If you want to blame anyone, blame Tom Rafferty."

Lucy nodded. "You're right. Oh, Mary, I'm so confused at the moment. First, Ma shot down in a fight between cattlemen and railroad workers, and now Pa because he was trying to do his job."

"I'm sorry," was all Mary could think to say.

"Will you sit with me?" Lucy asked. "You know, until..."

She didn't finish. Mary nodded and squeezed her. "Of course, I will."

* * *

It was mid-afternoon when Quade rode into Sagebrush Creek, leading the horses with bodies draped over them. As he rode past a group of women, he was curious when he heard one say, "Not again."

Paying the comment no mind, he was about to learn different. He eased to a stop outside the jail and dismounted.

"You're wastin' your time, Quade," a man said from the boardwalk. "No one there."

He stared at the man. "They gone somewhere?"

"Could say that," came the reply. "Deputy is dead, and the sheriff will be afore the day is out."

The news was shocking. "What happened?"

"Sheriff Carter took himself a bull by the tail is what happened. Thought he could lock Hunk Dawson up. Dawson shot him, and one of his men killed Tobin."

"No law at all?"

"Nope." The man looked at the horses Quade was leading. "Say, ain't that them surveyor men?"

"Yeah," Quade replied grimly.

"Someone sure don't want the railroad comin' to town."

"It would seem that way. You said the sheriff was dyin'. Where is he?"

"At his home."

"Do me a favor?"

"Depends on what it is."

Quade pointed at the corpses. "Find the undertaker and have him get rid of these."

"I can do that."

"Thanks."

Quade left the horses tied to the hitch rail and rode over to the sheriff's home. He knocked on the door and was surprised when Mary answered it. Alarm came to her face, and she stepped out, pushing her brother back. "Jack. No. You shouldn't be here."

"What's goin' on, Mary? I just came to see how the sheriff was gettin' on."

"He's dying, Jack. He hasn't got long left. Lucy is with him."

"What happened?"

"Rafferty and his hired guns brought in the bodies of Sampson and his wife."

"What?"

"Yes. They claimed the ranchers tried to shoot them and Hunk Dawson shot them both down. Sheriff Carter knew Dawson was wanted elsewhere and tried to arrest him and hold him until a marshal got here. Instead, he and Chuck Tobin were shot like dogs."

"Darn it, I knew there would be trouble when they hit town."

"It started already."

"In more ways than one," Quade said.

Mary looked puzzled. "What do you mean?"

"Franks and Grimshaw have been killed."

"Oh no," Mary gasped, clutching at her chest. "How?"

"They were shot by the same gunman. Sometime yesterday."

"What are you going to do?" Mary asked.

"Send a telegraph to Mr. Faraday," Quade replied. "Tell him that Franks and Grimshaw are dead, and I have no idea who done it. But first, I'd like to see Carter."

"No. You can't."

"Why not?"

"Because she's confused and hurting at the moment. You will only make it worse."

"But—"

"No buts. Go and send your message." Mary started pushing him away. "Now."

Reaching out, he hugged his sister. She looked at him quizzically. "What was that for?"

"Just because."

"Get."

* * *

Quade went to the telegraph office. Vern Moss looked

up when he entered and started to shake. "I—I didn't know, honestly."

"Know what, Vern?"

"That they were goin' to kill the sheriff."

"Why would you?" Quade asked.

"Because—because Mr. Rafferty pays me for certain things."

The Faraday man nodded slowly. "Do you know about the herd?"

"Yes."

"When will it get here?"

"A few days."

"How many riders are with it?"

"Twenty maybe."

"What else do you know, Vern?" Quade asked.

"Not a lot. Honest."

"I need to send a message."

"Yes, sure."

After the message was transmitted, Quade said, "I'll be gettin' a reply. Anythin' happens to it, I promise you, Rafferty will be the least of your problems."

"Yes, sir."

* * *

Amos Dent almost fainted when Quade entered and locked the door. He turned as white as a ghost and started to stammer. Quade's face grew hard, and he snarled, "Shut up."

"Ah—ah, yes, sir, shutting up."

"You are goin' to tell me what is happenin', and when I'm satisfied, I might let you leave town. If not, you'll stay here. Permanent."

"What do you want to know?"

"Start from the beginnin'."

"Mr. Rafferty came to me just after I came to Sage-brush Creek. He said he needed land to start ranching. I told him there was nothing, but he said that we could make some available."

"What did he mean by that?" Quade asked.

"He looked at the map." Dent pointed to the one on the wall. "He pointed at the Broken J. He said that he would start with that one."

"I told him that Bob Jenkins owned it."

"What did he say to that?"

"His exact words were, not for long."

Quade nodded. "What do you think he meant by that?"

"You figure it out. Not long after that, Jenkins was dead. Supposedly, his cows had stampeded over him. Soon after that event, Rafferty owned the Broken J."

"Are you sayin' that Rafferty killed Jenkins?"

"He's too smart for that," Dent said with a shake of his head. "More like Holiday."

"Holiday?"

"Yes, but that's not his real name. I overheard him and Rafferty talking one time. His real name is Silas Grubb."

Quade had heard the name before. Grubb was wanted for a bank robbery in Kansas, where the teller and manager were killed. He'd been part of a gang who'd got away with thirty thousand in cattle buyers' money. The gang simply vanished after the robbery, and the money was never found. There were four others. Cain, Bodie, Stroud, and the gang leader, Red Talbot.

The Faraday man had an idea. "How long has Grubb been with Rafferty?"

"Since the beginning," Dent replied.

"I guess it's possible," Quade muttered.

"What is?"

"Never mind. Just a thought. Tell me about Bobcat Springs and the creek."

"Bobcat Springs is all legal. The creek boundary, Rafferty had me adjust the lines on the map so he could fence the creek and cut your father off. Put more pressure on him."

"The dam?"

"He needs the water for his cows. But you already knew that."

"Yeah."

"What are you going to do?" Dent asked.

"I'll give you an hour to get out of town. But first, we're goin' to see the judge and you can tell him all you know."

"What? Rafferty will kill me."

Quade shook his head. "No, he won't. You won't be here. Now, move."

The Faraday man followed Dent out onto the street, and the pair set off for the courthouse. Within moments, things fell apart. The shot when it came, hammered out of an alley. The crash of gunfire was followed by a grunt of pain from the land agent. He staggered and fell when a second shot hit him hard.

Quade's hand streaked to his Colt as he threw himself flat in the dirt. A third shot roared, and the bullet passed through the air above where Quade lay. He returned fire. Two shots rang out, splintering wood from the building at the alley mouth.

Townsfolk started running, clearing the street.

Quade came to his feet and raced toward the boardwalk on the same side as the alley.

Two more shots came from the drygulcher. Dirt

kicked up at Quade's heel before he threw himself on the boardwalk and rolled against the front wall of the saddlery.

The impact jarred his body, but Quade had no time for pain. He came to his feet and moved forward, pressed against the wall.

No more gunfire followed. He quickened his pace, but by the time he reached the alley, the shooter was gone. "Damn it."

Quade reloaded and holstered his Colt. By the time he had finished, Mayor Jerry Price had arrived on the scene. "I should have known," he growled bitterly.

Quade was in no mood for his bluster. "Go away, Price."

"No, mister. You don't tell me to go away. I tell you. Now, get out of our town."

Quade ignored him and walked over to where Dent lay. The man was dead, and so was what he had to say.

"Is that Amos Dent?" Price asked.

"Was Dent."

"Who would shoot him? Was this you?"

Quade turned on the mayor, a dark pall of rage descending on his face. His hand dropped to his Colt. Price took two steps back, uncertainty on his face. Quade followed him.

Fear replaced the uncertainty, and the mayor turned and ran.

"Damn, it's Dent, the land agent."

Quade turned and saw a crowd starting to gather around the dead man. "Someone get the undertaker. He's goin' to be busy today."

"Who shot him?" another man asked.

"I don't know, but I aim to find out."

"Out of the way," a harsh voice sounded, and a man

pushed his way through. Quade recognized him instantly. It was Judge Hamilton. "What the hell happened here?"

"Someone didn't want him talkin'," Quade said.

"What do you mean?"

The Faraday man looked around at the gathering. Every eye was locked on him in anticipation. "Maybe we should talk somewhere else. The sheriff's office?"

"Sure, but the sheriff ain't there."

"Yeah, I know that. But there's somethin' I want to do while I'm there."

"Sure, sure."

Hamilton turned to the others. "Get this damn corpse off my street."

Pushing through the door of the sheriff's office, Quade closed the door and locked it behind them. Hamilton frowned. "There a reason for that?"

"You'll see. I'm Jack Quade."

"I know who you are."

"I work for Matthew Faraday."

Hamilton nodded. "I heard that too."

"Then you'll know why I'm here."

"That is a bit vague, Quade," Hamilton allowed. "Are you getting' involved in a range war or investigatin' the murder of a man?"

"Three," Quade replied.

"What?"

"Three men. I brought in two more, Franks and Grimshaw, not long ago."

Concern etched the judge's face. "I hadn't heard that."

There was a reason for that. He'd been upstairs in the saloon with one of the girls while his wife was at her weekly sewing meeting.

"I'm assumin' that their killer was the same one as before."

"Good Lord. Do you have anythin'?" Hamilton asked.

"Just a bullet casin'."

"They're a dime a dozen," the judge remarked.

"Not like this one. It has a distinct strike on it. But that's my problem. You have another."

"Don't I know it. There is a range war startin' up and I don't have any law in town." Hamilton's eyes narrowed. "Say, you don't want to do the job while we're lookin' for a new sheriff?"

"No. I have a job."

"Just thought I'd ask. Now, what is my *problem* that you speak about?"

"Dent was paid by Rafferty to move the boundary line between the Rockin' R and the Double Q. There were other things which we were on our way to tell you when he was shot. Now, I have almost nothin'."

"Almost must mean you have somethin', son."

"Dent told me he overheard a conversation in which Bren Holiday was actually Silas Grubb, the outlaw."

"Are you sure?"

"No, I can't be—" Quade had an idea. "Where does Carter keep his wanted dodgers?"

"In the bottom drawer of his desk."

Quade grabbed a sheaf of papers out and started going through them. After a minute or so, he removed one and passed it to Hamilton. "No picture, but read the description."

The judge did so and looked up at Quade. "Could be anyone."

"But it isn't. It matches Holiday."

"What if it does?"

Quade started going through the flyers again. "At the

259

time of their last robbery, Grubb was ridin' with Red Talbot."

"Okay."

A second flyer came from the pile. The Faraday man gave it a quick read and handed it over. Hamilton read it and looked up. "This is Red Talbot."

Quade nodded. "It's also Tom Rafferty."

The judge gave a slow nod. "It could be. But without proof, we have nothin'."

"My proof is layin' on a table at the undertaker's."

Hamilton said nothing.

"At first, I thought this was all about the railroad, Judge, but it isn't. It's about the land. Rafferty has a large herd comin' in and not enough land to put them on. That's why Sampson and his wife were killed and why he wants the Double Q."

"All right, what can I do to help?"

"Put a court injunction on Rafferty so he can't take my pa's ranch."

"I can do that, but I haven't got anyone to enforce it."

"You need to appoint a sheriff."

"You. You could do it."

Quade shook his head. "Me puttin' on a badge will just give them somethin' to shoot at."

"You're the only one with a hope in Hades of standin' up to them."

"I'll do it my way, Judge. Besides, I still have a killer to find. But you'd better find someone before that herd gets here, or they'll burn the town down."

* * *

Before leaving town, Quade returned to the telegraph

office to check for the reply he'd been waiting on. It had arrived and he read it twice.

Got message. Don't blame self. Have sent help. Will be there soon. Just thought you should know, Elijah Pike trail boss of herd. Expect trouble.
M.F.

Elijah Pike. A damn rustler in charge of a trail drive. He'd no doubt have a tough crew with him. The lid was about to come off, and all hell would break loose.

"You think it's goin' to be bad?" asked Vern Moss, lifting a quizzical eyebrow.

"What do you think, Vern?"

"Yeah, stupid question."

"Yeah, stupid damn question."

* * *

That night, Rafferty and Abigail sat eating supper at the long dining table. One at each end. The food was good, but Abigail only toyed with her meal. It was something that hadn't gone unnoticed by her husband-to-be. "Is there something wrong with the food, Abbey?"

She dropped her fork onto the plate and looked up. "No, the food is fine, it's just everything else that's happening."

"Let me worry about that, Abbey. With Dawson and his men, everything will fall into place. The dam will be finished tomorrow, and the herd will be here the day after."

"Quade isn't about to let you push thousands of cows onto his land."

261

"He won't be around to stop me. I have given that old coyote enough chances. So, tonight, we will fix that problem once and for all."

"What if the town sends for a marshal? What then?"

Rafferty placed his knife and fork onto his plate, side by side. He took up a napkin and wiped his mouth. "As I said, Abbey, let me worry about that."

"But I'm worried about you," she said. "What if that land agent gets nervous and spills everything?"

"He won't. Bren Holiday took care of that problem today before he could."

"He's dead?"

"As dead as dead can be."

Moments later, Dawson appeared. "Boss, we're ready to ride."

Rafferty dropped his napkin beside the plate and got to his feet. He walked to the other end of the table, kissed Abigail on the forehead, and said, "I'll see you in the morning."

"Be careful, Tom."

"That's why he has us, Miss Abbey," Dawson said. "We do the shootin' and he does the livin'."

I hope so, she thought. At least until we are married.

CHAPTER 21

Jack Quade had a sixth sense about trouble, and that night, with a full moon and clear skies, he had that feeling. It was just the men at the ranch. Mary had stayed in town, sitting with Lucy. Word had reached Quade before leaving town regarding the sheriff's passing.

Now, with the Henry in his hands, he sat on the front porch waiting, listening. Over in the bunkhouse, he could hear the hands making a noise.

"You want somethin' to eat, boy?" Charlie Brown asked, walking up beside him and looking out into the yard.

Quade glanced up and saw the cook holding a plate of stew. "Beef or chicken?"

"Beef. Went and killed one of your pa's cows. Just don't tell him."

The Faraday man grinned. "Your secret is safe with me."

Charlie handed him the plate and the fork. Laying the rifle down, Quade started to eat. "Your stew is just as good as I remember, Charlie."

"Tell that to your father. He complains every time I make it."

They talked for a while as Quade chewed through large chunks of meat and gravy, and then Charlie went back inside to clean up. The night was cool but clear. Quade remembered nights like this when he would wander away from the ranch house and into the night. He'd sit somewhere and listen to the silence, stars sparkling overhead. As a kid, it had been wondrous.

Then there were the rustlers. They came one night and stole a hundred head of Double Q beef. His father had taken five hands with him the next day to bring them back. After three days, they found them. The ensuing gun battle had killed two rustlers. The remaining three his father had hung from a tree. They had been left there as a warning to any others thinking about taking Double Q cows.

Thunder!

Quade looked skyward. It was clear, no clouds, no rain. But the thunder grew louder. Nearer.

Horses!

Quade came to his feet and saw the dancing lights in the distance. He jacked a round into the breech of the Winchester and called over his shoulder. "We got riders comin' in."

Vince appeared beside his son. "Who could it be?"

"Get your rifle, Pa. They're carryin' torches."

"Burn me out, will they?" the old rancher snarled. "I'll give them a bit of Quade justice."

"Here," Charlie Brown said as he emerged from the house carrying two rifles and a couple of boxes of ammunition. "Just keep your fool head down, Old Man. Don't be stubborn."

Quade said, "Charlie, warn the men in the bunkhouse."

Brown started to jog across the yard. He disappeared inside. Meanwhile, the riders were almost there. Quade could now hear the riders urging their mounts onward. "Find yourself some cover, Pa."

"Cover be damned."

"Charlie was right, you are stubborn."

"I never built this spread up by hidin' when the times got tough."

"Old fool."

"I heard that."

Then the riders were there. The two lead ones carrying torches broke away and made for the barn. Two more headed for the bunk house, while the others came at the house. Gunfire rattled from other riders. Quade figure there were a good dozen of them. All wore flour sack hoods.

He fired at a rider who was about to throw a torch onto the barn. The man toppled from the saddle and hit the ground hard.

The second man dismounted, placing his horse between himself and Quade. He opened the door of the barn and threw the torch inside. The floor was covered with straw, and it caught alight instantly.

Quade aimed and fired. The man staggered but stayed upright. Quade levered another round in but never fired. A bullet snapped past his head, and he turned to look for the shooter.

Beside him, his father worked the lever of his rifle and kept firing. He saw a rider come off his horse and changed his aim, looking for another target.

Men tumbled from the bunk house. Some of the

riders turned their guns on them. A hail of bullets brought three to the ground before they could even begin to shoot. One of them was Charlie Brown.

A torch was thrown onto the bunk house roof, which was sufficiently dry to begin smoldering. Eventually, it caught alight while the shooting continued.

Two riders charged the house with torches held high. Their friends covering them with gunfire.

Quade managed to knock one from his saddle, but the second threw his torch onto the roof of the ranch house.

Lead was swapped back and forth as the attackers held their ground and their nerves. Beside Quade, he heard his father grunt under the impact of a bullet. He glanced at his father and saw him falling to the ground. "Pa!"

Crouching beside him, ignoring the bullets flying around him, it took only moments to realize that the old man was dead. Throwing the Winchester aside, Quade brought up his Colt and started firing. He stepped out into the yard and knocked two riders from their saddles.

Behind him, the ranch house roof was starting to burn. The fire from the barn, now well ablaze, threw an orange glow across the scene of carnage. Quade fired once more before he felt the impact of a bullet. He fell to his knees, his strength leaving him. Then, as he looked up, he saw a horse coming straight at him. Then everything went black.

* * *

About the same time, Elijah Pike stood next to the campfire, drinking an almost-cold mug of coffee. A big man, he bossed by strength and a fast gun. He figured violence would keep any man in order if you beat him enough. If it didn't, then you killed him.

He tipped out what remained and threw the mug on the ground near the fire. The sun had been down for two hours, and he was getting ready to turn in. It would be another early start tomorrow if they were to reach their destination in a couple days.

"Hello the camp!" The voice came from out of the darkness. Men scrambled for their weapons. "We're comin' in."

"Come ahead," Pike called back. "Slow and easy."

The two riders moved to the edge of the light. The man on the left asked, "Mind if we climb down, friend?"

"Come ahead."

Both men dismounted and left their horses ground hitched.

"The names are Boone and Harlan," Coltrane said. "We smelled your coffee from about a mile out and followed the scent in."

"Elijah Pike," the trail boss replied. "Coffee's on the fire. Help yourselves."

If either man had heard the name before, they gave no indication of it. "Thank you. Mighty appreciate it," Baines said with a nod.

"You're a bit late for grub, gents."

"Coffee will be fine," Coltrane said, grabbing a mug from near the fire.

"Where you gents headed?" Pike asked.

"Sagebrush Creek to get some supplies," Baines replied. "Then we might head further west."

"Sagebrush Creek?"

"That's right. What about you gents? Mighty large herd you got out there."

267

"Why don't you mind your own business?" a stocky hand said from where he sat.

"Now, Jeremiah, these gents are just makin' friendly conversation." Pike turned back to Baines and Coltrane. "Matter of fact, we're headed that way ourselves. Goin' to deliver this here herd."

Coltrane nodded. He held up his cup and said, "Coffee's good."

Pike shook his head. "You're a liar. It tastes terrible."

With a shrug, Coltrane said, "Been drinkin' grounds too long."

"You're welcome to ride in with us, if you like."

"Thanks for the offer," said Baines. "But we'll keep moseyin' on. Reckon we can reach town by mornin'."

"Could be," Pike allowed.

Both men tossed out what was left of the coffee in their cups and put them beside the fire. "Thanks for your hospitality."

The two men climbed on their horses and disappeared into the night.

One of the trailhands turned to Pike and said, "Somethin' odd about them two. It was like they were checkin' us over."

Pike nodded. "Yeah. Double the night hawks. Just in case."

* * *

"Mean lookin' bunch of sonuvers," Baines said.

"Outlaws all," Coltrane replied.

"Where you figure they got that herd from?"

"Who knows? Mexico, Texas, rustled some from somewhere and put a runnin' iron over them. It would all add up."

"Looks to be about twenty hands with Pike, possibly more with night hawks."

Coltrane nodded. "I was fugurin' on that myself."

"Make things mighty tough when it all kicks off in Sagebrush Creek," Baines said.

"Mighty tough."

"You figure we should do somethin' about it?"

"What have you got in mind?" Coltrane asked.

"Them cows have been on the trail for a while. They look mighty edgy."

"Mighty edgy."

"Wouldn't take much to start them runnin'."

Coltrane took out his six-gun. "Nope, I guess it wouldn't at that. Might make things easier for us in the long run."

Baines followed Coltrane's lead and took up his Colt. "Let's get them runnin' then."

The pair raised their weapons and opened fire.

* * *

"*Stampede!*"

The cry of alarm had quickly followed the gunshots. Pike let out a curse and shouted, "Get mounted. Forget your damn saddles. Just get the herd stopped."

Men scrambled for their horses. Some threw themselves across their backs and were riding away from camp in a heartbeat. The warning was always the last one any trail hand wanted to hear. It spelled danger and death.

An hour later, the herd was scattered to kingdom come. Pike gathered in most of his hands and asked, "How many men are we missin'?"

"Forbes went down. I saw that," one man said.

"I saw Henry go under," replied another.

A third said, "Potter and Nelson are missin'."

"So are Granger and Zeb."

Pike grunted. "Six, we lost six men. Leaves us with fourteen."

"Still, could have been worse," a man said.

"Anyone see who started it?"

They all agreed that they'd been too busy to worry about looking. It was Daniels, the one who'd voiced his concerns earlier, who spoke. "Seems mighty convenient them two strangers ridin' out and the stampede startin', Pike. You think it was them?"

"I don't know. But if it was, their lives won't be worth livin'. Daniels, you need to ride into Sagebrush Creek and let Rafferty know we struck trouble. Then get your ass back here. I don't want you gettin' drunk in no saloon while you're there. The rest of us will start gatherin' the herd."

"Hell, boss," one of the hands moaned. "They're scattered to hell an' gone. We'll be lucky to find anythin' in the dark."

"Then open your darn eyes. Move, the lot of you!"

Not one man grumbled about the task at hand. They knew if they did, Pike would possibly make them out of a job. Permanently.

* * *

Coltrane and Baines rode into town mid-morning under the watchful gazes of the folks of Sagebrush Creek. To them, the newcomers appeared to be just another couple of hired guns riding in.

They stopped at the jail to announce their arrival to the sheriff but found the door locked. As they turned away, a thin-faced man stopped and said, "Law office is closed."

"Kinda figured that," Coltrane said. "When will the sheriff be back?"

"Won't unless he can come back from the dead."

"What do you mean?" Baines asked.

"He was shot along with his deputy. If I was you, I'd keep on goin'. You've rid into a dang range war."

"That bad, huh?" Coltrane asked.

"Then some. Tom Rafferty brought in some hired guns. Since then, the Sampsons were killed, and so was Vince Quade. His ranch was burned to the ground."

"What about his son?" Coltrane asked, afraid that they might be too late.

"He got shot too. But the ranch hands—what was left of them—brought him in for the doc to patch up."

"So, he's alive?"

"Sure is."

"Could you point us toward the sawbones?"

Just keep headin' that way. There's a sign out front."

"Thanks, friend."

Walking their mounts along to the doctor's house, they tied them to the hitchrail out front. Both men strode up to the front door and Baines rapped on it hard.

"No need to knock the door down, Harlan," Coltrane said.

"He might not hear too good. Most doctors I know are old men."

"He'll sure hear it if his door falls off."

The door opened and Julius Ferdinand answered. "Yes?"

Coltrane said, "We hear you got a friend of ours here. Jack Quade."

"Who might you be?" the doctor asked suspiciously.

"Boone Coltrane and Harlan Baines. We work for Matthew Faraday."

"How do I know that you are telling me the truth?" Ferdinand asked.

Coltrane took out his credentials. "Will that do?"

Ferdinand squinted and then nodded. "Come on in."

CHAPTER 22

Quade had awoken that morning to find his sister sitting beside his bed. At first, he didn't know where he was until Mary said, "You're at Doc Ferdinand's."

Quade frowned. Then he remembered. "Pa?"

Mary grew suddenly sad. "He's gone, Jack."

The Faraday man nodded. "I remember. Charlie too."

"Yes."

"How did I get here?"

"Lucas and Lefty brought you in. Doc Ferdinand took out the bullet. He said you should be up and around in a few days."

"The ranch house?"

"Gone. They burned it all."

Quade's face grew dark. "Damn it."

"Who was it, Jack?" Mary asked.

"I don't know, they wore hoods. But I could guess."

"That's what Lucas said. They took their dead away with them. But like you, I'd say it was Rafferty."

"Talbot."

"What?"

"Red Talbot, that's his name. He's an outlaw."

"Really?" Mary looked surprised.

"Holiday's real name is Silas Grubb. He was part of Talbot's gang."

Mary went quiet.

"What is it?" Quade asked.

"Lucas said he saw Rafferty moving cows onto the Double Q early this morning. He went back out to check on things but was stopped by Rocking R riders."

"They can't do that," Quade said. "Besides, their new herd hasn't arrived yet."

"I guess they're making room."

Quade started to sit up. Mary placed a hand on his chest. "Where do you think you're going?"

"I have things to do."

"No, you don't. You don't even get out of bed for a few days."

"But Pa—"

"Pa is dead. You've been shot. You can't do anything while you're like this."

"Hell, Mary."

The doctor entered the room. "There are some men here to see you, Jack."

Ferdinand stepped aside and two men entered. Jack looked at Coltrane and said, "Howdy, Boone."

"Jack. I guess I've seen you look better."

"Probably felt better, too."

Quade had never seen Baines before, so the introductions were done. Then Quade filled them in on what had been happening.

"Sorry to hear about your pa, Jack," Coltrane said.

"The worst part is, I'm laid up here and there are

things to do. They need to be done before Elijah Pike gets here with the herd."

"Yeah, about that," Coltrane said. "He'll be a bit longer than expected. Harlan and me came across them last evening. Shared a coffee with them and then stampeded the cows across half of the state."

"That's great," Mary said.

"That's just one part of the problem," Quade said. "With no law, Talbot has no one to stop him."

Baines frowned. "I thought his name was Rafferty?"

Quade explained.

Coltrane nodded. "Okay, we'll hang around town until you're back on your feet, Jack, and then we'll come up with a plan."

"That won't be for three days," Quade growled.

"Nothing will happen before then," Coltrane said. "If anything, Rafferty will get comfortable."

"You mean Talbot," Baines said.

"Let's just call him Rafferty to save the confusion. Meanwhile, Harlan and me need to put our broncs up at the livery."

"I'll take care of them, Boone," Baines said. "Then I'll find us somewhere to sleep."

"While you're in town," Quade said. "Ask around about Franks and Hamish Grimshaw."

"What about Hamish?" Baines asked.

"Didn't anyone tell you?"

"No, we've been hard pushed to get here."

Quade told them. "That was the reason I was sent here. The first surveyor was shot down too."

Baines shook his head. "That dang sidewinder. I knew Grimshaw was goin' to dupe me out of that five dollars he owed me."

Coltrane nodded. "Jack, tell me what you've found out so far."

* * *

Having the shorter distance to travel, Daniels reached the Rocking R long before Coltrane and Baines reached Sagebrush Creek. When he rode into the yard, Holiday stopped him. "What do you want, mister?"

"This is the Rockin' R?"

"That's right, an' you're trespassin'."

"No, I'm right where I should be."

"Say again?"

"Name's Daniels. I'm with the herd Pike is bringin' in. I need to see Mr. Rafferty."

"Why?"

"I'll tell him."

Holiday's face grew hard. "No, you'll tell me."

Daniels was tired and not in the mood for Holiday's trash. "Fine. I been ridin' all night. Last evenin' someone stampeded the herd to hell an' gone. It's goin' to be a while before they're all back together and on the trail."

"Damn it. Fine, you'd best come in."

Daniels shrugged and followed the foreman into the house. Rafferty was sitting up to a hearty breakfast, pleased with the previous night's work. He saw Daniels and asked Holiday, "Who is he and why is he here?"

"Pike sent me," Daniels replied. "It's about the herd."

For Pike to send someone on ahead, Rafferty knew that the news couldn't be good. "What about it?"

Daniels told him about the stampede. Rafferty growled, cursed, threw his breakfast across the room, and then calmly said, "Tell Pike that I expect the herd to be on my range within the week."

"It'll possibly take that long to gather them all back in."

"I don't care. I want those cows on my range by then."

"I'll let the boss know."

"Now, would you care for some breakfast?" Rafferty asked. "My fiancée should be in shortly, but I'm sure we can stretch to a third plate."

Daniels shook his head. "Kind of you, but no. I'm to head straight back. But I need to stop off in town first."

"The saloon?"

"Man has been ridin' all night. I'm sure one drink won't hurt."

"I think I can help you there," Rafferty said. He pushed his chair back and stood up. "Come with me."

Moving into the living room, the men followed Rafferty to the sideboard, where he took a glass and a bottle of whiskey. Pouring a drink, he passed it to Daniels. "There. Try that."

The liquor went down without touching the sides. Daniels handed the glass back and said, "Thank you, Mr. Rafferty. That hit the right spot."

"Now there will be no need for you to go into town."

"No, sir, I guess there won't."

A couple of minutes later, Daniels was on his horse... and headed for town.

And trouble.

* * *

Baines led both horses along to the livery where he met Silas Holmes. "Help you, mister?"

"Got room for a couple of horses?" Baines asked.

"No, all full up. Can put them in the corral out back.

They won't have a stall, but they'll get treated the same as the others."

Baines nodded. "Fine, that'll do."

The hostler took the reins of one horse while Baines led the other to the corral. Removing the saddles, Silas said, "I'll store them inside for you. I have a tack room."

"That would be great."

"I didn't get your name."

"Harlan Baines."

"Pleased to meet you," Silas said. "I'm Silas Holmes."

Before leaving the livery, Baines grabbed both their Winchesters then began the trek back to the saloon. Pushing through the batwings, he found the bar empty apart from the barkeep and one of his working girls.

Glancing over at Baines, Foley said, "We're not servin' yet."

Baines nodded. "I don't want a drink, just a couple of rooms."

Foley nodded. "For how long?"

The Faraday man took out a couple of notes and threw them on the bar. "For as long as that will get me."

"You say two rooms, but there is only one of you."

"My friend will be along later."

Taking the keys from Foley, Baines climbed the worn stairs and went in search of his room. Finding the appropriate number halfway along the hall, he opened the door and looked around the small room. Crossing to the bed, he dropped the saddlebags and the rifles on the stained coverlet. Then he locked the door behind him and headed back down the stairs.

As he reached the midway landing, Baines saw that there was now another man in the saloon. The Faraday man started down the stairs and heard the man say, "All I want is a drink before I go."

"We're not servin' yet, friend," Foley replied.

Daniels slapped the money on the bar and said, "There, now get me that drink."

"I already told you—"

"I don't give a hoot what you said," Daniels snarled. "Get me the drink, or the next thing that goes on this bar will be my Colt."

"You heard what the man said," Baines said quietly.

Daniels turned and saw him coming down the stairs. "This don't have anythin' to—well, well, look who it is."

Baines remembered him from the trail herd camp. He kept walking down the stairs.

"It was you an' your friend, wasn't it?" Daniels made it more an accusation than a question.

"Me and my friend what?"

"Scattered our herd last night. Killed six of our riders."

"Don't know what you're talking about."

"Sure you do. You an' your friend came into our camp, had coffee, an' then stampeded the herd. Ain't that right?"

Baines shrugged. "If you say so."

Daniels straightened and stepped away from the bar. "Some of them that died were friends of mine."

"Rustlers too, were they?"

"Now you're just askin' for it, mister," Daniels snarled. His hand hovered just above his six-gun. "Anytime you're ready, pilgrim. Pike will pay me extra for killin' you."

"Only if you're alive to collect it. What's your name?"

"Les Daniels. Why?"

Baines's face remained deadpan. "Just need to know for the monument on your grave."

With a snarl of rage, Daniels went for his gun, wrapping his hand around the butt and dragging it clear of its holster. But he was painfully slow. His face turning pale, he immediately regretted the error he'd just made.

Baines's six-gun roared and Daniels felt the impact of the bullet in his gut. He doubled over and sank to his knees. The Faraday man thumbed back the hammer on his Colt and, without so much as a second thought, shot Daniels in the head.

Baines holstered his weapon and looked over at Foley, the acrid smell of gun smoke thick in the air. "I guess you'd better find the undertaker."

Foley nodded. "I guess I'd better."

* * *

Hunk Dawson was in the Rocking R stables when Abigail found him. She'd been pondering her best option in replacing Cable as her ally since his demise. Her decision had been the outlaw killer. Who else was better?

"Anythin' I can help you with, ma'am?" he asked, glancing sideways at her.

"I don't know, Hunk. Maybe you can."

"Yes, ma'am."

"It seems to me you are a man who likes money. Is that correct?"

Dawson nodded. "Would be fair enough to say, I guess."

"And with the new herd coming in and the railroad, there is going to be a lot of money to be had."

"I guess so."

"Maybe you would like a little extra?" Abigail suggested.

"What exactly are you gettin' at, Miss Abigail?"

"Just suppose that after Tom and I were married, something happened to him."

Dawson stared at her, his mind working. Then he asked, "Are you sayin' that you want me to kill him?"

"I'm just saying that if something were to happen to Tom, then—well, there could be some extra money in it."

He stared at her before saying, "I'll think about your proposition."

Abigail smiled. "You do that."

* * *

Later that day, news came from town. One of the hands had gone in to order some wire. When he returned, he went to Holiday and said, "Quade is still alive."

"Damnit, we thought he was dead along with his father."

"Well, he's not. He's at the doc's."

"Fine, I'll let the boss know."

"You might want to let him know that the fella that was here this mornin' went into town and got hisself shot."

"How?"

"From what I can gather, he just picked the wrong man. A stranger."

"Okay."

* * *

He found Rafferty at the corral checking out a colt that had been brought in. "Boss?"

The rancher turned. "What is it?"

"Quade is still alive."

"He died with his father," Rafferty said emphatically.

"No. He's at the doc's."

"Christ."

"What do you want to do?"

Rafferty shook his head. "Nothing. He'll be laid up for a while. By then, the herd will be here."

"There is somethin' else. That rider who was here this mornin' went to town and got shot by some stranger."

"What stranger?" Rafferty asked.

"No idea."

"Leave it with me. Are the cows moved onto Double Q?"

"Yeah. There are some men ridin' herd on them. Just in case."

"Good."

* * *

Holiday went about his business leaving Rafferty with his thoughts. Hunk Dawson approached him. "Problem, Tom?"

"It seems our little escapade last night failed to get rid of Jack Quade."

"Where is he? We'll take care of it."

"No, leave it. He's laid up. But there is something else. A stranger arrived in town. He killed a man this morning," Rafferty explained. "Send one of your men into town and see if they can find out who he is."

"You afraid he could be a marshal?"

"It's possible. Though I doubt it. Best to be sure."

Dawson nodded. "I'll send Utah."

"Good. Find out who he is and if he's going to be a problem. If he is, get rid of him. Also, I think it's time to get rid of some other problems. Namely the mayor and the judge."

"You want them dead, or moved on?"

"Make them disappear. Then we'll need a new sheriff and deputy."

"You're goin' to take the town?"

"Yes."

"I'll tell him. I'll send Jesse too." Dawson paused. "By the way, there's somethin' you should know."

"Oh?"

"Yeah. You ain't goin' to like it."

CHAPTER 23

Mayor Jerry Price threw his cards onto the center of the table and muttered a curse. He'd lost the last four hands, and it was starting to eat into his winnings. He was seated with John Haskell from the barbershop, and Greg Brown from the bank. It was dark outside and he needed to go home.

"Mind if I sit in?" a voice asked.

Price looked up and hesitated. "Table's full."

Utah sat down. "That's why there's a spare seat here."

He took out a wad of notes and placed them on the table. Price licked his lips. There had to be at least two hundred dollars there. "I—I guess that's okay."

All thought of who the man was had disappeared with the appearance of the money. With the introductions done, they got down to playing cards.

For the next hour all seemed civil and the three men began to relax. Each man was winning some, losing a little. Then came Utah's deal and he went to work. He dealt himself two aces and Price two kings. The others were dealt rubbish too.

The others dropped out right away, which left the two, just as Utah had intended. Both men took three cards each. Price checked his cards. He had two more kings. Utah was holding three aces.

With bets made, the pot was soon up past one hundred dollars. When it was time to show, the cards lay there face up and Utah played his part.

Price, grinning from ear to ear, started raking the pot toward him. Utah's expression changed. "Mister. You cheated."

Price froze. "I beg your pardon?"

"I said you cheated. I threw out the king of diamonds. There's no way you could get four. You cheated."

"You're mistaken, friend."

Utah reached out and turned the cards up. The king of diamonds was there. Price paled. "I—I don't understand."

"The hell you don't," Utah snarled. "You blame well cheated. Where did you hid it? In your sleeve or inside coat pocket?"

In desperation to clear himself, Price showed Utah his sleeves. "No. See, nothin'."

"Then it was inside your coat pocket."

Price's hand moved inside his coat. It was what Utah was waiting for. His Colt snaked out of its holster and poked above the table. He fired and Price lurched up and back. A second shot sent him to the floor. In the sudden silence, Utah said, "He was goin' for a hideout gun."

No one said anything. The killer looked at the other two men at the table. "You saw him reach."

They nodded dumbly, not wanting to incur the man's wrath. Utah stood, holstered his weapon, scooped the money up, and stuffed it into his pockets. Then he turned and walked out of the saloon.

As soon as he was gone, Brown sank down beside the mayor. "He's dead."

Then he checked his pockets and looked up at the gathering crowd. "There's no gun."

* * *

While Utah had been playing cards, Jesse Crow knocked on the judge's door. The old man opened it and stared at the grinning man. "Can I help you, son?"

There was a blur of movement and suddenly Crow's Colt was prodding the judge in the belly. "Back up, old man."

"What do you want? Don't you know who I am?"

"I won't tell you again. Back up."

Once Crow was inside, he closed the door. The judge suddenly looked scared. "What—"

"Turn around."

Hamilton did as he was told. Crow's face took on a harsh expression and the six-gun rose and fell. The old man grunted and fell to his knees as Crow hit him again, sending him sprawling onto his face. But the killer wasn't satisfied. The six-gun rose and fell five more times until he was sure that the judge was dead.

"Who is it, dear?" Hamilton's wife called from the kitchen.

Crow grinned coldly, gripping his Colt as he strode down the hallway toward the kitchen. Shortly after, a voice was heard, then a sudden scream that was cut off immediately.

* * *

The following morning, Coltrane rode out to the Double Q to check on things. Quade had asked them to because he'd been told that Rafferty had moved cattle onto the range. "That ranch still belongs to my family," Quade had said. "They shouldn't be there."

Baines had already been to the telegraph office to send a wire to Faraday to inform him of what had happened and where they were in the investigation.

"Can't send it," Vern Moss had told him. "Wire's been down since yesterday mornin'. The mayor was goin' to send for a marshal after no one wanted to be sheriff but couldn't."

"Did he send a rider?"

Vern had shrugged. "It would take at least two days to the next town with a telegraph and then another week for the marshal to get here. By then the wire could be fixed."

When Baines had told Coltrane, he'd nodded and said, "Someone is trying to bottle things up. You hang around town and see what you can dig up on the railroad murders. Just watch your back."

Before the detectives left, Quade had warned them both about Pike Miller. "He's out there somewhere."

"We'll keep an eye open for him," Coltrane replied.

On arriving at the ranch, Coltrane checked out the house area first. He sat his horse overlooking the yard in a stand of sycamore trees. The yard was clear. Only the charred ruins were visible of where the buildings had once stood. All the hands had moved into town, not wanting to incur the wrath of the Rocking R gunfighters.

From there Coltrane moved out along the valley until he found the cows. There were three riders with them. The Faraday man figured that the Rocking R herd was mixed in with the Double Q.

Coltrane's next stop was the creek where the fence was—had been. Quade had given him instructions to check it. He had a feeling that there would be nothing to be found, and he was right. It was gone now. The Rocking R crew had pulled it down.

Suddenly two riders appeared on a ridge overlooking the creek. Coltrane saw them as they took rifles from their scabbards and rode down. "Here we go," he muttered to himself.

Bren Holiday and Joe Trent were on the Double Q sweeping for unwanted guests. And they had just found one.

They two men drew up in front of Coltrane. "You're tresspassin', mister," Holiday growled.

"This is Double Q range, isn't it?"

"Not anymore," the foreman replied. "All this belongs to the Rockin' R."

Coltrane nodded. "My mistake. I'll be riding on."

"Who are you anyway?"

"No one special," Coltrane replied.

"Never seen you around here before."

"No, just passing through."

Holiday's eyes narrowed. "If you're just passin' through, how come you know this was Double Q range?"

Coltrane made a clucking sound with his tongue. "Well, you got me there. I lied."

"You got about ten heartbeats to tell me who you are or I'm goin' to fill you full of lead."

"My name is Boone Coltrane," he replied. "And I work for Matthew Faraday."

Holiday muttered a curse and went for his gun. He might have considered himself fast, but he was molasses slow. Coltrane's first shot hit him in the chest and blew him out of the saddle.

Not waiting to see the result, Coltrane turned his attention on Trent. The kid had his .44 out and was lining up for a shot. But he fired too fast, shaken by the speed of Coltrane's actions.

The Colt in the Faraday man's hand thundered again. Trent dropped from the saddle onto the ground with a thud before forcing himself upright to his knees with a groan. Coltrane shot him again. This time the young gun rolled down the bank and into the creek and didn't move.

Dropping the empties from his weapon, Coltrane reloaded it with fresh rounds. He gave the bodies one last look then turned and rode away.

* * *

Lucy eventually plucked up the courage and came to visit Quade. Although hesitant at first, she entered the room and asked, "How are you feeling, Jack?"

"Sore," he replied. "How are you doin'?"

She shrugged. "We bury Pa tomorrow."

"I'd come but the doctor says I have to stay in bed."

"Probably for the best," she said. "I'm sorry about your pa and Charlie."

"Thanks."

"What are you going to do?" Lucy asked.

"I'm goin' to get better and then take the Double Q back."

"It might be a little harder now."

Quade frowned. "Why do you say that?"

"Two of Hunk Dawson's men have taken over the law."

"What? How did they manage that?"

"I don't know. They just did it."

"What about the judge and the mayor? Surely—"

Mary burst in, her expression a mix of fear and concern. "Oh, Jack, it's terrible. Terrible."

"Whoa, Mary. What is terrible?"

"I just found out that Mayor Price was killed in the saloon last night."

Quade glanced at Lucy. "Really?"

She nodded. "He was accused of cheating at cards."

"But that's not all," Mary said. "They just found the judge and Mrs. Hamilton in their home. Both are dead."

"Oh, no," Lucy gasped, placing a hand on her chest. "Why would someone do that?"

"So they could take over the law," Quade said. "And the town."

"Yes."

"This will be Rafferty," Quade theorized. He looked at Lucy. "Be careful."

"They murdered my father. They don't have an interest in me. Which is their mistake."

The Faraday man frowned. "What do you mean?"

"Yes," said Mary. "What do you mean?"

Lucy shrugged, swiping a stray hair from her face. "Nothing. I don't know why I even said it. Mary, meet me for coffee?"

"Sure, be there soon."

For the first time since meeting her, Quade noticed a different side to Lucy Carter. Her eyes disclosed something that warned him there was more to her than face value. And he didn't like it.

Turning away, she walked off. Quade looked at his sister. "Mary, how well do you know Lucy?"

Mary was unprepared for the question. "What do you mean, Jack?"

"She's different somehow, but I think she's showin' somethin' that was already there."

"What are you thinking?" Mary asked, giving her brother a skeptical look. "I think getting shot has affected your brain."

"Tell me about the death of her mother."

"I don't know much at all. But she did see it happen. I know that much."

"Did it affect her?"

"She was young, Jack. It would affect anyone."

Quade nodded slowly.

"Jack, talk to me."

"I remember somethin' she said not long after we met. She said she could shoot."

"A lot of women can, Jack," Mary replied. "Are you suggesting that she shot the surveyors?"

"I'm not suggestin' anythin'."

"Good. Keep it that way. Now, I have to go and meet my friend."

Not long after Mary had left, Baines returned. "Find anythin'?" Quade asked.

With a shake of the head, Baines replied, "No."

"I need you to do somethin' for me. It has to be done now."

"I'm listenin'."

Quade told him what he wanted done.

"I'll get to it."

* * *

Baines lifted the open window and climbed through. He landed catlike inside the small home and listened for any signs of life. Hearing nothing, he began moving furtively around the house, searching each room.

He found the rifle in the bedroom leaning against the wall within reach of the bed. Baines picked it up and worked the lever. He ejected every round from the magazine onto the bed so he could find them. Then he took out a bullet casing from his pocket. It wasn't loaded. Everything had been done to make it safe. Opening the breech, Baines slid it into the chamber. Then he pulled the trigger.

There was an audible click after which the Faraday man worked the lever and ejected the casing. When he picked it up, he examined the end where the pin had struck. It was off.

Baines grunted and after reloading the Winchester, began looking around in the room drawers. He found nothing and was about to look elsewhere when he heard the front door open.

Dang it!

Baines hurried back to the window. Before climbing out he gave the room one last look to make sure that it was as he had found it. Satisfied, he climbed out and closed the window behind him.

* * *

Returning to the doctor's house, Baines found Quade sitting on the side of his bed, looking out the window. His head turned. "How did you go?"

He reached into his pocket for the shell casing. Quade looked at it and said, "Where was the rifle?"

"In her room."

"Doesn't mean it's hers. Could have been her father's."

"It could have," Baines agreed. "But the question remains, even if it was her father's, did she know?"

Quade remained silent, contemplating the answer. Deep down, he knew but wished he didn't. Then he thought about what had happened so far. The body count was building, and only promised to get worse.

CHAPTER 24

It was late in the afternoon when one of the hands brought in the bodies of Holiday and Joe Trent, draped face down over their saddles. "What happened?" Rafferty demanded through gritted teeth.

"Found them both over at the boundary of Rockin' R and Double Q," the man said.

"Bushwhacked?"

The hand shook his head. "Both have been shot in the front. Their six-guns were on the ground near them. There was sign of another horse."

"Are you sayin' that someone beat both of them in a standup fight?" Dawson asked.

"Yes, sir."

The outlaw looked at Rafferty. "It can't have been Quade. He's laid up at the doctor's."

"Then who?" He looked around for the rider who'd brought the news about Daniels. "That stranger you said was in town. Did he look like law to you?"

"I didn't see him, Mr. Rafferty."

"Then get a horse saddled and find out who he is. I

want to know by the time we ride into town in the morning."

"Yes, sir."

"Does it really matter if he's law?" Dawson asked.

"It does if he's a damn marshal."

"They still die the same."

"Yeah, and then they breed, and before we know it, we're up to our ears in them."

Dawson nodded. "You're the boss."

* * *

Utah stood on the boardwalk looking across the street at the dry goods store. His right index finger was tapping the butt of his six-gun. Deep in thought, he was unaware that Crow had appeared at his shoulder. "What's up?"

Startled, Utah replied, "Don't do that. I was just thinkin' is all.".

"What about?"

"That dry goods store across the street. People have been comin' and goin' quite regular. Seems to me that the owner is makin' him some money."

"So?"

"Seems that someone makin' a lot of money should be payin' taxes."

Crow nodded slowly, his mind getting the inference. "Yes, they should."

Both men crossed the street and entered the store. There was a distinct aroma of leather and tobacco in the dim room, along with a hint of soaps in the air. A woman was at the counter about to pay for her goods when the pair entered. Taking one look at them, she abandoned her purchases and abruptly left. As she hurried past with her head down, Utah touched his hat brim. "Ma'am."

295

All his greeting did was hasten her retreat.

As they approached the counter, the man behind it had already gone pale.

Utah asked, "What's your name?"

"E—Elias Dowd."

"Things look reasonably busy today, Elias."

"They're reasonable."

Utah placed a hand on the top of a glass display case. "Good, good. Then you won't mind payin' taxes."

"What taxes? I already pay taxes to the town."

"Don't worry about that anymore," Utah said. "From now on, you pay your taxes to us."

"But why would I do that?" Elias asked.

"Well, you never know when someone might come in and start bustin' up your store," Crow said. "You'll be needin' the law to take care of everythin'."

"But that's your job," Elias pointed out.

"So it is."

A sound somewhat like a gunshot echoed through the store, followed by the unmistakable tinkle of shattering glass. Crow looked at Utah, who had drawn his six-gun, using the butt to smash the front of the display cabinet.

"Oops," Utah said, unable to conceal the hint of amusement in his voice.

"What are you doing?" Elias's voice came out as little more than a squeak as his throat constricted.

"Just showin' you what could happen if you don't pay your taxes and someone comes into the store lookin' for trouble."

Elias swallowed hard. "What—how much?"

"Fifty dollars."

"Fifty!" Elias's eyes bulged. "That—"

"That what?" asked Crow.

"Ah—is more than fair."

"I think so."

The storekeeper opened his cash drawer and counted out the money. He passed it over to the two men and closed the drawer.

Utah held the money up and said, "We'll be back next week."

As Elias watched the pair leave, a thin bead of sweat trickled down his brow. If they kept this up, he would go broke within a couple of months.

* * *

The next stop was the saloon. Emboldened by their success, Utah and Crow decided to try their luck again. Watching their approach, Jasper Foley knew they looked like trouble. With only a few customers in the saloon, he couldn't afford to be choosy. Maybe all they wanted was a drink.

"Get you gents a beer? On the house." Foley smiled, trying to be friendly.

Crow nodded. "That would be right friendly of you."

The two men got their beers, and before Foley walked away, Utah said, "We're out collectin' taxes."

Foley nodded. "I see. Enjoy your beers."

He was stopped again when Utah said, "Which is the reason we're here."

The saloon owner stared at the two men.

Crow continued. "You need to pay your tax."

"I already do. But just not to you."

"Yeah, we're changin' that."

"The hell you are," Foley snapped.

Like a bolt of lightning, Utah reached across the bar and slapped the saloon owner across the face, splitting his lip.

297

With a backward stagger, Foley ran into the shelf behind him.

However, Utah wasn't finished. On the back wall of the bar was a large mirror. The killer's six-gun came free of its holster, and he placed a bullet dead center of the mirror. Shards rained around Foley to the floor. He jerked back and waited for the shower to stop.

"What the hell?"

"Just a sample of what can happen if you don't pay your taxes."

"Damn it, how much?"

"Fifty dollars."

"Fifty?"

"Each week."

"Each week?"

"Is there an echo in here, Utah?" Crow asked, cupping his left hand around his ear.

"Sure do sound like it."

Foley went to the cash drawer and retrieved the money before handing it across the bar to Utah.

"Thank you kindly, sir."

The two outlaws left the saloon and stood on the boardwalk. "Where to next, Utah?"

"Let's try the general store."

The pair filled the following two hours visiting various establishments in Sagebrush Creek. By the time they were finished and had returned to the jail, they'd scraped together five hundred dollars. The pair divided it up, and Crow stuffed his share into his pocket. He grinned. "Hell, this is easier'n robbin' banks."

"Yeah, all we have to do is go straight to the source. Wait until Hunk hears."

* * *

The rider's name was Moffat. He'd been with the Rocking R long enough to know how Rafferty and the rest operated. That was all right with him because he was paid well, and had a place to remain out of sight from the law.

Pushing his way into the sheriff's office, he found the two new lawmen lounging around, reveling in their new income. He told them about Holiday and Trent.

"Dang it, the kid was fast," Utah said.

"Not fast enough," Moffatt replied. "Mr. Rafferty sent me here to find out about the new stranger in town."

"There are two," Crow said.

"Two?"

"There's that echo again. Yeah, two."

"Mr. Rafferty wants to know if they're law."

"No idea," Crow said with a shake of his head.

Utah said, "I know someone who might know. I saw one of them comin' out of the telegraph office. Maybe the telegrapher knows."

"Let's go and find out."

As they left the boardwalk and entered the telegraph office, Utah locked the door behind them. Vern Moss looked up and all but had heart failure. His face paled and a tremor started in his hand. He stared at all three and waited for one of them to speak. It was Crow who broke the silence. "The two strangers in town, who are they?"

Vern shook his head. "No idea. But there are three."

"Three?"

"Yes."

"Who is the third?"

"I don't know."

"Utah saw one of them come out of here."

"I—I'm sorry, I'm not allowed to give out personal information."

Crow took out his six-gun and placed it on the counter. "Try again, telegraph man."

"He—he is a Faraday agent."

Crow glanced at the two other men. Then he said, "He's a detective?"

"If you want to call him that?"

"What was he sendin' the message about?"

"He couldn't, the line is still dead."

"But where was he goin' to send it?"

"His boss."

Utah stared intimidatingly at Vern. "Tell me, why are the Faraday people here?"

"Lookin' for the one who murdered the surveyor."

"Was he the one who killed the stranger in the saloon?"

"Yes, I think so," Vern replied.

"What about the third stranger? Is he a Faraday man?" Crow asked.

"I don't think so."

"Marshal?"

Vern shook his head. "He don't look like any lawman I've seen. If I had to guess, I'd say he's a hired gun."

"Well, isn't that interestin'," Crow said. He turned to Moffat. "You can go tell Mr. Rafferty what he wants to know, now."

"Yeah, but the only issue is that he's goin' to have more questions than I've got answers."

* * *

On his return, Coltrane told Quade what he'd found and what had happened. In return, Quade and Baines informed him about finding the rifle. "What are you going to do?" Coltrane asked.

Quade opened his mouth to speak but the distant sound of thunder interrupted. He waited and then said, "That should be self-explanatory. I have to question her to find out if it was her or her father."

"You really think it was her?"

"It's possible."

"Who would have thunk it?"

Just then, the door opened and Mary arrived. Once again, there was a concerned expression on her face. "What is it this time?" Quade asked.

"Our new lawmen are collecting taxes from the town."

Quade threw back the covers. "That's it. Time to do somethin' about it."

"No!" Mary said. "Stay right there."

"I've lain around long enough," Quade growled. "It's damn well time."

The doctor appeared. "What's all the noise? What are you doing up?"

Thunder crashed. "Fightin' back, Doc."

Ferdinand shook his head. "I wouldn't advise it."

"Is there a solid reason why not?" Quade asked. "I'm stronger than what I was. While I'm layin' around, Rafferty is takin' over the town."

"Damn it, Jack. Just take it easy."

"I promise I won't leave town, Doc."

Ferdinand shook his head again. "You're a fool."

"Been called worse than that before too. Now, Mary, get me my clothes and my gun."

* * *

Once the three men were outside, Quade stopped them. It was almost dark and the rain had started. "We'll head over to the jail."

When they walked up to the sheriff's office, they could hear Crow and Utah laughing. When they entered, they found the pair finishing off a bottle of whiskey. The surprise on their faces was evident. "What are you doin' here?" Utah growled.

"Tellin' you to get out of town," Quade said evenly.

"You can't do that. We're the law."

"Take the badges off and git," Coltrane growled. "Or you'll wind up like your friends."

It suddenly registered what Coltrane was talking about. "You killed them?"

"That's right."

"Damn you," Crow snarled and went for his gun.

It was an expected response, and Coltrane had his gun out in a flash. It crashed loudly in the office and Crow dropped his gun after the bullet smashed into it. Crow rubbed his hand, glaring at the Faraday man.

"You should have killed me," he snapped.

The hammer went back with an audible click. "I still can."

Utah took off his badge and tossed it onto the desk. "Come on, Crow, it's time to retreat."

Crow followed his friend's lead. Glaring at Coltrane, he snarled, "You an' me have got unfinished business."

"I won't be too hard to locate."

"Before you go," Quade said. "Empty your pockets."

Utah's eyebrows shot up. "What?"

"All the money you stole from the good folk of Sagebrush Creek. Leave it on the desk."

With more than a few grumblings, they followed the orders. Then Crow made to pick up his six-gun.

"Leave it there," Baines said, speaking for the first time. "You might stay alive that way."

Crow straightened and followed Utah out the door and into the storm.

Quade turned to Coltrane and Baines. The latter said, "This is your territory, what do you want to do?"

"I need to talk to someone. How do you men feel about takin' a ride tonight?"

"In this weather?" Baines asked.

"No better time."

"I'll bite," Coltrane said. "What for?"

"You're goin' to blow up a dam."

CHAPTER 25

Elijah Pike rode out of the storm and into the Rocking R ranch yard with two other men. Both were trail hands that doubled as hired guns. Temple and Foster. All three were wringing wet.

When Pike hammered on the door, Rafferty answered and frowned. "Elijah. Weren't expecting you until tomorrow at the earliest. Come in."

Once they were in the living room in front of the fire, Pike said, "We gathered the herd in. We were lucky, they were too tired to run too far."

"When your man came—"

"Where is he? He never came back. Probably holed up in the darn saloon."

"He's dead," Rafferty said bluntly.

Pike's face darkened. "What happened?"

"He went to town and was killed in the saloon after confronting a stranger."

"What stranger?"

"We think the man was from the Faraday Security Service. There are three of them in town."

"Damn it. Why are they here?"

"Looking into the murder of a surveyor—three murders now. The kicker is, one of them has gone to war with me because I was trying to squeeze his father out."

The front door opened, and Hunk Dawson appeared. He saw Pike and nodded. "Elijah, you're early."

"Hunk. Plying your trade for Rafferty, I see."

"Tryin'."

"Trying?"

"That's why I'm here." Dawson turned to Rafferty. "Utah and Crow just came back from town. They were run out by Quade and the other two."

"Damn it. Couldn't they do something about it?"

"They had them cold."

Rafferty nodded stiffly. "Then tomorrow we go to town and end this once and for all. Care to join us, Elijah?"

"Damn right. I owe them for Daniels. He might have been a pain, but he was a good worker."

"Then that settles it."

* * *

Rafferty was sitting in front of the fire nursing a glass of whiskey when Abigail appeared. "I'm going to bed, Tom. I just came to say goodnight."

"We are going to town tomorrow, Abbey. You will be with us."

"I will?"

"Yes. And pack your things. You won't be returning to the Rocking R."

Abigail was surprised. "But why? We're to be married."

"Not anymore. Do you think I would marry a woman who would see me dead?"

"What on earth do you mean?"

Rafferty threw the glass at the fireplace, where it shattered. He came to his feet. "Don't play games with me, Abbey. I know what you planned to do. Dawson told me everything."

"But, Tom, why would you believe him? He—"

Two steps were all it took for Rafferty to close the gap between them. His right hand flicked out like the strike of a rattler. The sound of the slap filled the room. Abigail took a step back and raised her hand to her face. The stunned look on her face said it all. "Tom, what—"

"You are lucky that I don't kill you for what you've done. There was a time when I would have done just that."

Abigail's expression changed yet again. Her face was filled with bitterness and anger. "You shouldn't have done that, Tom."

"It's what you deserve."

"You can't make me leave. I know your dirty secrets, remember. All I have to do is go to the marshals and your world will come crashing down."

Rafferty stared at her then nodded. "You're right."

He walked toward her, arms extended, hands searching for her throat.

* * *

It had stopped raining when Quade stepped up to the door of the dining room attached to the saloon. He found a table and sat down, waiting for Lucy to come and take his order. "What are you doing out of bed?"

Quade was tired. Surprisingly so. He grinned and said, "I come for some of your cookin'."

"I could have brought it over to you," Lucy replied.

"I'm tired of bein' in bed."

"You look tired, period."

"Startin' to wear down. But what about you?"

"Keeping busy."

"Yeah."

"Will the other two gents be joining you?"

Quade shook his head. "No. They're off doin' somethin' for me."

Lucy nodded. "What would you like to eat?"

"Steak and fried potatoes and gravy."

"We can do that."

"How about you join me?"

She looked around the dining room. Quade was the only one there. "I think that might be possible."

When the food was ready, Lucy joined Quade at the table. They made it through most of the meal in silence before it got too much for Lucy and she had to ask, "What's wrong, Jack?"

"Who said there is somethin' wrong?"

"I may not have known you that long, but I think I know when there is something wrong."

Quade stared at her before sighing. Then he reached into his pocket and took out the casing. He turned it upside down on the table so the pin strike was facing up.

"Are you still carrying that around?"

"It's the only clue I had to do with the murders of the surveyors and another Faraday agent," Quade explained.

"Faraday agent?" Lucy asked. "I thought they were all surveyors."

"No, Grimshaw was one of us."

Lucy stared at the casing.

"Is the rifle yours or your father's, Lucy?"

Her eyes gave it away.

"Why, Lucy?" Quade asked.

"The railroad killed my mother. I saw her die. Can you imagine what that does to a young girl?"

"No."

"It tore me apart. She was as close to me as you are now. When the bullet hit, I was sprayed with her blood. I was trying to get her up when Pa found me."

"But why?"

"Don't you understand, Jack? We can't have the railroad here. More people will die."

"So, you thought killin' the surveyors would stop it?"

"I had to try," Lucy said.

"What about Jimmy? He was just a kid."

"He might have remembered something and told you." Her voice was cold, distant.

"You ambushed Mary and me on the trail. I thought Mary was your friend."

"That was just for you. When you were asking questions, I needed to stop you."

"But you had feelin's for me."

Lucy nodded. "They were real. At first, I figured if I got close to you, I could control it all. But then you stopped it. But I couldn't bring myself to try again. With all the trouble with Rocking R, I thought maybe they would take care of you instead." She shook her head. "But you just wouldn't die."

"Crosby? Was that you too?" Quade asked.

"Yes. That was easy. Mary was asleep. I just crept in and used my razor to finish him."

"Because he witnessed somethin' out there. I'm guessin' it was a rider. And that rider was you."

"Yes. When he said he had seen something, I knew I had to stop him from telling."

Quade shook his head. "Tell me about Franks and Grimshaw."

"No one ever takes notice of a girl going out for a ride. Except when I found them, my father was there. I had to wait for him to go before I shot them."

"And you took them to the line shack? I find that hard to believe. You had to put them on their horses."

"I'm stronger than I look."

"No."

Lucy thought about lying again, but realized it was futile. "A man came along. He was riding a bay. I thought he was going to turn me in, but instead, he asked if I needed a hand."

"What was his name?"

"Pike Miller."

Quade nodded slowly. "Why did he help you, Lucy?"

"He knew I needed help."

"No. People like Miller don't do anythin' for nothin'," Quade said. "What did he get out of it?"

Lucy glared at Quade. "I'm a woman, he's a man, you figure it out."

He could figure it out all right. He leaned back in his chair. "Finish your meal, Lucy."

"What are you going to do, Jack?" she asked.

"Once you've done with your food, I'm goin' to take you over to the jail. Then send for a marshal. If one isn't already on the way."

"I figured as much." Lucy gave a sad sigh, and moments later, a straight razor appeared in her hand.

Quade went for his Colt, expecting her to lunge across the table and attack him with it. But she didn't. He watched on in horror as she brought the razor up and ran it across the exposed flesh of her throat.

At first, there was just a thin red line.

Then came the blood.

Lots of blood.

"Ah, Christ."

* * *

Coltrane and Baines arrived at the dam after the storm had cleared. The clouds had blown away, and now the moon was out, its silvery glow reflecting off the water. The two riders eased their horses forward and stopped at the edge of the dam, not far from the creek. Coltrane grabbed his saddlebags containing the dynamite.

They wrapped two bundles together and placed them against one of the main supports. Baines said, "This ought to do the trick. I'll cut a length of fuse."

"Not too short. I want to be well clear when this lot goes up," Coltrane said.

Within minutes, they had it set up and were ready to light the fuse. Putting a match to the cord, they got on their horses and ran headlong into trouble.

"Freeze!"

Baines and Coltrane glanced at each other in the moonlight.

"Turn around."

Both Faraday men turned and stared at a man holding a rifle. "What are you two doin' here?"

"You want to answer that?" Baines asked Coltrane.

"Sure. We're going to blow the dam."

"Yeah, right. Try again."

"No, he's tellin' the truth," Baines said. "But if you want to find out for sure, just stay standin' there."

The man started to get nervous, licking his lips indecisively.

Coltrane said, "Don't take too long to make a decision. I'd like to know soon if I'm going to die."

"I don't believe you," the man replied.

"Damn it," Baines said. "I'm not standin' here waitin' to die." He hurried past the man and kept moving.

"Hey, stop!"

Coltrane started to follow Baines. "Wait up, Harlan. I'm coming too."

"Wait, hell. You can catch up."

"Hey, stop!" the rifleman called after them. When they didn't stop, he said, "Ah, the hell with it."

Then he started running.

Only minutes later, the dynamite exploded, releasing a torrent of water into the valley.

* * *

The rider pulled Rafferty out of bed in the middle of the night to break the news to his boss. The longer the story went, the angrier the rancher became. "Who were they?"

"Don't know. A couple of strangers."

"And the dam is gone?"

"Yes, sir. Blew it to hell."

It was the news he received shortly after that that tipped the rancher over the edge.

* * *

Three of Pike's riders rode in a couple of hours before dawn. They found their boss sleeping in the bunkhouse.

"What are you doing here?" he demanded. "You're meant to be with the herd."

"What damn herd? It got washed away," one of his men said.

"What do you mean?"

"That's what I mean. A great, dang wall of water came along and washed them away. The only reason we made it is because we were ridin' night hawk."

"What about the others?" Pike asked.

"Gone."

"Damn it. I'll have to tell Rafferty."

"What's goin' on?" Dawson asked, dragging himself awake.

"The herd's gone. Someone blew the dam."

"Rafferty is goin' to go crazy."

"Ain't that the truth."

CHAPTER 26

Coltrane watched Quade thumb rounds into the Winchester '76. The three of them were in the sheriff's office. Once he was done, Quade jacked a round into the breech. "You figure they'll come?"

Quade nodded. "Rafferty will come. We've pushed him too far now. He'll be so worked up, he won't be able to help himself."

Baines checked a shotgun. "I need some cartridges for the street howitzer."

"Try the desk."

Baines looked and found a box in the second drawer. He loaded and snapped the weapon closed. Then he loaded his pockets.

"You won't need anymore," Coltrane said. "Fire both barrels and throw it away. It'll be six-guns and rifles from then on."

Baines grumbled and scattered the shells onto the desktop. "There goes all the fun."

It was just before daylight, and the main street was laced with puddles from the previous night's storm.

313

None of them had slept, and outside was as quiet as a church. Which was why they heard the approaching rider.

He must have seen the light on in the jail because he stopped at the hitchrail and climbed down. The sound of him clomping across the boardwalk to the door was loud in the silent morning air. As he opened the door, he stopped suddenly, finding himself staring down the barrels of loaded guns.

"Who are you?" Quade asked.

"Fletcher. I'm from the Rockin' R. You want to point them guns somewhere else?"

"Maybe after we find out why you're here."

"I'm leavin'," Fletcher replied. "But before I do, you need to know what's comin'."

"What might that be?" Coltrane asked.

"Hell."

"You need to be more specific."

"Rafferty and everyone with him. After the flood washed away most of the herd he brought in, he's just gone crazy."

"The herd?"

"Yeah, it was along the creek in the valley. Pike lost most of his crew too. He'll be comin' as well as Hunk Dawson. They're goin' to burn this town to the ground."

"I guess he's not happy," Baines said.

"That's not all," Fletcher said. "What made me pull out was that Rafferty killed that woman of his."

Quade was stunned. "What?"

"He found out she was tryin' to get Dawson to kill him. So he killed her with his bare hands. Buried her out back of the house."

"Damn him."

Fletcher nodded. "You got a war comin', Quade, and

the Devil is leadin' the charge. If I was you, I'd cut and run."

"That's not goin' to happen."

"Then I wish you luck. I surely do."

He started toward the door. "Wait," said Coltrane.

"Why?"

Coltrane turned to Quade. "If this gets as bad as he says, we need to get everyone out of town."

"And go where?" Quade asked.

"The cemetery on the hill," Fletcher said. "It's out of the way."

"It'll have to do," Quade said.

"You know anyone who will fight?" Baines asked.

"I guess we'll find out."

* * *

It took until an hour after dawn to get the townsfolk out of their homes and onto the hill where the gravestones and crosses sprouted like wildflowers after the rain. Men, women, and children. They gathered and talked in hushed whispers among themselves.

Quade heard one woman say, "Why should we suffer for what he has done?"

Then he heard Mary reply, "You would rather Rafferty and his outlaw friends take over, Mrs. Harrison? Because that's what he was going to do well before this."

"There was no trouble before your brother came."

"You silly woman. Trouble started before he came. Now stop your wailing and go sit with the children."

Quade smiled. His sister came over to him. "You got a rifle for me?'

"You'll be here, Mary. You won't need one."

"Worth a try, I guess." There was a period of silence before she said, "I can't believe that it was Lucy."

"She was head sick," Quade replied. "Had been for a while would be my guess. She just hid it well."

"I guess watching your mother die as a child might do that to some."

"Might do." Quade turned to the crowd on the hill. "All you men, listen up. I'm lookin' for some volunteers to help out."

A murmur ran through the crowd, but no one came forward. Each man looked around, looking for any indication of who would be the first to step up and volunteer to defend their town.

Then the crowd parted, and a voice said, "I'll go with you."

Fletcher emerged from their midst. "I know what I said before, but I guess I can't go."

"I'll help." This was from the saloon owner, Foley.

Next to come forward was Silas Holmes. "I'll help you."

"Thanks, Silas," Quade said.

"Don't forget us."

Lucas Howard and Lefty Powers.

"Glad to have you."

"Time to get some of our own back," Howard said.

"Here they come," someone called out.

Out across the flat land on the other side of town, they could see the riders coming. Quade guessed there were around twenty of them, being led by Rafferty. They disappeared as they entered the town. Within minutes, smoke started to rise above Sagebrush Creek.

Quade glanced at Coltrane and Baines. "Let's go."

* * *

By the time they reached the town, the smoke was hanging like a storm cloud above it. Dark and gray from the buildings already on fire. They split up. Some circled around the town while Quade and the two Faraday men went straight in.

As they walked along the main street, they saw riders milling around in the distance while others set fire to another building. "That's the saloon," Coltrane said.

Quade brought up his Winchester and sighted on a rider. He stroked the trigger and the rifle roared, hammering back into his shoulder. The rider straightened and fell from the saddle.

Moments later, there was a shout, and another rider pointed in their direction. Coltrane and Quade fired, and he joined his friend flat on the muddy street. Jacking another round into the breech, Quade said, "See you both when it's over."

As the trio split up, Quade disappeared into an alley. He tried to break into a jog, but his bullet wound slowed him up. Gunfire sounded from another part of Sagebrush Creek. Savage at first, then sporadic. Then it stopped.

Then came the deep-throated roar of the shotgun.

* * *

Baines waited in the mouth of an alley for the charging rider. Coltrane had disappeared behind him somewhere to circle around to a better position. Gunfire erupted further along the street, closer to where the fires were burning.

The thunder of hoofs grew louder until the horse and rider filled Baines's vision. He let go with both barrels of the shotgun and the rider was flung from the saddle. He hit the ground, and the horse bolted toward the end of town.

Discarding the shotgun, Baines ran back along the alley, emerging onto the narrow street behind the main one. Although there was no sign of Coltrane, Baines knew he'd be about somewhere.

* * *

Coltrane had run until reaching the rear of the blacksmith's. Making his way through the back and past the forge, he could hear yelling from the riders out on the main street. Gunfire erupted, and he saw Lefty Powers up on top of Mrs. Hamblin's boarding house.

Lefty fired at a rider and the man jerked but was only wounded in the arm. Coltrane saw Dawson and Jesse Crow bring their six-guns to bear and fire back. Splinters flew from the bullet impacts near where Lefty was, making him duck for cover. Then, as he came back up, a bullet took him in the forehead, just to the right of his nose. He slumped back out of sight and never reappeared.

Coltrane heard the deep-throated roar of the shotgun further along, where Baines had been. One of the Rocking R hands cried out and heeled his mount forward along the street. The Winchester in Coltrane's hands came to life and the saddle emptied.

"In the blacksmith's," someone shouted, and guns turned and opened fire.

Throwing himself to the dirt floor, Coltrane began crawling toward the rear exit. Meanwhile, outside, the riders started to dismount, and cutting through the staccato gunfire, he heard Rafferty shout, *"Kill them! Kill them all!"*

* * *

Rafferty's shout came to Quade as he entered the rear door of the newspaper office. The door had been locked, but a swift kick had remedied that issue. Ignoring the smell of ink and paper, he made his way past the presses, reaching the front of the building and the office area.

Through the large window, he could see horses but no riders. They were working their way along the street. The wind had swung around, and the smoke was blowing down the main street. Quade unlocked the front door and stepped onto the boardwalk.

Gunfire was regular and steady now, and he looked along the street at three men firing up high. Through the smoke haze, he caught sight of a figure on the roof of the bank. The smoke cleared a little and he saw Howard.

The Double Q foreman was firing a Winchester at the men on the ground. Quade saw dirt kick up around them. The Faraday man raised his rifle and sighted on the closest shooter. He realized it was Utah just before he fired.

The bullet smashed into the killer's back, thrusting him forward. He fell face down and didn't move. One of the other shooters turned and opened fire. Bullets cracked as they whizzed past Quade's head.

He stepped back into the doorway and more bullets peppered the thin wall. A cry of pain made Quade look in time to see Howard topple forward from the bank roof to the ground below.

"Damn it," Quade growled.

He opened fire again, this time, one of the shooters fell screaming as a round took him in the leg. He lay in a puddle, writhing in pain. Another bullet from the '76 put an end to it.

The third shooter used the smoke as cover, forcing Quade to come out onto the boardwalk. He couldn't see the shooter anywhere.

Behind Quade, the growing conflagration was framing him in a wall of orange. Sagebrush Creek was fast becoming an inferno.

* * *

The only thought on Silas's mind was to save his livery stable. It was all he had. The horses had all been turned loose and the air inside was thick with smoke from the approaching fires. Armed only with an old Spencer Carbine, he had gained access past the corrals at the back. The barn out there burned like Hades, fed by straw and dry wood.

Seeing the double front doors open, Silas hurried forward to close them. He was almost there when confronted by a man with a lit torch. Both men were surprised by the other and fired at the same time.

The .44 slug from the torch holder's weapon ripped into Silas's gut, shredding everything it touched.

The Spencer's round did the same, but through the chest. With one final effort, the torchbearer threw it into a stall filled with straw. Then he fell onto the floor and died.

"No," Silas gasped.

Upon being shot, the hostler dropped to his knees, pressing his hand to his stomach, trying futilely to stanch the blood. It poured through his fingers.

Silas looked up and watched the flames begin to spread rapidly. Overwhelmed with a sudden sadness at his failure to save his livery, he felt as though he'd redeemed himself slightly with the death of the man with the torch.

Silas tried to stand, but his effort was no good. Quickly losing his strength, he began to crawl, pulling himself forward. He managed a couple of body lengths before stopping. This was it. He'd die here. Either from the gunshot or the flames.

Burning fiercely, the fire spread rapidly, hungrily devouring the seasoned wooden structure, fueled by straw and hay stored in the loft. Silas could feel the heat start to burn his face. Soon, the whole livery was engulfed in flames and smoke. But Silas didn't see it. He was already dead.

* * *

Foley watched on in horror as what remained of the saloon and dining hall started to collapse in a shower of sparks after being gutted by the fire. He gripped the shotgun in his hands as ire began to consume him. This place had been his life. Now it was gone.

"Bastards," he growled. Foley turned and looked at the smoke-shrouded street.

A figure emerged from the haze. At first, he couldn't identify them, but when the man was almost on top of him, he recognized Crow. Foley's anger surged as he remembered what he and Utah had done.

When Crow saw who it was, his face registered surprise. The shotgun was already leveled at the killer, who tried to bring his Colt into play. The shotgun roared once, and the load of buckshot smashed into Crow's chest. The killer was thrust backward, arms and legs flailing like a rag doll. He landed in a puddle, muddy water creating a large splash.

Foley walked over and stared down at the dead man, a halo of red staining the dark water in which he lay. The saloon owner spat on the corpse. "Steal my money, you sonofabitch."

A gunshot sounded close by. Real close. Suddenly, Foley felt as though he'd been kicked by a horse in the center of his back. He fell to the street. As he did, he turned so that he landed on his back. He was now staring up at the sky, his mouth opening and closing as he tried to suck in breath.

A figure loomed over him, the face swimming into focus. It was Hunk Dawson. The killer's six-gun aimed at Foley's head, and the last thing the saloon owner saw was the glare on Dawson's face.

* * *

Dawson looked down at Crow. The shotgun blast had ripped his chest to shreds. Earlier, he'd found Utah, which made him the last of his men left. "Son of a bitch."

The killer turned on his heel and stalked off through the smoke. It seemed as though half the town was on fire. The heat from the flames was intense. He'd seen Rafferty angry before, but this time he'd lost it completely. His last words to Dawson as they started the fires were, "The townsfolk are up on cemetery hill. We burn the town, and then we burn them."

The crazed look in the rancher's eyes gave him pause, but as he was being well paid, Dawson shrugged it off. Losing his men was another matter. And someone would pay.

Up ahead in the middle of the street, he saw Rafferty. The Rocking R owner was standing beside another man and had someone kneeling in front of him. Rafferty saw Dawson and called out to him, "Dawson. You're just in time to see how we deal with damn traitors."

Dawson looked at the kneeling man and saw that it was the one they called Fletcher. The hand gave Dawson a defiant look. Glancing at Rafferty, the killer responded, "All my men are dead."

The gun in Rafferty's hand crashed, and Fletcher flopped to the ground. "That's how we deal with traitors."

"Didn't you hear me, Rafferty? I said all my men are dead."

"That's what they get paid to do, Hunk. They get paid to die."

Elijah Pike appeared. "I can't see nothin' for all this blamed smoke."

Rafferty turned to Dawson. "Have you seen Quade?"

"No sign."

"Then damn well find him. I want him dead."

"You can't see nothing, Rafferty," Pike growled. "I already told you that."

"Are you saying you want to quit?" Rafferty asked.

"Not by a long sight. I'm just saying, with all this smoke, we can't see anyone until we're on top of them."

"It's the same for them. Now see to it."

Rafferty disappeared into the gloom. Pike turned to Dawson. "He's lost it."

"Maybe so, but we're gettin' paid to fight."

"Not me. I was paid to get a herd together and bring it here."

"What about your men?"

"What about them?"

Shaking his head, Pike turned and walked in the opposite direction to which Rafferty had gone. He managed three steps before a gun fired and he turned back to face Dawson, a hole in his chest.

Out of the gray-brown shroud, Baines emerged. He held a Colt in his hand. Because of the smoke, he failed to see Dawson until it was too late. The outlaw fired at Baines and hit him. Baines spun around and fell to the ground before starting to move, reaching for the gun he'd dropped.

Dawson took careful aim and was about to fire when a voice said from behind him, "Hold it there."

Dawson froze. "I guess you got me."

"Holster your gun and turn around," Coltrane growled.

"If you say so," Dawson replied.

Dawson began to pivot without holstering his gun. His movement was swift, designed to take Coltrane by surprise. However, the Faraday man had fully expected him to do just that.

Coltrane squeezed the trigger, and his bullet bit deep into Dawson's side, making him lurch sideways. But the killer wasn't done. He fought to bring his six-gun up and train it on Coltrane.

The gun Coltrane held roared once more, and this time Dawson went down. But not before he managed a shot of his own. The bullet from the killer's gun clipped Coltrane's left arm, burning a bloody furrow through the flesh it found there.

The Faraday man braced himself for another shot, but none was forthcoming. Stepping up to Dawson, he watched as the killer breathed his last.

"Just in case you're wonderin', I'm fine by the way."

Coltrane looked over at Baines. He was up on his knees. "You okay?"

"Bullet went straight through my side. Didn't hit nothin' vital."

"Then get up, we're not finished."

* * *

Two men appeared in front of Quade and opened fire at him, their shots too hasty, and both bullets missed. Quade, on the other hand, made sure that his bullets didn't miss. Both men fell. One was shot through the gut, the other through the right side of his chest. Both were hit hard, which put two more out of the fight and of no further threat.

Quade walked farther along the street. Most of the main street was on fire now. A large explosion of black powder up ahead signaled the death knell to the gunsmith's store. The livery was gone, and there were bodies scattered around. The jail burned fiercely as well as the newspaper office. The bank was now on fire as well. It was just good forethought that the bank manager had taken out the money when they evacuated the town.

Quade took a moment to assess the devastation. The whole town was almost gone as each building was devoured by flames. Then he saw the boarding house. Mrs. Hamblin's stood alone like a sentinel in the holocaust that was Sagebrush Creek.

An alleyway on either side had acted as a firebreak, leaving the building untouched. Even the church was aflame. The Lord hadn't saved His house from Satan's grasp.

A familiar voice spoke. "Now I have you, Quade."

Turning quickly, Quade saw the sweating face of Rafferty. "So, this is it, Rafferty? Or should I call you Red Talbot?"

"You figured it out," Rafferty said. "Too bad it was too late."

"Why did you kill Abigail?"

"The bitch couldn't keep her mouth shut. She was planning to kill me and got caught out in the process. Intending only to send her away, I reconsidered when she said she was going to talk. Well, she ain't talking no more."

"You know you won't get away with this," Quade said. "It's gone too far."

"Maybe so, but I will have the pleasure of killing you before I go."

Quade braced himself. All he had to do was beat the drop of a hammer. But the Winchester was in his gun hand. No one was that fast.

The sound of a gunshot rocked the street and Rafferty stiffened and lurched forward. Quade quickly realized that it wasn't Rafferty's gun that had spoken. Then came a second shot, and Rafferty fell dead in a puddle of muddy water.

The rancher's last act revealed the gunman who had been standing behind him. The one who shot him dead. The hired gun, Pike Miller.

Miller holstered his gun and stepped closer, but not too close. He said, "I couldn't let him kill you, Quade. That's my job. He would have cost me two thousand dollars. That money is mine."

"I was wonderin' when you'd get around to it," Quade replied. "Thanks anyway. Was it Colin Doyle who hired you?"

Miller nodded. "You got under his skin, Quade. He takes that kinda personal."

"Blame his son. Lucy told me about you helpin' out."

Miller grinned. "She sure is a fiery one, that."

"Was," Quade said. "She's dead. By her own hand."

"Damn shame," the killer replied. "I would have liked to get acquainted with her again before I left."

The Faraday man just stared.

With a shrug, the hired gun said, "They say you're fast. Shall we find out?"

"Not goin' to backshoot me like Rafferty?"

Miller shook his head. "No, a man of your reputation deserves to go down in a style befittin' him."

Quade changed his rifle over to his left hand. Behind Miller, a pall of smoke drifted across the street. "Call it."

Miller showed a mirthless grin and then snapped, "Draw!"

As soon as Miller's lips moved, Quade commenced his draw. It was smooth and fast. Miller's was fast too. Both weapons snapped into line. One was a mite slower than the other. Hammers fell and Colts boomed.

Quade's bullet smashed into Miller's chest a heartbeat before he fired. The impact was sufficient to deflect his aim, and the bullet from Miller flew wide. The hired gun took a couple of steps back and looked down in shock. There was a neat hole in his shirt. Around it, blood was spreading, being soaked up by the stained fabric. Then, when the shirt could take no more, blood commenced its downward trajectory along Miller's torso. He looked up, eyes full of respect for the man who'd beaten him to the draw. "Damn you're fast."

Then he fell, dead before he hit the ground.

From the drifting smoke emerged a bedraggled pair. One was supporting the other. Coltrane and Baines. "You two men okay?"

"Yeah," Coltrane nodded.

"Speak for yourself. You ain't the one with a hole in you."

"I been shot too," Coltrane pointed out.

"Damn scratch if'n you ask me."

"You right to go on?" Quade asked, walking toward them.

Coltrane looked at the dead bodies on the street. "Looks like you been busy."

Quade nodded. "Let's get the rest of them."

As they walked around the burning town, they found no men willing to continue the fight. Any remnant of the criminal crews had hightailed it, bringing the battle of Sagebrush Creek to an inauspicious close.

By the time the fires ran out of fuel, there was little left of the town except for charred debris and ash. And Mrs. Hamblin's boarding house. Cemetery Hill had several new rows of fresh-dug graves. Howard and Lefty Powers had been interred on Double Q range alongside Vince and Charlie Brown.

Those townsfolk who'd been killed in the takedown were buried in the main section of the cemetery, while the outlaws and those of the Rocking R crew were relegated to a corner reserved for their kind.

Until Baines was fit enough to ride, Quade spent the next few days watching as people left the burned-out shell of a town. Then there were others who set about rebuilding their lives.

On the Rocking R, all the remaining hands had left. They'd completely abandoned everything, including cows and horses.

Mary and Quade stood on a hill overlooking where the Double Q ranch house had once stood. She looked at her brother and asked him, "Do you think that the railroad will still come?"

"I can't see why not. Remember Ma tellin' us about that beautiful bird that rose from the ashes?"

"The phoenix?" Mary asked.

"That's it. Well, Sagebrush Creek could be that phoenix. It'll be tough to rebuild at the start, but I think they can do it."

"They? What about you, Jack? There needs to be someone to run the ranch. I can't do it on my own."

"I've been thinkin' about that, Mary. Maybe I'll take some time away from my work and get this place back on its feet. The town should sell the Rockin' R and the other ranches that Rafferty had control over and use the money to help rebuild."

"I think that is a great idea. But I have a feeling that you're leaving."

"One more thing to do."

"In Kansas City?"

Quade nodded. "In Kansas City."

Mary hugged her brother. "Just come back alive, Jack."

CHAPTER 27

Colin Doyle hadn't heard from Miller for over a week. Which meant he was either dead or he'd taken the upfront money and vanished. The hour was late, and he was having his evening meal at The Palace, a gentlemen's club on the corner of 4th and Grand.

Sitting across from him was his son, Marion. The young man slurped the soup from his spoon. Becoming increasingly annoyed after listening to it for several minutes, his father finally hissed, "Must you do that?"

Marion looked up. "What?"

"You sound like a damn foot coming out of a bog."

Marion shrugged but continued with his slurping.

A gray-haired man appeared at his side then sat down at their table. Doyle did a double-take, thinking he was seeing things. After all, no one who knew him had the audacity to sit at his table without being invited.

Marion leaned back and waited for the explosion.

"Who are you?" Doyle asked. "And the answer better be preceded by an apology for interrupting my meal."

Faraday stared at him before answering. "My name is

Matthew Faraday, Mr. Doyle. I believe we have a mutual acquaintance. Jack Quade. Mr. Quade happens to be one of my employees."

"Aye. What can I do for you, Mr. Faraday?"

"It's what I can do for you. A little advice."

"And what might that be?"

"Leave Kansas City. Better still, go back home to Ireland. Before it is too late."

"Are you threatening me, Mr. Faraday?" Doyle asked, taking a linen napkin and wiping his face.

"Not me, Mr. Doyle. I don't threaten. I do. A man doesn't get to be where I am on threats."

"And if I don't do as you suggest?"

"Then I do believe you shall die, Mr. Doyle."

Doyle put down the napkin he was using. "Again with the threats, Mr. Faraday."

A shake of the head. "No. Giving you a chance to live. You see, Quade is in Kansas City. Ah, I see this surprises you. Your man is dead. He failed. Now Quade is here to make sure no one else comes after him. And to do that, he has to eliminate all threats."

"I'll get the men, Pa," Marion said.

"Just shut up," Doyle snapped. "Why would you warn me, Mr. Faraday?"

"Not warning, Mr. Doyle. As I said, I'm giving you a chance to live."

"I'll think about it. Now, if that's all, get the hell away from me so I can finish my meal."

Faraday nodded and got to his feet. As he walked away, Marion asked, "What are you going to do?"

Doyle forked some more food into his mouth. "Finish my supper."

* * *

Faraday had met men like Colin Doyle before. He knew talking to him would prove fruitless, but it gave him a chance to gauge the man. His take was that due to the man's arrogance and carelessness, he deserved everything that was coming to him.

Walking down the steps, Faraday climbed into the enclosed carriage that was waiting for him. It rocked with the transfer of his weight, and he sat down. With a sigh, he stared at the man on the seat opposite.

"Well?" Quade urged.

"He's going to keep coming after you until he's stopped. His pride has been hurt, and he can't have that. Do what you need to do, Jack."

"You're not goin' to try and talk me out of it, sir?"

Faraday shook his head. "The only thing you can do with a rabid dog is kill it."

Quade stared at his boss. "Yes, sir."

* * *

The residence had been constructed with substantial financial resources, featuring three floors and twenty rooms. Its foundation, however, had been established on the bones of others.

When Doyle arrived home, he was alone, apart from his two bodyguards, whom he quickly dismissed. They retired to their own purpose-built residence out back.

Thunder crashed outside as a storm rolled in from the west. The flashes of lightning illuminated the inside of the mansion even though the houseman had already lit some of the oil lamps in the reception area and on the stairs before leaving.

Using an oil lamp, Doyle made his way into his study where he sat it on the desk. The walls were lined with books, and there was a hardwood desk with hand-carved scrollwork and a leather chair. He sat down and reached for the brandy decanter and a glass.

Lightning flashed again, casting a momentary illuminating in the room. Doyle froze, unsure whether what he'd just seen was real or imagined. Then Quade stepped out of the shadows and into the weak circle of light. "Enjoy your drink, Doyle. It's goin' to be your last."

Placing the glass onto his desk, Doyle looked up calmly and said, "I can pay you money, Quade. More than you can imagine. Ten thousand. Twenty."

"I don't want your money, Doyle. What would stop you from sending someone else after me?"

"So you are going to murder me."

"You were given a chance to leave and go back to Ireland. You didn't take it. You call it murder, I call it self-defense."

"You won't get away with this, Quade," Doyle snarled, his hand below the desk where he had a sawed-off shotgun fixed. The Irishman was nothing if not careful.

A crash of thunder coincided with the sound of the shotgun. Buckshot ripped through the desk, spraying Quade with splinters. He fell to one side, body burning from multiple thin slivers of razor-sharp hardwood.

Doyle sprang to his feet and raced for the door.

Ignoring the pain in his body, Quade drew his Colt and fired at the running man, hitting the door jamb instead. Quade muttered a curse and got to his feet. A thin trickle of blood ran through the stubble on his jaw from a splinter cut.

He brushed at the ones lodged in his left arm and the side of his chest. They came away, some breaking off, leaving embedded tips. He'd worry about them later.

Quade walked toward the door. Out in the reception

area, he heard Doyle running up the stairs. He followed the kingpin upward.

Upon reaching the second floor, Quade stopped to listen. He heard footsteps and then a slamming door. Doyle was on the third floor.

Below Quade, loud voices could be heard coming from the reception area. He turned and saw Doyle's bodyguards step into view, guns searching. With a shout, they lifted their weapons to the second level. The Colt in Quade's hand fired twice, hamming both bodyguards backward under the mortal blows. As they tumbled to the oak floor, their blood began to stain the hardwood.

Quade turned back toward the flight of stairs and started to ascend.

The third and top floor of the Doyle mansion had a lengthy hallway lined with dark wood. Several oil lamps barely banished the dark shadows along it. The flickering orange light bringing to life the artworks hanging on the walls.

The corridor had six doors: three to the left, the others opposite them. A one in six chance of being right. Approaching the first door on the right, Quade tried the handle, swinging it open with a loud creak. The room was dark and empty. The lack of gunfire attested to that fact.

He tried the door on the left. A timely flash of lightning illuminated the room, revealing that it was also empty.

Quade moved along to the next door. Beneath his boot, a floorboard squeaked as he reached out and turned the knob. The door swung free, and once more, nothing happened. The room opposite was the same. That left two.

Approaching the next door on his left slowly, Quade

tried the knob. The door was locked. Stepping into the middle of the hallway, the Faraday man raised his boot. With all the force he could muster, Quade kicked the door near the lock.

Wood splintered and the door flew wide. The report of a gunshot filled the room, and Quade felt the bullet burn past close to his cheek. He threw himself through the opening, landing on the floor. He rolled to the left and brought his Colt up just as lightning flashed once more.

Doyle was framed against the room's window, a veil of blue light illuminating him. Quade fired twice. The bullets hammered into Doyle, knocking him backward.

Glass shattered as the kingpin fell through and disappeared. Quade came to his feet and hurried to the window. A curtain was blowing in the wind coming through the opening, bringing with it great drops of rain.

Quade peered down into the darkness. Once more, lightning flashed, lasting longer than the others as though knowing what the Faraday man wanted. He saw Doyle lying in a puddle of mud and blood. On his back, one leg twisted at an odd angle, quite dead.

Raindrops splashed across Quade's face, diluting the blood from the cuts. He grunted. It was over.

*   *   *

Quade tossed his identification onto the desk and stared at Matthew Faraday. "I'm done."

"What do you mean, done?" Faraday asked, looking up at one of his best detectives.

"I need to go home and help Mary build up the ranch. She can't do it on her own."

335

Faraday leaned forward and pushed the wallet back across the polished hardwood. "Keep it, son. I may need you again one day. Take all the time you need and do what you have to do."

Quade shook his head. "Sorry, Mr. Faraday, but I'm done with it."

"Maybe so, but look at it this way. While you have that wallet, you still work for me. While you still work for me, you will be getting paid. Understand?"

"I understand, but I can't take your money for nothin'."

"It won't be for nothing, Jack. Like I said, I may need you again one day. Until then, go home and work your ranch."

Retrieving the wallet, Quade said, "Thank you, Mr. Faraday."

"You're welcome."

Quade turned and started toward the door. He hesitated, then turned back. "Sir, do you know if the railroad is still comin' through to Sagebrush Creek?"

Faraday smiled. "It is, Jack. It most certainly is."

"Thank you, sir."

Quade left his boss's office, and Faraday watched him go, rising and crossing to his window. Staring out at the scene before him, he smiled, knowing he would need him again one day. A man of his specifics would always be needed. "I'll be seeing you, Jack."

* * *

Jack stopped the roan on a rise overlooking the Double Q ranch yard. It was a hive of activity. The barn had been rebuilt, and the framework for the house was up. He kneed the horse forward down the slope.

As he rode into the yard, Mary spotted him. She ran over to him. "Jack, you're back."

"Yes," he replied.

"To stay?"

He nodded. "For the moment."

He climbed down and she threw her arms around him. "Oh, Jack, you wouldn't believe it."

"I'm lookin' at all the work that's been done and it's amazin'. Where did the money come from?"

"The money from Rafferty's safe. He had Pa's payment inside and other money that will go to rebuilding the town. Also, the railroad has agreed to pay the rest when the bank has been rebuilt."

Quade smiled. "You'd better show me what's been done then."

Mary smiled excitedly and they walked arm in arm to where the new ranch house was being erected. "It's going to be bigger than the other one, Jack. If we're both going to live here, it'll need to be. Do you think Pa would approve?"

It was Quade's turn to grin. "He'd say, *what the hell do we need such a big house for*. Then he would approve."

They both laughed and Mary said, "Come with me and I'll show you the kitchen that Charlie always wanted."

"Lead the way."

A LOOK AT: THE CROCKETTS'
WESTERN SAGA ONE

During the Civil War, Will and Gid Crockett sought justice
outside of the law, paying back every Yankee raid with one of
their own. No man could stop them, no woman could resist
them…and no Yankee stood a chance when they rode into
town.

After their parents are murdered by a band of marauding
Yankees, the Crockett brothers join William Quantrill and his
gang of bloodthirsty raiders to seek revenge on the attackers.

But someone's about to mess with the Crocketts', and that
means someone's about to be messed with back. Will and Gid
don't like getting shot at—especially by varmints who don't
have skill enough to kill them.

Readers are sure to be captivated by this pulse-pounding tale of
revenge and survival as they immerse themselves in the action-
packed world of the Crockett brothers, where bullets fly and
justice is served with a side of vengeance.

AVAILABLE NOW

ABOUT THE AUTHORS

Robert Vaughan sold his first book when he was 19 and penned early 500 books in his career. He was a retired army officer, helicopter pilot with three tours in Vietnam. He received the Distinguished Flying Cross, the Purple Heart, The Bronze Star with three oak leaf clusters, the Air Medal for valor with 35 oak leaf clusters, the Army Commendation Medal, the Meritorious Service Medal, and the Vietnamese Cross of Gallantry.

Brent Towns self-published his first book, a western, in 2015. Since then, he has written 26 western stories. In the past, he worked as a seaweed factory worker, a knife-hand in an abattoir, mowed lawns and tidied gardens, worked in caravan parks, and worked in the hire industry.

Brent's love of reading used to take over his life, now it's writing that does that; often sitting up until the small hours, bashing away at his tortured keyboard where he loses himself in the world of fiction.

A country town in Queensland, Australia, is where Brent lives with his wife and son.